Praise for *Holly Hernandez and the Death of Disco*

"A teen mystery set in an elite public school in 1970s New York City. The novel alternates between Holly's and Xander's perspectives as the danger mounts and the two investigate the case in parallel. This fast-paced, skillfully developed murder mystery offers equal billing to both characters, their separate lives and their individual problems while also examining gender inequality and social injustice and providing an interesting look at the history of disco as a safe place for queer people and people of color. A fun murder mystery with a side of disco fever."   —*Kirkus Reviews*

"Readers will find plenty of action and suspense, a complex mystery, as well as humor and a slew of interesting characters. The 1979 setting—with the absence of current technology such as cell phones and laptops—sets a refreshing stage where the characters use other methods to uncover information. Readers will appreciate the detailed world created, enriched by the addition of appendices following the story which give additional insight to some of the characters. VERDICT: A complex, exciting mystery that will leave readers hoping for a sequel."   —*School Library Journal*

"This twist on the classic whodunit brings to life the end times of disco as two early '80s–New York City teenagers attempt to unravel a cryptic murder that has rocked their high school. As the clock winds down and the killer prepares to strike, Narvaez expertly juggles several parallel plots. From glittery discotheques to strange passages between classrooms, mystical mysteries are infused into a fun, historical murder case that takes a fresh approach to teenage angst, anxiety and the need to belong."   —*Booklist*

HOLLY HERNANDEZ

AND THE

DEATH

OF

DISCO

RICHIE NARVAEZ

PIÑATA BOOKS
ARTE PÚBLICO PRESS
HOUSTON, TEXAS

Holly Hernandez and the Death of Disco is funded in part through a grant from the National Endowment for the Arts. We are grateful for their support.

Piñata Books are full of surprises!

Piñata Books
An imprint of
Arte Público Press
University of Houston
4902 Gulf Fwy, Bldg 19, Rm 100
Houston, Texas 77204-2004

Cover design by Mora Des¡gn

Names: Narvaez, Richie, author.
Title: Holly Hernandez and the death of disco / by Richie Narvaez.
Description: Houston, Texas : Piñata Books, Arte Público Press, [2020] | Audience: Ages 15-18. | Audience: Grades 10-12. | Summary: In New York in 1979, high school sophomore Holly accuses her academic rival, Xander Herrera, of murder, but quickly realizes her mistake as they both set out to find the real killer.
Identifiers: LCCN 2020011580 (print) | LCCN 2020011581 (ebook) |
    ISBN 9781558859029 (trade paperback) | ISBN 9781518506222 (epub) |
    ISBN 9781518506239 (kindle edition) | ISBN 9781518506246 (adobe pdf)
Subjects: CYAC: Murder—Fiction. | Hispanic Americans—Fiction. | High
    schools—Fiction. | Schools—Fiction. | Disco dancing—Fiction. | New York
    (N. Y.)—History—20th century—Fiction. | Mystery and detective stories.
Classification: LCC PZ7.1.N3725 Ho 2020 (print) | LCC PZ7.1.N3725 (ebook) |
    DDC [Fic]—dc23
LC record available at https://lccn.loc.gov/2020011580
LC ebook record available at https://lccn.loc.gov/2020011581

The paper used in this publication meets the requirements of the American National Standard for Information Sciences—Permanence of Paper for Printed Library Materials, ANSI Z39.48-1984.

Printed in the United States of America
Versa Press, Inc., East Peoria, IL
May 2020–July 2020

5 4 3 2 1

This is for my teachers. I hope I won't be graded on this.

Table of Contents

VICISSITUDE

The body lay on the pink rug in the pink room. Brown skin, teen-aged, barely more than a boy, really. Head slightly askew, arms and legs splayed out. Green checkered shirt, blue jeans, black Pro Keds, very dirty. That explained the stains on the pink rug.

"A gun or knife would leave a wound," said Holly Hernandez, adjusting the tinted, tortoise shell, oversized glasses on her nose, "depending on the caliber or size of the weapon."

"Of course."

"Nothing on the victim's front side. We would have to turn him over to see if he was shot or stabbed there."

"I'm not turning him over. That would be dangerous."

"Agreed."

On the pink walls were posters of ponies, *The Wiz*, Lynda Carter as Wonder Woman, Shaun Cassidy, Jimmy Carter, the Periodic Table of Elements and the FBI's most wanted.

Holly bent down to look closer at the victim. "If the killer used a wrench or a candlestick, the head would be cracked opened."

"Like an egg. *Koosh!*"

"There would be blood all over the floor. And brains."

"Grrross."

Holly stood up and crossed her arms. "That's the reality of this kind of work, Melissa. You're going to have to accept that, if you really want to be a police detective."

"Columbo never has brains all over the place."

"That's because Columbo is not real. Now, a rope would leave *gross* ligature marks around the neck. But all this body seems to have is a big ol' hickey."

"He wishes!"

Holly giggled, and Melissa snorted, which caused the corpse on the floor to finally lose its composure.

"That's not funny. I could totally have a hickey."

"From who?" Melissa said, lisping through her braces. "Daisy Duke? In your dreams. Holly, you should see the poster he has on his wall of her. It's obscene."

Marcelo the corpse moved to get up, which made Bandit, Holly's Doberman Pinscher, get up too and begin licking his face.

"Holly! Get your rabies dog away from me."

"You're supposed to be dead already. Rabies can't kill you if you're already deceased."

"I don't like this way of playing Clue," Marcelo said, lisping through *his* braces and nudging the dog away.

The twins were alike in skin tone and hair color but most of all in the way they laughed, big, opened-mouthed laughter, which Holly knew she would miss. They had all graduated junior high school the Friday before. She feared they would never see each other again.

"I thought the game would be more interesting this way," Holly said. "With three people, it's too easy to guess who the killer is. I thought some forensic pathology would be neat."

"Okay, *Quincy, ME*. Can we play some tunes now?"

"Yes, Marcelo," Holly and Melissa said at the same time.

"Sweet!" He jumped up and went over to Holly's record collection, sorted by category and then alphabetical order, with the albums in one and the singles neatly stacked above them. "You need some new records," he said. "There's almost nothing from before 1976. No Donna Summer. No Bee Gees?"

"Marcelo!" his sister said.

"Oh, yeah. Sorry. Say, how about 'We've Only Just Begun?'"

"I love that song, but," Holly said. She flopped down on the floor and put her legs on top of her Funky Junk Trunk, which had belonged to her dad in the war.

Melissa flopped next to her and did the same. She said, "Maybe we heard it enough at graduation and all the rehearsals?"

"Agreed," Holly said. "How about John Denver?"

"But he always makes you cry."

"Does not."

"Does too," both twins said.

"I already feel sad."

"But we're going to visit," Melissa said. "It's not like California is on the other side of the world."

"Just the other side of the country," Holly said, "which is actually a considerable distance."

"We'll come back for Christmas. Our parents promised we would."

"ABBA!" Marcelo took a vinyl single out of its sleeve, popped in a plastic adapter and threaded it onto the spindle of the record player. He turned the player on and there was a burst of static from the speakers. As the 45 began to spin, he set the needle at the start of the record.

Melissa got up to dance and sing with her brother. Holly watched her friends from the floor. They knew she didn't like dancing, hadn't danced for a long time anyway.

Eight 45s later, Marcelo sat on the floor. Bandit immediately sat next to him, placing his head in Marcelo's lap. "You should be psyched you get to go to a new school. Flatbush Tech! You'll get to be with a lot of other brainiacs like you."

Melissa snorted at that. "Yeah, so how did snot-faced Brandy Vega get in?"

"Brandy's smart," Holly said. "She might be mean and sarcastic, but she did do better in math than I did. She won that award at graduation."

"I beat she cheated!" Marcelo tried to push Bandit away, but the dog just moved closer.

Flatbush Tech was the best specialized school in the city, and students had to take a difficult entrance exam to get in. Holly wanted to go to Flatbush Tech because that was where her father had gone. Her plan was to study science, like her father did, to become a scientist just like her dad.

"How are you going to avoid her, Holly? She hates you to pieces."

"A million people must go to Flatbush Tech," Marcelo said. "She probably won't even see her once, if she's lucky."

"Eight thousand. But it doesn't matter. I don't care about Brandy. I'm just sad that you two won't be there. I won't even get to spend the summer with you because you have to move this week."

"Think of it this way," Melissa said. "No one will know anything about you, about your past. They won't think of you a certain way, you know? And a new school means you'll have a chance to make new friends and have new adventures."

"My mother said the same exact thing to me this morning! Using the same exact words!"

"So did ours!" the twins said.

They laughed for a while. Then Melissa put on the *Grease* soundtrack she had bought for Holly. They all sang along, Marcelo doing his best John Travolta imitation.

Hours later, after the twins had left to go home to finish packing, Holly's room felt gigantically empty, cathedrally hollow. All the light, all the life had been sucked out of it. Holly plopped back on the floor, scooted next to Bandit, and cried.

HAPLESS

Outside at the B61 bus stop, Xander Herrera stood alone in the rain, under a broken umbrella that barely covered him. After a brief heat wave over the last few days, the sky had cracked open that morning and was pouring down seven seas worth of water. *A fitting end to a summer of no smiles,* thought Xander. His brown Pumas with yellow stripes were soaked through. He knew without having to look that his white tube socks were now also brown and yellow.

No person stood nearby in either direction on that block. All the buses had ceased to exist as well, apparently. Xander looked far down along Driggs Avenue, where cars and trucks sliced back and forth across the wet blacktop. There was not a single bus in sight.

This did not bode well.

He took his old Timex watch out of his pocket—its strap had disintegrated years ago. Was the second hand not moving again? *By Odin's furious beard!* He tapped it and, with a hiccup, it ticked back to life again.

According to several calls he had made to the MTA, the bus was due at 6:45. If it stayed on schedule, he would arrive at Fort Greene Park at 7:20. He could have taken the G train, but it was a half a mile walk in the rain, always

6

exceedingly unreliable and, worst of all, he would have been trapped in it with a lot of gawking fools.

He checked his watch again. Exasperatingly true to form, the bus was late. Definitely, defiantly, distressingly late.

An infinite amount of time later, it lumbered into view through a curtain of rain.

Sneakers squishing with every step, Xander climbed aboard, putting in his token and making a show of not looking at the driver—in order to communicate his disapproval of the driver's tardiness. Now, if only there were no traffic or traffic incidents on the streets of Brooklyn would Xander arrive at his destination in good time.

Excelsior! A seat by itself! He plopped into it, tucked the wet umbrella into the side pocket of his heavy pleather briefcase, and set the briefcase down on the seat next to him. He immediately turned his gaze outward, so that no person claiming infirmity would plead for him to give up his spot. He watched the drenched nonsense of the world go by.

Slowly go by.

He made a mental note to add fifteen minutes to the start of any school day with inclement weather. That was what this practice ride was for, after all. To gauge mass transit. This was to be his routine, Monday through Friday, throughout high school, starting in just two weeks. He wanted nothing to affect the unblemished record of punctuality or excellent attendance he had accumulated since kindergarten.

Bored by the monotony of the borough out the window, Xander risked a look around at his fellow passengers. They seemed like lethargic sheep, traveling unwittingly to the slaughterhouse of the responsible grownup world. *Get used to me,* he mentally told his fellow passengers. *You'll be seeing me every day for the next three years, except for summers and religious holidays, of course.*

He pulled a Robert E. Howard book from his briefcase and began to read, while enjoying the space he and his briefcase maintained from the others. A few stops later, however, a dozen people got on, and he had to surrender his briefcase's seat. *Very well, then.*

Finally, after what seemed like several hours but what was in fact—he tap-tapped on his watch—sixty-three minutes (twenty-two behind schedule!), the bus arrived at his stop across the street from Fort Greene Park. Xander checked the time again as he alighted from the bus. The rain had slowed to spittle from the heavens. The school was on the other side of the park. He could, of course, walk *through* the park. The entrance to it stood in front of him. The walkway was littered with beer bottles, wet newspapers, pigeons, mud puddles. It curved into the unknown, shielded by dark, drooping trees. He checked his watch. It was twenty to eight. He decided it would be a good idea to see how long it would take to walk not through the park but *around* it.

Many commuters rushed hurriedly along the broken concrete and shambolic cobblestones ringing the park. Several men, covered by garbage bags, dozed on benches. Perhaps these were his future teachers. The Board of Education's finest.

As Xander turned the northern corner of the park, the school towered ahead of him. An impressive symbol of Depression-era federal spending, Flatbush Technical High School stood nine stories tall, a borough-sized skyscraper that took up most of a city block. Xander admired its mix of Art Deco and Collegiate Gothic styles, as he walked up to the front door.

It was, of course, closed for the summer, but he checked the lock anyway. School would not start for another month. Flatbush Tech was one of the few specialized high schools in New York City, a refuge for the best and brightest. Xander had been the only student in his junior high school graduating class to pass the entrance exam, so no one here would know anything about him at all, which pleased him immensely.

He checked his watch and calculated that his commute would be approximately one hour and seven minutes, door to door. Taking into account the average time of his morning ablutions, which were not inconsiderate, he would have to arise each day at 5:45. Which meant that in order to get his absolutely essential eight hours of sleep, he would have to be asleep by 9:25 p.m. That could prove difficult, but he would manage.

Xander decided to have a look around, since he was in no hurry to get back home. There wasn't much to see. Regal, imperturbable, large-stooped brownstones lined the street across from the school. The street itself was empty, silent.

He walked to the back end of Flatbush Tech and saw a narrow alley behind the school that led to the street on the other side. He decided to walk through it to get to the front, to get a full 360-degree view.

He took stairs down into the alley. Nothing much to see. High fence on one side. Two small windows of the school, gated. Closed rear exit doors. Puddles. In front of him was a steep ramp going up to the street. He walked toward it.

But suddenly, at the top of the ramp, stood a man.

The man wore a long coat and had long hair and a squat hat. His hands were stuffed in his pockets. Then he took one hand out. In it there was something metallic.

Xander felt a deep cold in his bowels. He tried to move his feet but found he could not. The rear exit door—he was right in front of it. He moved to turn the handle, but of course it was locked. *Of course!*

He had to run. *Feet, you must start working.* He had to get back up the steps. And then onto the street, the street where he had seen no one. Where this man could pursue him. But at least he'd have a chance.

Still, his feet would not work.

The man walked to a space in front of Xander and roughly pushed him back to the exit door.

Xander dropped his briefcase. He knew death was imminent. And there were so many books still to read.

"Give me your money," the man said.

"I don't have any," Xander said, his throat feeling tight and dry, as did his sphincter.

"I don't want to use this."

Xander saw that the sharp object was one-half of a pair of scissors, just one of the blades. The man held it close to Xander's throat. The tip of it bit into his skin.

Xander reached in his pocket. All he had was less than fifty cents, one token for his return-trip home and his watch. "That's all I have," he said.

"Give me the watch, bro," the man said.

"I can't."

"I don't want to cut you."

"No."

"Come on! Let's go."

The scissor blade touched Xander's skin. With a shaking hand, he handed the watch to the mugger.

"Thank you," the man said. He took his blade and walked away, up the ramp.

Xander's feet tentatively began working again, allowing him to walk very slowly back up the stairs. He remembered his briefcase and slowly stepped back to pick it up.

He had lost his watch. He had no money to go home.

Xander walked a few feet, when suddenly the man was there again, at his side.

"Hey, kid," the man said.

Xander had nothing to say to the man.

"Say, kid, was that your last token?"

Xander nodded.

"Here, bro." The man handed the token back to him. "This is so you can get home."

"May I have my watch back?" Xander said.

"Nah, my man, I need that."

Xander kept walking and the mugger kept walking next to him.

"You should be more careful where you go, kid. Things happen to you, ya know." The man rolled his sleeves and showed a tattoo. "See this? I got this in prison. I went down the wrong road and did some bad things. Trust me, you don't want to end up in prison. It's a heavy place."

Xander nodded. Did the man expect sympathy? Xander thought of a thousand deadly oaths but didn't utter a single one.

"Take care of yourself, kid. Don't let people pick on you. Watch where you go, like I said, okay? Get home safe."

It seems a little too late for that advice, Xander thought. He watched the mugger turn and walk back into the alley.

Xander walked a little more quickly—his legs worked well again. *Finally!* He walked back around Fort Greene Park, back to the bus stop. It had started to rain again. He shoved his hands into his empty pockets and stood there waiting with his broken umbrella.

⤜ ⤝

When Xander got home he was tired and his feet were soaking wet. He stood there, shocked, silent, sad. His grandmother saw him enter and unfolded a newspaper for him to stand on.

"*M'ijo,*" she said, squinting at him through thick glasses. "*La lluvia te besó fuerte.*"

She helped him take off his shoes and peel off his wet socks. They were fecal brown, indeed.

She was tall, but still she had to pull his head down to wrap her big arms around it. "*Pobrecito niño,*" she said. "*¿Quieres algo de comer?*"

He didn't have to answer. There was already a cup of hot chocolate and a small plate of *sorullitos de maíz* at the kitchen table waiting for him. And she was already moving to the refrigerator, getting stuff together for a sandwich.

"Yes, please, Abuela, very much."

He plopped down into a kitchen chair with a *squish.*

3

FORTUITOUS

Holly moved as stealthily as she could. Surrounded by a grove of fragrant *pinus rigida,* she could still smell the salt of Napeague Bay nearby. The day was cloudless, and she could just see the water sparkling through the trees. She crouched low and then remained as motionless as possible. Bandit stood right by her, and when she cocked an eyebrow, the Doberman immediately dropped to the ground with a crunch. She checked to see if the sound the dog made had disturbed the brilliant thing, the magic thing perched high atop a bare tree twenty yards ahead.

"What is that?"

"Shhhh, Mom," Holly said.

She was grateful and amazed that her mother had been as quiet as she had been so far. She could move stealthily—she used that skill on the police force every day. But she wasn't always good at keeping the peace off the job. Especially at times like this.

"Is it an eagle?" she said.

"It's a great egret. A fledgling."

"What makes it so great? Huh? See, I made a joke."

Holly gave her mother her best disapproving squint, but she couldn't help smiling back. Her mother's corny jokes

13

were a good sign. It meant she was feeling relaxed, care-free. It was a state of mind Holly hadn't seen in her moth-er's face for a long time.

Holly had the same brown hair, big brown eyes and tiny teeth her mother had. But her mother had a beauty Holly didn't think she would ever achieve, what with her gangly limbs, fat nose and the forest of hair that was growing that very minute up and down her arms.

"Sorry, Holly. Do you want me to take a picture of the big bird?"

The last thing Holly needed was for her mother to start snapping pictures and scare off the egret. Besides, Holly didn't need to preserve this moment on film to enjoy it later. She wanted to enjoy it now.

Miles away, a Long Island Rail Road train noisily pulled into the station. The egret looked up quickly but then went back to cleaning its feathers. It was probably used to the sounds of trains by now.

Holly loved being out in nature, embraced by the gold-enrods, kissed by the orange-blossomed butterfly weeds. Give her a canteen, a flashlight, a pocketknife and her dog, and she could stay there forever. Not even mosquitoes would spoil it.

But she could feel the weight of her mother's impatience behind her. This wasn't her kind of scene. Her mother pre-ferred looking at boats and fireworks and baseball games. But Holly she didn't want to just sit back and observe. She wanted to live those things, be a part of those things, sail the boats, set off the fireworks, hit the homerun.

"These mosquitoes sure are hungry, aren't they?" her mother said.

"They sure are, Mom. It's lunch time for us, too. Let's go." She wasn't hungry at all, but she knew her mother would be.

"Great idea. I'm a starvin' Marvin. Are you sure you want to leave? I don't want you to have any *egrets*."

"Ha ha, Mom. You should have been a comedienne. You missed your calling."

They walked back along the path to the car and drove to the bungalow they were renting in Montauk. There, Marta had made them a lunch of roast beef on toasted baguette. Her mother had to remind Holly to wash her hands, something she had always been lax at. A habit, her mother said, that she got from her father. As they sat down to two heaping plates, Marta told them that Mr. McGuire had called.

"The commissioner called?" her mother said, and just like that the relaxed look on her face was gone. "I gotta call him back." She popped up from the table and went to the telephone in the living room.

Holly remained in the dining room, eating her sandwich. Bandit stood nearby, carefully watching her progress. She would normally wait for her mother to sit with her, but calls from work could take forever. She wondered why the commissioner called during her mother's day off. Would her mother have to rush back into the city? Holly didn't mind being alone. What bothered her most was her mother's dangerous job. She was an excellent officer and detective, Holly knew, but criminals could be unpredictable, and when her mother went to work there was always a chance she wouldn't be coming back.

"Um, lucky us. Turns out, Commissioner McGuire is staying in Southampton, a few miles down the road," her mother said when she sat back down at the table. "So we're having dinner with him tonight."

"Why do you need me to go? I'm not a child. I can stay by myself. And I have Bandit."

"Some day I'll explain to you why I like you to go along with me to see the commissioner. But this time his son will be there, so you can talk to him. How does that sound?"

Oh no, Holly thought, but she tried not to let her face show it. The commissioner spoke like a gangster from an old movie, and he told very interesting, if long-winded, stories about old police cases. But his youngest son, Brendan, had a terrible crush on her and he wouldn't stop trying to sit in her lap. And trying to steal baby kisses with his milk breath.

"Sounds like fun," Holly said. She didn't have much choice. She was the only family her mother had and knew her mom wanted to go.

If only she could understand that she would have preferred to stay in, to read her books, to have the windows wide open and listen to the water and the lonely sound of the trains coming and going in the night. She had tried to explain it to her, but her mom would only say that it was bad for a young girl to be so weird. Her mother thought she was doing what was best for her.

After lunch, she went to her room and wrote in her journal about what she had seen on the forest trail. She made notes about the wildflowers and the great egret. She hoped she would get to hike the trail again before they went back home, but she knew it was unlikely. If she couldn't, well then, she wouldn't mind if summer ended already. Despite her mother's motherly advice and the knowledge that she would miss her best friends, she had decided to think positively, to look forward to new adventures and to meeting new people at Flatbush Tech.

This made Holly think of her father and she had to resist the urge to get sad. She lay on her back on the floor and stared out the window at the bright blue ceiling of the world. Bandit inched his way over to her, yowling and yawning.

"Thanks for reminding me, Bandit!" Holly said. She had to get ready to go to the commissioner's house. Sky blue blouse for summer, matching slacks instead of jeans because it was Mom's boss, and sky blue socks. Thinking of little Brendan McGuire, she made sure to put a Smile button on her sky blue sweater.

Little Brendan McGuire ran crying down the hall, rubbing his butt. That's what you get for constantly trying to sit on a girl's lap when she says, "No."

Holly was grateful none of the grownups had noticed the scene.

Perhaps they were distracted by the steady beat of music coming from the house across the street. A party had been going on when Holly and her mother had arrived. Through the open windows, she saw dozens of people dancing inside that house, and pulsing, multicolored lights playing off their bodies. People danced on the stairs, on the lawn, on the roof. The music was so loud the living room windows in the McGuire's house vibrated.

The commissioner and his family were staying in a huge white house right next to the beach, very different from the modest bungalow Holly and her mother were renting. The grownups were gathered around a long, white dining table in the middle of a gigantic room with a two-story ceiling. Holly sat apart from them, at the end of the giant room, sunk down into a large beanbag. Little Brendan's attempts to park his rear end on her lap had sunken her deeper into it.

Just then the doorbell rang. Commissioner McGuire's maid Lupe got the door, which faced the living room. When the door opened, loud, thumping music poured into the room.

At the door was a male, pale, skinny, mid-30s, curly hair (possibly a wig), in a shiny purple shirt, white vest, white slacks.

"Ha! Is the commish here?" he said. Without waiting for an answer, he walked past Lupe.

"Denny Shabat," Commissioner McGuire said, getting up to face the man. Holly noticed they didn't shake hands. "That's some swell shindig you've got going over yonder."

"Ha! Commish! I wanted to make sure we weren't making too much of a racket."

"Tsk tsk. Course not. Why, we can barely hear it above the rumble of the air conditioner. And anyway, my wife Meredith loves this new-fangled rhythm. Don't you love it, darling? Course she does."

McGuire's wife looked horrified. She didn't say a thing.

"You and your guests are free to join us after you're done here. Ha!" the man named Denny said. He looked around the big room and spotted Holly. "I'm sure this gorgeous little number would love to go. Ha!"

Holly half-smiled, not sure what to say. She looked at her mother, who was halfway out of her seat and looking upset.

"Thank you, no," Commissioner McGuire said. "Our little group is set for a quiet evening of cards. But you lot enjoy yourselves, only not so much you make me call the local sheriff."

"Oh him? He's already in the jungle room upstairs at the party. Well, listen, I better let you get back to your cards. Ta, Commish!" the man said, and then he looked at Holly and added, "Good night, lovely thing."

After he left, Holly's mother said, "So that was Denny Shabat?"

"Yes," the commissioner said. "Owns Mission Venus, the number one discotheque in the city."

"Haven't we busted him and his place a dozen times?"

"We have, indeed," the commissioner said proudly. "These discotheques, they're nothing but clip joints. But they're great for policing. All the drug takers and the drug dealers in one spot. We swoop in like eagles and net the lot of them."

"Hasn't he been implicated in the dealing?" Holly's mother asked.

"Mr. Shabat? Yes, he's in it up to his fancy necklace."

Holly couldn't believe what she was hearing. Before she could stop herself, she said, "So why hasn't his placed been closed?" She felt silly asking a question while half-sunk into a beanbag, and she knew this man was her mother's boss, so she had to watch her tone. But she couldn't stop herself.

"Good question." The commissioner winked at her. "I'll tell you something, young lady. It seems in this brave new world there is no such thing as bad publicity. It seems that bad publicity is, for all intents and purposes, good publicity, if you get my meaning. We bust Mr. Shabat, and his discotheque gets more hoofers than ever. Lupe, I think it's time for dessert. Where's young Brendan? Mercedes, maybe your Holly wants some ice cream? I know I do."

Holly did not want ice cream. She wanted to know why this drug dealer, who was having a wild party right across the street from the police commissioner's house, hadn't been brought to justice. She didn't understand and wanted to ask questions, but she knew now was not the time. She would try to ask her mother in the morning. After she had had her coffee, of course.

It took Holly a minute or two for her to free herself from the beanbag and, standing up and straightening her sweater, she realized she actually did want ice cream.

INSURGENT

The school hallways smelled like school hallways always do on the first day, a not unpleasant mingling of floor cleaner, wood polish, fresh paint. Give it a few days, Xander knew, and the scent would be replaced by the stink of grease, cheese, armpits.

Xander followed signs to the auditorium, although he had already researched and memorized the layout of the building.

The auditorium of Flatbush Technical High School was the largest auditorium in New York City, besides Radio City Music Hall. The entire incoming class of freshman and sophomore students filled only one quarter of the front of the space. Knowing this, Xander was still impressed. It was the biggest room he had ever been in.

But Xander hated crowds because crowds were full of people, and he didn't like people. On the other hand, crowds were useful because he could disappear into them and be noticed. Most of the time.

He found a seat as far back as the school authority figures would allow, on the aisle farthest away from the entry door. He took out a paperback from his schoolbag, Isaac Azimov's *Caves of Steel,* and began reading. Other students filed into his row. He ignored them all as they passed, keeping his eyes fixed on his amusing reading.

Unfortunately, his peaceful idyll was soon interrupted. A very short woman with curly hair, in a brown pantsuit and a mustard blouse, walked to the front. She introduced herself as Principal Schnitger and seemed to enjoy showing off her yellow teeth.

Xander placed a finger in the book to hold his place. He would stoop to paying attention for a while. A short while.

In a high-pitched voice, the principal blathered on: " . . . so glad to see all the new, shiny faces. . . . You all worked so hard to be here today. . . . My father used to say to me if you work hard you will go far. . . . Hard works always pays off. . . . You can be anything you want to be." On and on, cliché after cliché. He'd heard it all before. In seventh grade.

She introduced her minions, saying something that was supposed to justify getting to know them. Several of them were clearly hippies who had forgotten the '60s were over. One was a tall Peggy Fleming clone, another a geek with a pocket protector. The most alarming of all of them was the security chief, a man named Licata who resembled a sewer rat in a velour tracksuit.

The principal finally wound up her gassy chatter. The students were told to follow their prefect teacher to their homerooms. As each prefect called their names, they got in line and then filed out of the auditorium like so much cattle.

Upstairs, on the third floor, Xander passed students gathered outside of the first classroom on the left.

A teacher was crouched in front of the classroom door. He kept trying to fit a key into the lock. "It's the right key but I can't make it work," he said to the students surrounding him like sheep. They blinked in comprehension.

In front of the next classroom on the right, a similar scene: students gathered around another teacher, who solemnly told her class, "I don't know what to tell you. The door won't open."

This scene played out again and again in front of every classroom down the hall. Students standing around a flummoxed teacher in front of an unassailable door.

Finally, Xander came to his homeroom. The prefect, a slope-shouldered man with wild hair and a ginger beard, had his hands up, addressing the students but not looking them in the eyes.

"Listen, the door appears to be jammed," he said to the floor, "and it looks like it's been done on purpose."

He yelled across the dense crowd of students for someone named "Bob!"

A bald-domed teacher across the hall, who wore a striped shirt that was stretched across his belly, and who was no doubt this "Bob," yelled back: "Glued shut. Am I right?"

"I concur," said Ginger Beard, then he muttered to himself. "Vandals. We're being sacked by vandals."

The students stood outside the classroom, some talking to each other, taking the opportunity to make new friends. Xander opened his Asimov novel.

Eventually, Principal Schnitger appeared. She walked down the hall saying, "Please, will you return to the auditorium until we have this situation resolved."

So Xander went back downstairs, found his seat near the back of the auditorium and returned to reading *Caves of Steel*. Smiling, he held the book with one hand and slowly rubbed the fingertips of his other hand to remove any last bits of glue.

5

ORATION

A hulk, ruddy-skinned, scarred face, balding, about 6'4", waited in the hallway.

"I don't need a bodyguard, Mom," Holly said.

"He's not a bodyguard. He's just a driver," her mother said. "No offense, Victor."

In the hallway, Victor nodded. On him, it was a big movement.

"He's as big as that Cadillac out there. Bigger!"

"Look, Holly, Victor is a good guy. He's half-Puerto Rican, half-Irish. I knew him from my early days on the force. He was a mentor to me. He was at your first birthday party."

"Hmmm," Holly said, arms crossed and not convinced.

"He was security at Attica for years."

"Oh? I can ask him about prison! He must have great stories!"

"Hang on." Her mother turned to Victor. "Do not tell my daughter any of your horror stories, not about the war, the police force, Attica, *nada. ¿Comprende?* I don't want her getting nightmares."

Victor nodded. It was a lucky thing the dishes didn't fall off the shelves.

"But, Mom! Why do I need a driver? I wanted to take the train to school."

"A bunch of teenage hoodlums."

"Or I can take the bus."

"A bunch of senile hoodlums. C'mon, do this for your mom. Think of how nice it'd be to get dropped off in that nice car. I know I would've loved it when I was a girl."

"And how can we afford this *and* Marta?"

Her mother looked embarrassed. She knew the answer before she said it.

"Leftover from your dad's. . . . Now come on . . . "

Holly felt ashamed. She knew not to say anything else. "Okay, Mom."

The next day, on the first day of school, Victor was waiting outside in the Cadillac. As soon as she slid in, Holly greeted Victor and then asked him to tell her a story about prison.

"Sorry, Ms. Holly. Your mom said I shouldn't."

"But I bet your stories are fascinating."

"You wouldn't believe half of 'em."

"I bet I would. Try me."

"Sorry, your mom's orders."

Holly tapped her chin with her finger and, as they drove, watched the buildings change in architecture, from the gorgeous homes in her Kensington neighborhood to tenements. She then remembered that Marta was an engine of efficiency and had packed her a second breakfast, two snacks and a full lunch.

"Are you hungry, Victor?"

"Matter of fact, I'm starving."

"Didn't you eat breakfast? Scrambled eggs, bacon? Pancakes, waffles? French toast? Sausages? Steak? Bison? I bet a big man like you eats a big Fred Flintstone breakfast."

"When I can. But I was running late."

"I have a sandwich here. Looks like a chicken BLT." She took the sandwich out of the bag and the smell of the bacon filled the car. "Would you like half?"

"Oh, I couldn't . . . "

"Tell me a story, and you get the whole thing."

As they turned onto Atlantic Avenue, Victor was finishing a story about his early days on the police force, before he went into security. " . . . we were booking pretty hard, fast as we could," he was saying, "you should have seen this guy coming after us, and his ear is barely hanging onto his . . . . Hey, are you okay, Ms. Holly? You seem a million miles away."

"I'm okay. I'm listening."

"I know what it is. First-day-of-school jitters."

"Maybe a little. But your story is helping. I want to hear more about the ear man."

"You don't worry, Ms. Holly. You'll make new friends right away. Treat it like prison. Look for the biggest person, and then you walk right up and knock his teeth in. You'll make plenty of friends. Works every time."

"Is that how you got through school, Victor?"

"You're assuming I ever went to school, Ms. Holly."

She laughed. "Well, that might get me murdered on the first day," she said, and after he laughed, she added, "But that doesn't mean I won't try it."

"Want to borrow my brass knuckles?"

"I have my own, thank you."

She briefly considered asking Victor about her outfit. Her mother was always too busy to ask about silly things like clothes and had been so super busy that summer that Holly had had to shop for her new school wardrobe with Marta. Holly had on her brand-new royal blue skirt, white blouse with a blue vest, white socks and blue shoes. Marta said she liked the outfit, but Marta said she liked everything Holly wore. The first day of school was always a bit of a fashion show, everyone wearing brand-new clothes and trying to impress each other. She was curious to see what the other girls would be wearing, and she wanted to make sure she made a good impression. She had spent an hour that morning blow-drying her hair straight, hoping that it looked right. She didn't know. She had wanted to ask her mom, but she had already left for work. Holly wanted to look approachable but not snobby, stylish but not pretentious. Maybe the vest was too much?

"Victor, do we have time to turn around?"

"We're here."

Flatbush Technical High School loomed before her. The nine-story building, constructed by the Public Works Administration in 1930 in a dramatic Gothic Revival style, rose up from the humble pavement, dwarfing all the brownstones surrounding it. Unlike most city high schools, FTHS had specialized programs of study, in architecture, engineering, mathematics and science, and it had an enrollment of students equal in size to a small college.

Here it is, Holly thought, *a fresh start.* No one here would know her as the valedictorian, the one voted Miss Bright of '79, the *brainiac* who knew the answer to every question and who could feel everyone sighing (sometimes with jealousy, sometimes with relief) every time she raised her hand. But more importantly, no one would feel bad for her or look at her differently because of what happened to her father. She would be lost in this school. One among thousands, anonymous.

Holly walked down the hall to the assembly, smiling and saying, "Hi" to friendly faces. One girl said, "Nice hair."

Another: "I love your vest." *Great!* She was going to love this school. No more dirty looks and whispers. She was here to be just another student. She was here to be regular, plain Holly Hernandez.

She followed the signs and the flow of students into the auditorium. It was a massive space, with two balconies, and a gorgeous proscenium arch framed by intricate detail work. She couldn't wait to see it close up.

Because she was busy admiring the arch, she almost bumped into a boy in front of her. He was walking very slowly, as if there were no one else in the world. She had to go around him and passed him closely. *5'11", very thick glasses, curly hair, heavyset.* Smelled a little bit of sweat and sour milk. He stared into a book. She wondered what it was.

"Hello," she said to him. "What book is that? I love to read. I have a million books."

The boy grunted. Literally grunted. And gave her what distinctly looked like the stink eye.

Not knowing how to react to that, she decided she'd better take a seat before the good seats were taken. She liked to be in the front, but the first few rows were filled. *Ah well.* She just followed the crowd and found herself near enough to the front. The girl to her left was talking to the girl to her left, and the boy to her right was talking to the boy to his right, so Holly just smiled and looked forward.

In front of the stage, a woman was standing and talking to other adults. *Fortyish, medium height, big, round glasses, straight back, gray hair, unkempt.* The principal.

A minute later, the woman turned around and addressed the students. She introduced herself as Principal Schnitger and then she introduced the staff members around her: Head Coach Carl Kartoffel—*40s, thin, blond, thick blond mustache,* Coach Diana DiGeronimo—*40s, tall, red hair bobbed, seemed stoic.* Assistant Coach Stephanie Gorney—*30s, medium-height, athletic build, ponytail*—also an assistant gym teacher, in charge of something called Safety Order Service, or SOS. John Licata—*50s, pomade-haired, seven o'clock shadow*—was in charge of security. Linda Barkley—*late 20s, brunette, feathered hair, button nose, chubby cheeks*—who was the guidance counselor.

"You'll all have to come see me," Ms. Barkley said. "Sooner than later."

After the assembly, the students were supposed to follow their prefects directly to homeroom. They had three minutes to get there. Just as Holly was filing out, she saw Brandy Vega off to her right.

The twins Marcelo and Melissa liked to call her "snot faced," but actually Brandy had been voted Miss Vogue of '79. She seemed as tall as Holly, but it was hard to tell her real height because she wore heels and her hair somehow grew supernaturally high. Brandy also wore make-up, which Holly couldn't understand because this was school, and she carried only a single spiral notebook, which Holly also found hard to comprehend because she needed a bookbag to carry all her school necessities.

They had never been friends but had known each other since kindergarten. Maybe it was time they did become friends.

"Hi, Brandy! Isn't it great here?"

Brandy looked straight through Holly as if she didn't exist. Then she kept on walking.

"I'm such a doofus," Holly whispered to herself.

6

UBIQUITOUS

"What makes a hero a hero? Hmm?" Mr. Baci, the English teacher who, Xander concluded, was over-enamored of the 1960s aesthetic, stood at the head of the class and tossed a piece of chalk up and down in his hand. "We all need heroes, don't we? So what are they like? Do heroes have to be righteous and rockin'? I wonder. What does a hero have to do to be a hero? Does a hero win the day by slitting the throats of his enemies? Does he—or she, let me be fair—trample on and crush the skulls of their antagonists and emerge, covered in bits of brain and blood and gore, victorious? Hmm?"

Mr. Baci's shoulder-length hair bounced wildly as his voice grew manic. He stomped hard on the floor. "Like this: 'Die! Die! Die!' Just like that!" He paused and drew a breath. On the board, he wrote the word "Hero."

Xander knew only one true, real-life hero: his grandmother. She could cook a full dinner in five minutes, could take the stains out of anything, could make any day better and her only kryptonite was boiled Brussels sprouts.

Turning back to the class and tossing his hair back, Mr. Baci told them: "Or does a hero mean someone who uses his wits to win the day? Keeping his own brains in his head.

29

Someone clever and cunning who doesn't need to cut out the hearts of his enemies. He can convince them to defeat themselves. To cut out their own hearts, if need be. Hmm? How about this: Does a hero do things that are evil for the sake of an ultimate good? Is that okay? What do you think?

"How about this? Where do we find these heroes? Do we still have any? Are any of them here? Is one of you here in this classroom secretly a hero? Or not so secretly?"

Mr. Baci glanced at Holly Hernandez when he asked that last question.

Which made Xander roll his eyes.

When Xander came to this, his first class after home-room, he saw that the girl who had tried to speak to him at the assembly was walking in the same door. There was something he did not like about her, but he could not quite name it. Seeing her again, her smile beaming, he found the word for it: perky. Xander hated perky.

Not wanting to have to interact with her again, he turned and walked down the hall. Then he circled back and walked into the class and away from where she sat (at the head of the class) to the back of the room, his preferred seating area. Sitting in the back allowed him to leave last leisurely after each class.

But this Mr. Baci had insisted on the archaic system of having them seated in alphabetical order. *So much for this being a free country,* Xander thought. Now he was jammed into the ancient, pew-like desk, fastened with cast iron legs to the floor, in the exact middle of the room and, by an accident of alphabetics (Hernandez, Herrera), that perky girl was sitting right in front of him, her mane effectively blocking a small but no doubt significant portion of the blackboard.

Baci himself had long, scraggly hair, a thick, scraggly beard and wore faded jeans that might also be described as scraggly. Also, sandals. *Sandals on a teacher! What had become of the public school system?*

"How are heroes in literature different from the heroes we see in real life? What does one have to do to become a hero? Does it require bravery, sacrifice? Or are you a hero if you just do your job well?" the scraggly, Serpico-haired teacher continued. "Which would disqualify people who run the New York City subway system."

Xander snorted. *That was funny.*

"What's important for this term, for this class," Baci went on, "is the idea of the archetype."

If Xander's nostrils were correct, Baci gave off trace hints of patchouli. Not that he could smell it above the strawberry cloud that emanated from Ms. Perky Hernandez in front of him.

"A pattern that is followed by all or nearly all things of the same kind is called an archetype," the hairy, hectoring hippie continued, "a concept developed by Carl Jung. You've all heard of Carl Jung, right? 'Fairy tales can come true, they can happen to you, if you're Jung at heart.' No? That's okay. You don't have to know him. The word 'archetype' comes from the Greek word for 'model.' By which I do not mean people like Jerry Hall or Marisa Berenson. I once saw Jerry Hall at a, um, well, never mind. Never mind that."

As he spoke, Mr. Baci thumbed a dilapidated paperback of Edith Hamilton's *Mythology,* a book Xander had read and reread as a child.

"There are some marvelous stories in here, stories many of you have probably heard, like Androcles and the Lion, or the Labors of Hercules. But does anybody know the story of Atalanta and the three golden apples?"

Of course, Xander thought. *Atalanta bets her hand in marriage.*

Ms. Strawberry Cloud's hand shot up in front of him. "Yes," she said, without waiting to be called on. "She didn't want to get married, so she challenged all her suitors to a footrace. Whoever beats her gets to marry her."

"Brilliant. Holly, right? Holly. And then what happened?"

Brilliant? Why was that brilliant? She had only recalled a story. A trick of memory! The girl has a good memory. So does an elephant. This is brilliance?

"Hippomenes cheated."

"Cheated? Honestly?" said Mr. Hirsute Hands-Out-Accolades-Like-Candy. "But who told Atalanta to get distracted by golden apples?"

"It was still cheating," Holly answered. "She was still faster than he was."

They were skipping the whole part about Aphrodite's interfering because Atalanta was against love, which was Aphrodite's superpower, so she colluded with Hippomenes. They got turned into lions anyway. Xander bet they wouldn't mention the lion part.

But by then, the scraggly teacher had already moved on to the Titans.

After the class drained away, Xander walked out of the room and into the hallway and was immediately touched—touched!—by one of those students he had seen standing, just standing in the middle of the hallway.

"No more than three squares," this student said. He was thin as a ruler and pizza-faced and stood ramrod-straight like a soldier with his hands behind his back. On his checked shirt was a large button that read "SOS" and in smaller letters around it: "Safety Order Service."

"Pardon?" Xander said.

"No more than three squares," this SOS person said, indicating the tiles on the floor.

He realized that these people controlled the flow of traffic in the hallway. No one was allowed to walk, run or meander anywhere outside of a lane that was three tile squares wide. They wanted him to stay in place, like a car on a highway, a widget on a conveyor belt, a duck in a row.

"Pardon?" Xander said. They actually expected him to count the floor tiles every time he walked up and down the hall?

"No more than three squares."

"Pardon?" *Who made up this absurd rule? Who gave this stick of a sentinel the authority?*

"No more than three squares."

Xander gave up the parrot act. This was a rube, a rank-and-filer, a robot. But the robot had moved on, his attention drawn to the flurry of other students walking by, flagrantly disobeying the three-square law. "No more than three squares." The robot seemed about to self-destruct. "No more than three squares." Perhaps he would short-circuit and explode. *Wouldn't that add a fun edge to the day?*

Xander took the opportunity to stomp away. With every other step, he put his foot down squarely into a fourth square.

7

CAMARADERIE

Holly walked into her first class of the day, English, filled with anticipation. She loved books: classics, horror, science fiction and—not a little—whodunit mystery stories. But she really genuinely loved poetry. And she hadn't had anyone to really share her love of poetry with, not in a long time. She couldn't wait to get started.

In her first English class, she saw that biggish boy from the auditorium walking toward the same door she was headed for. She had a slight lead on him and picked up her pace to get into class before him. She didn't want a repeat of his grunting. It was too bad. He made her want to laugh, but not at him. Despite or maybe because of the stink eye he gave her, he seemed so unlike anyone else she had ever met. He didn't seem to notice or care when the other kids were pointing and laughing at him as he walked slowly down the hall. He was in his own world. She liked that. So much for new friends.

She sat down and was immediately drawn to a series of posters above the chalkboard and around the room. They were depictions of the Nine Muses from Greek mythology. Holly recognized Terpsichore right away. *Nearby, Erato and Melpomene.*

Before she could get them all, Mr. Baci began speaking. *5'10", thin, hooked nose, mole right cheek, bearded.* He had dark circles under his eyes, which made for a very intense stare. He was well versed in mythology, and he looked like he would be a challenging teacher. And he said they would be discussing poetry, a lot of poetry. The rest of the class groaned, but she was ecstatic.

Lunch was next, so Holly took the elevator to the lunchroom on the seventh floor. The car was crowded, and she kept getting jostled until she was almost at the back. Facing her was a short student, *5'5", with straight, black hair, wearing a gray polo shirt on top of a red polo shirt over a T-shirt.* The look in his eyes reminded her of the way Brendan McGuire looked at her, but at least this boy wasn't trying to sit on her lap.

She said, "Hi." But he immediately stopped looking at her and went back to scribbling in a notebook. *Okay,* she thought.

When the elevator stopped at the 7th floor, he disappeared in the rush of students into the lunchroom. It seemed to take up the entire floor.

Holly still had half the sandwich Marta had packed, but she wanted to eat what the other kids were eating. She wanted to experience high school just like everybody else. But the question of the hour was: Where would she sit?

Students were crowded around long white tables on wheels, and she could see cliques right away. Freshman, sophomores, juniors, seniors, athletes, deadheads, cheerleaders, nerds. But either because there wasn't enough seating or they didn't belong in cliques, many students hung out at the fringes of the room, by the windows, holding their lunches with one hand and eating with the other.

As Holly walked toward the food stations, she smelled something strange. It was like cologne, a mix of citrus, rubbing alcohol and neglected hamper. *Ugh!* She realized it was emanating from a group of boys cluttered around a lunchroom table. Some stood on the sides, some sat on the benches, some sat on the table. The table was covered with the leftovers of dozens of devoured meals. She didn't see a book or bookbag in sight. She had met many of their type before. *Jocks.* She sighed.

Two of them saw her looking, and one said, "Sweet freshman meat," while another boy made kissing sounds. How did they expect her to react? Their behavior seemed so primitive, so predictable. They reminded her of the officers at her mother's police station. The loudness, the overuse of cologne. Except these young boys didn't have the potbellies. Yet. She worried that even at FTHS their conversation likely would consist of little more than sports commentary and dirty jokes. She wondered if she should correct them and tell them she was in fact a sophomore who had transferred in? *No,* she thought and walked away.

Boys fascinated Holly, but not in the way they did her cousin Zenaida, who spent eight months at home last year with mono. Boys were certainly something her mother worried about. She warned her at least twice a day about boys. "Boys are dangerous, bad news. They can't control themselves," she would say. Holly would remind her mother that she had met her father when he was a boy, and her mother would say, "That's exactly why I keep warning you."

Despite her mother's fears, Holly was looking forward to getting to make new friends with boys her age. Marcelo was her age, of course, but to her, he would always be the fingerpaint-splattering child she met in second grade. This would be like researching a new species. So far none of the boys would talk to her. She had tried to make friends with that Xander boy, and that hadn't gone so well.

Now she was being called "meat" and catcalled. Which did not reflect well on them. Which meant these jocks weren't concerned with overcoming their poor image.

Just then, one of the boys from the troop of jocks stepped in front of her.

"Sorry if those spazzes were bothering you," he said. *6'1", straight brown hair, crooked teeth, hazel eyes.* He wore a blue varsity bomber with white leather sleeves and the Tech logo on the front.

"They weren't," she said, curious now. "Hi. I'm Holly." She held out her hand.

He seemed puzzled by the gesture, but then he gingerly took her hand and shook it.

"You can call me . . . Dragon," he said.

"Okay."

It seemed that he expected her to ask a follow-up question.

He pointed to where "Dragon" was sewn on his bomber. "See."

"Yes, I can read."

"Why don't you come over and hang out at our table?" He added a laugh to the end of his sentence, which made him seem insecure.

Probably not his intention, Holly thought. She smiled and said, "Thank you so much for the invitation. But I'm looking to meet new types. Thank you very much though." As soon as she said it, she wondered maybe if she should have given a more diplomatic answer. But it was too late.

The boy's mouth had dropped open. "Oh. Okay, catch you on the flipside. I guess," he said, walking backward to his troop.

She turned and immediately almost bumped into some-one. A very short girl with a plaid blouse, designer jeans, and the cutest purple shoes. *Brown eyes, one slow, mild acne, braces, black hair feathered like Farrah Fawcett's.* She was in a few of Holly's classes. As the girl sat down, she turned and complimented Holly on her blouse.

"Thank you," Holly said. "I love your shoes."

"Hi, I'm Tina."

The girl was bouncing with energy. Holly liked her on the spot.

"My name is Holly."

"Oh, I know! That guy's cute, isn't he?"

"Yes, but not in the way he thinks he is."

"You think so? To me, he defines 'cute.' Are you going to lunch? Of course, you are. You're here. Come with me. Let's find a seat. Have you noticed how cute the boys are? Not that I'm going to do anything about it. But after junior high, it's like a whole new crop to gush over."

She and Holly laughed, and then she led Holly to the lunch line, where Holly got milk and a slice of lukewarm pizza.

"I like your hair," Holly said.

"Do you? I don't know if it works. I just want to be part of the cool people. I bet you never have that problem."

"Me? I don't even know who the cool people are."

"I was born in Hong Kong. I came here when I was three, but I still feel like I have to work to fit in. I'm so happy to be in a new school, to try again."

They took a table near a window facing the park.

"I'm sure you'll be great," Holly said.

"I know. It's exciting. All then there's all the boys!"

At that moment, Brandy Vega walked by. It was hard to miss her. She was flanked by two other girls about the same height and wearing similar outfits. She must have seen Holly, who was in her line of sight. Holly half-raised her hand to say hi. But again, Brandy gave no sign of recognition.

It didn't matter this time. Holly turned to Tina, her new acquaintance (and potential friend) and asked if she'd thought about declaring a major yet.

At the end of the day, Victor was waiting in the car right outside the entrance. This slightly embarrassed Holly. Would the other students think she was a rich snob?

When she got in the car, her curiosity overcame her shame. A question popped into her mind.

"How was your day, Victor?"

"Can't complain, Ms. Holly."

"What did you do after dropping me off?"

"What did I do? I waited for you."

"All day?!"

"All day."

"Don't you get bored?"

"Nah. I, uh, did the *Times* crossword."

"And then?"

"And then? That takes all day. I just finished."

After Victor dropped her off at home, Holly ran upstairs to do all her homework. Around dinnertime, she listened for her mother's arrival. She wanted to tell her all about her first day, the interesting teachers she had, the students she'd met.

She didn't hear the sound of her car. *Mom must be working late again.*

Holly plomped down the stairs to the dining room. It was Tuesday night, which meant wiener schnitzel and fried potatoes, which her mother and she both adored. Holly sat down at the dining room table to eat alone.

Marta zipped from the dining room to the kitchen. As she zipped, she said, "Your mother called. She is working late on a case, so she said not to stay up. Right? And she said, quote, 'This time I mean it.' Good? Right?"

"Okay, Marta. Thank you."

"Good. Remember to listen to your mama."

Holly ate without thinking. The schnitzel had no flavor, the potatoes just existed.

8

DISSIPATE

What was Xander going to do with a "pawl"? It was apparently a tapered piece of wood that was important in the fascinating world of cogwheels and other such machine parts. At least in junior high school when he had been forced to make something it was practical. In fact, the desk set he had made in Wood Shop still proudly held his dictionary and thesaurus at home, and the World's Greatest Grandma plaque he had labored over still hung in the kitchen. But the poor, paltry pawl, who in the world would ever use one, let alone spend valuable minutes of valuable energy making such a useless, pointless object? Here they were in a shop full of fools using tools. Why not make sets of nunchucks or—better idea—as a class, build a trebuchet!

Alas, no. It was to be the pawl for each and every one of them. But first, of course, professed Mr. Kugler, the shop teacher (a short Teutonic man with a pencil-thin mustache and lacquered hair, suspiciously jet black), they would have to draw a pattern for the worthless thing.

It was the third day of what was already proving to be a very long semester for Xander. Standing around large wooden block tables, each student bent over a manila folder and drawing desk set patterns in color pencils. Once that was done to Mr. Kugler's "ultimate satisfaction," as he put it, then and only then would students be allowed to actually make the thing using the saws and drills.

Mr. Kugler circled the shop in his immaculate lab coat (it seemed starched), grunting approval here, slinging one-liners there. Xander could see that the patternmaking shop was Kugler's factory, and the students were his pitiful workers.

Xander stood near the back, far from the door. He was finding it utterly impossible to draw a straight line with the tiny metal ruler and pencils he had had to purchase in the GO store downstairs.

"Wrong pencil," said Herr Kugler. "That's a number 8. Too thick. Use a number two. Not that one. Nor that one. This one here." The teacher picked up a pencil and handed it to Xander. "You'd think you'd see better with those glasses," said Kaiser Kugler, who then cheerfully whistled the theme from *The Bridge on the River Kwai* and moved on to another student, one across from Xander.

This student wore three shirts for some reason. Perhaps he was chilly, or child-sized, or crazy

Mr. Kugler said to him, "Stop. Listen to me. Once more. This area in red pencil. Again. This area in blue pencil. Again. Get it? Got it. Good."

Xander didn't know how the student could "get it" when he kept his gaze squarely on the floor in front of him. The kid took out a rubber eraser, but the Kaiser said, "That will just make a mess. Best to start from scratch. You need the practice. Who knows? You might end up doing this for a living. And then where would you be? I'll tell you. You'd be in my shoes. And believe me you wouldn't want to be in my shoes because they're too tight and they squeak."

The teacher finally goose-stepped away in his tight shoes. Xander went back to his arduous patternmaking. He continued with his work until he came to an impasse. The pawl had circles in its design. In order to draw perfect circles, Xander needed a scribe. And he had spent the last of his money on his randomly numbered pencils and a T-square (which had turned out to be crooked). The scribe had not been a viable option economically.

The three-shirted student across from him had one and seemed to not be using it at the moment, being too busy starting from scratch. Xander abhorred having to address any of his fellow students, but he did need to do this idiotic work properly.

"Borrow the scribe?" Xander said.

"Oh Silver Tree, oh Silver Tree," the student said in a monotone.

What was that now? Xander thought.

"My dear old daddy came to talk to me."

He was forced to repeat himself and speak at length, two things he hated to do. "That," he said. "The scribe. Some call it a compass, but it's not. It's a scribe."

Seeing where Xander was pointing, the kid picked up the scribe and handed it to Xander. "Poor, hungry or sad I'll never be," he said.

"What?" Xander sighed. "I'll give it back."

The boy had gone back to his patternmaking, so Xander concentrated on his own work, hurrying to get the scribe back to the three-shirted kid. He drew circles, perfect, useless circles.

Xander jingled his keys into the door of his family's apartment. As he opened the door something smelled . . . different. Then he heard music blasting from the kitchen. He knew instantly what it was. Who it was.

His mother was home.

"Alexander!" she said. "Cop a squat. I'm cooking. I'm making *pernil*."

It was a small kitchen in a small apartment. The old stove generated massive heat that came at Xander in waves. In the sink was a two-foot-high pile of bowls and pans.

"Where is Grandma?" Xander asked.

"Chill out. She's still alive. She's just in the bathroom."

Xander began to slink toward his room, with a plan to knock on the bathroom door to make sure his mother was telling the truth.

"Where you going?" Xander's mother said. Her name was Carmen. He never called her "Ma" or "Mami," not that he ever tried to refer to her, at all, ever.

"I have to do my homework."

"Your homework? Uhuh. You come here and set the table, man. I need a ciggy, so I'm gonna cop a squat."

His grandmother never asked him to do the dishes. His mother, on the other hand, loved to make him work.

It had been two years since Xander had seen Carmen last. For the first ten years of his life, they told him that she was his sister. Xander figured out the truth by going through papers and pictures. One day while eating a grilled cheese sandwich he casually announced, "I know you're my mother." His grandmother said, *"Sabe más que un lápiz."* Nothing much had changed after that. She had always treated him as a little brother more than a son and continued to do so.

When his grandmother emerged from the bathroom, she blinked behind her thick glasses and hugged him. *"Mi reyito está en casa."*

Xander looked at his grandmother, then toward Carmen, who was lighting another cigarette with her previous one, and then back to his grandmother, who shook her head. She didn't know why his mother was there either.

At dinner, Xander had to cut through very dry *pernil* with a plastic knife and fork.

"Plastic?"

His mother said, "So there's less dishes for you to wash, you dig?"

The *arroz con habichuelas* was somehow mushy and burnt at the same time. The *plátanos* were undercooked and undersalted, exactly the opposite of his grandmother's culinary perfection.

"I hear you got into that egghead school," said Carmen.

Xander grunted.

"What's shaking there? I bet you're showing off with all your big words."

Xander grunted again.

"I know you're bugging. You're wondering why I'm here." His mother lit a cigarette in the middle of the meal, inhaled and exhaled. A cloud floated over the table.

"You're moving back in, I suppose," Xander said.

"Say what? You're such a mumbler, Alex. You don't get that from me."

"You're. Moving. Back. In."

"You wish. Nah, a friend of mine died, so I have to go to the funeral." She inhaled again, then added, "So sad."

Xander's grandmother asked, "*¿Quién murió?*"

"Hector Chevres. He was married to Marie. You remember them, Ma, they grew up around the block."

His grandmother asserted that Hector was young, too young to die.

"He got pushed onto the train tracks. They never found who did it."

Xander's grandmother crossed herself and told him that was why he must always take care in the subway.

"I seen Marie today," his mother said. "She's miserable without her man."

Xander felt her looking at him. "What's wrong with you?" she said.

He said nothing.

"You're bugging out thinking I'm going to take your bed and make you sleep in the kitchen, right?"

In fact, that is exactly what he had been thinking.

"Chill. I won't kick you out of your room. But if you were a gentleman, at least you would have offered."

She laughed long and loudly by herself, and Xander kept up the arduous job of chewing his dinner.

9

EMOLLIENT

Holly ran to the girls' gym, worried that she would be late. Gym class for girls was on the ninth floor of the building and getting there on time was a warm-up in itself.

The locker room was crowded and chaotic, per usual. She would be lucky if she could find a decent locker. Holly actually looked forward to gym. She liked finding out what her body could do, feeling her muscles grow stronger and her limbs more flexible. It took her less than a minute to put on her one-piece navy blue gym uniform, required by the school, but she had on matching sneakers, socks with matching stripes, and a matching barrette.

The girls assembled on the court floor for ten minutes of calisthenics, led by Coach DiGeronimo. Above and to the side, huge windows filled the space with light and heat. After they had worked up a little sweat doing calisthenics, they were allowed to play whatever games they liked for the rest of the period. Many of the girls went to play volleyball. Holly preferred softball or even basketball, but the gym was small and there weren't many options. (The rumor was that the boys' gym was ten times bigger than this one. Holly was curious to investigate.)

Holly joined a volleyball game. For a while, she thought she was playing pretty well, serving and returning just fine.

Until a ball suddenly went and smacked her in the face.

She was knocked to the ground, flat on her back.

Ponytail bouncing, Assistant Coach Gorney was suddenly standing above Holly. "Nice move. Did you make that up?"

"Paten'it myse'f," said Holly, intrigued by the stuffy sound of her voice.

"Funny girl. Nose is bleeding. Don'tcha have sense to dodge a moving object?" The assistant coach placed a towel that smelled moldy onto Holly's face and said, "Get to the locker room. Keep your head back."

Holly waddled as quickly as she could to the locker room. She had never had a nose bleed before and she was curious to see how much blood was actually coming out of her face.

The girls' locker room had its own specific unpleasant smell: sweat, perfume, feet. As soon as she waddled in, she smelled something different: Smoke.

Brazenly, in the center aisle, stood three girls. She could tell immediately by their hair that it was Brandy Vega and her friends. They were smoking cigarettes and giggling, as if no one would come along and catch them!

With her head tilted back and holding an increasingly bloody towel to her face, Holly had to think about which row was hers. Then she heard, "Oh shoot. What happened to you?"

Holly shrugged. "Wolleyball," she said.

Brandy grabbed the towel and peeked. "Eww."

Suddenly, Brandy and the other girls surrounded Holly and led her gently to the sink. One of them wiped her face.

Holly stuffily said, "Is it bwoken?"

"Nah," Brandy said.

"T'bad, I don't wike my nose."

"Hah! You got a cute nose. I got a schnozz. I guess I should go play volleyball." The other girls laughed at this.

Holly looked. Brandy did indeed have a large nose, sort of avocado-shaped. Funny she had never noticed that before. It didn't look bad on her.

"Just keep your head back," Brandy said.

"What, are they playing dodgeball out there today?" one of the other girls said, and they all laughed.

"Did it hurt?" another one said. "It looks like it hurt."

"I'm fwine. Just a bop in the face. I'm more embawassed tha' anyt'ing."

"Oh, don't be," another said. "That happened to me once, and when I landed I farted. It was so loud."

They all laughed for a while, and then Brandy and the other girls moved away, back to the center of the locker room, puffing away in full defiance of rules of conduct and not caring at all.

At lunch later that day, Holly sat at the window again with Tina. The Salisbury steak looked good. As they stood there, Brandy and her friends walked by and they all smiled or nodded at her.

10

CIRCUMLOCUTION

Aujourd'hui, it was Xander's turn. It was inevitable, of course. Xander had been dreading it since the first week of school. The problem with all language classes, of course, was that you were periodically forced to *speak*.

It had been Xander's adamantine policy since sixth grade to never raise his hand in class. Before then he had been a frequent question-answerer, but one day when Mrs. Ribak asked a question about fractions, he had raised his hand, and Artie Ramos, who already shaved regularly, shouted out, "He always answers the questions." Xander ignored him and confidently said, "Two-thirds," but Mrs. Ribak said, "No. That is incorrect." Artie Ramos exploded in quaking laughter (something like "Bwahahahahaha," which still echoed in Xander's nightmares), and since then Xander had decided that teachers could test the other students' grasp of the subject matter, but they would not test his, not aloud. *He knew* that he knew the answer to every question anyway, and he loved knowing them, especially when a teacher asked something crushingly easy and the class was struck dumb, crickets chirped, silence reigned. Xander refused to share his apple, and they would have to suffer in ignorance. And go home and really do the homework this time.

But in this French class, Xander knew that his turn would come eventually.

Mr. Bascanard made his way around the room, pointedly grilling students on basic questions and listening for weakness. The anticipation was torture for Xander.

It was just after Mr. Bascanard finished with the three-shirted boy from Xander's shop class whose name was apparently Daniel Calara. He sat two rows away.

Mr. Bascanard had said to Daniel: *"Ton accent est parfait. Très bon travail, Daniel."*

Mr. Bascanard then turned his watery eyes to Xander and said, *"Comment t'appelles-tu?"*

Language studies were for the most part simple memorization. So Xander could master the basics of grammar and spelling with ease. But making his mouth move the right way in order to pronounce the language correctly, that was another matter entirely.

"Je m'appelle Xander," he believed he said.

"'Je.' 'Je,' Ne dis pas, 'Juh.'"

"Juh."

"Je!"

"Je."

"Très bien. Prochain: Quel âge as-tu?"

"J'ai quatorze ans."

"'J'ai' 'J'ai,' Ne dis pas, 'Jay.'"

"'J'ai,'" Xander enunciated. Slowly.

"Très bien. Prochain: avais tu un parapluie?"

Xander could not help rolling his eyes. *When would this torture end?*

"Oui, j'ai un parapluie. En as-tu besoin?"

Mr. Bascanard smirked and said, "Ha!" Then, *"'J'ai' 'J'ai,' Ne dis pas, 'Jay.'"* He seemed about to move on to his next victim, but then he turned again to Xander and asked, *"Xander, dites moi: Combien de rayons sont sur le drapeau francais?"*

What? What kind of question was this? Something about the French flag. Xander had no idea what the teacher was saying, so he had no idea how to respond.

Out of the corner of his eye he saw Daniel. Daniel was looking at the teacher, but he had three fingers raised and wiggling.

"Trois!" Xander said. Of course. The stripes on the French flag. So simple! *"Trois!"*

"Très bien."

That afternoon, Xander was slowly making his way to Social Studies, stomping on every fourth square on the tiled floor and opening a Three Musketeers bar. As he took a bite he saw that Daniel fellow fumbling in his locker.

In all his score-and-2.5 years on the planet, Xander had never been rescued in a classroom situation the way Daniel had rescued him. Of course, he had never needed to be rescued before, but that was besides the point.

Xander approached Daniel and immediately took one more bite of the bar and then handed the rest to the three-shirted boy.

Daniel's eyes popped open. "Smiling, that boy was," Daniel said, "whistlin' Buck Owens."

As they walked down the hall to technical drawing class, Xander noticed that Daniel did not have a T-square sticking out of his backpack.

"Say, where is *ton* T-square?"

"There are things in life you just can't have."

"Hm, do you mean to say you don't have it? Did one of the troglodytes take it from you?"

Every freshman and sophomore at FTHS was required to take basic technical drawing classes, for which they were required to buy cheaply made wooden T-squares. These stuck out of whatever bookbag one carried, making it easy for the juniors and seniors to identify the lowerclassmen. Yelling "Frosh!," the upperclassmen would yank the T-squares away, out of bags, out of hands, and then smack the lowerclassmen on the heads or rear ends with their very own T-squares.

Xander had experienced this six times in three weeks already.

Usually the T-squares would be returned whole to the humiliated parties. But not always. Sometimes they were broken in half or tossed down the stairwell into oblivion.

Daniel never said why he didn't have his T-square, and in Drawing class, he was chastised by the teacher and given an inferior, crooked, chipped T-square. Xander watched as Daniel drew lines that varied five, ten and fifteen degrees from level. *Humiliating!*

The next day, Xander executed a plan.

He watched Wally Lau, a freshman, enter the bathroom. He counted to thirty. As he hoped, Wally was in the stall. Xander took the next stall and counted again to thirty. Then, stooping low, he peeked under the stall divider and, sure enough, there was a T-square hanging out of Lau's bookbag, which sat on the floor. Xander quickly yanked the T-square out and, yelling "Frosh!," walked briskly out of the bathroom. Wally protested, of course, but in his position, he certainly couldn't run after Xander.

This worked so well, Xander did it again, this time to a sophomore named Patrick Nelson. Xander knew his name because it was emblazoned on the T-square. It was one of the fancier, more expensive metal ones.

That afternoon, he presented Daniel with one of his new finds.

When Daniel took the wooden T-square, he said, "Johnny, roll your eyes once more!"

Xander didn't understand that at all. And he didn't bother to tell him from where it was procured, nor that he had taken Patrick Nelson's fancier T-square for himself.

BEGUILE

On the Monday of the fourth week of school, a cloud of epic poetry in her head, Holly was leaving English class and walking down the hallway when Tina suddenly popped up right in front of her. So much so that Holly almost dropped her books.

"Holly. I have been looking all over for you."

"You have?" Holly immediately felt suspicious and immediately felt bad about feeling that way.

"Did you just come from Mr. Baci's class?" Tina said.

Her friend seemed different, more subdued than usual.

"Yes," Holly said. "It's why I'm smiling. We were reciting discussing Beowulf to—"

"Mr. Baci is certainly an interesting person."

"Uh. Yes, yes, he is. He's really into his subject matter. You can tell he cares about it. That's a great quality in a teacher, don't you think?"

Holly took two steps toward the stairs, but she noticed Tina wasn't moving. *Why?* They both had to get to the same class in three minutes.

"Yes," Tina said. "But I would not mind if he cut his hair." She remained in the middle of the hallway. The exact middle. Students continued to walk around them, unstoppable ants on their way to class.

Suddenly, a boy appeared right beside them. *Black plastic-framed glasses, cloth tie, checked shirt, bumpy acne.* He kept his arms behind his back and stood like a soldier.

"Hello, Miss Hernandez."

"Hello," Holly said, not sure what was happening, because something seemed to be happening.

"Christina was telling me about you."

"Thank you, Tina," Holly said.

"'Christina.' Please, Holly," she said.

"Oh."

"This is Dharmesh Patel," Christina said.

"We think you would make a great part of the SOS squad," Dharmesh said. He had a rigid face that barely changed expression as he spoke. In fact, there was no expression in it, no lift of the eyebrows, barely any movement of the mouth.

"You mean the hall monitors who stand in the hallways?"

"Yes," he said, "we are the ones who make sure that everybody stays within the three squares and does not step out of three squares."

"My word. That sounds like it would be as easy as herding cats. In other words, *not*." Holly laughed, but she realized she was the only one laughing.

"It is important work. Sometimes we help with assembly or when students come in the building in the morning. We make sure that they walk in an orderly fashion. It is a very important job because there are over 3,000 students in the school, and we have to make sure that they get to and from class in orderly fashion."

"That sounds challenging. I'm not sure I'd have the time."

"It is challenging. But it is very important."

"What are the requirements? How do you turn into, I mean, how do you become a SOS member?"

"You must maintain a 95 average in order to be a SOS. If you go below that average, then you will be automatically ejected from the squad."

"So you must have some of the brightest students in the school."

Dharmesh's rigid face melted for a second, a hint of pride in the tiniest smile for a brief moment. "We do not like to brag," he said, "but, yes, yes, we are."

"Well, this is very sudden. I mean, I just started here. I don't even know what my average is going to be here."

"Christina has told me that you are a very good student."

"You're one of these SOSes, SOSsers?" Holly didn't know Christina that well at all, of course, but this SOS thing didn't seem to match up with the girl she had been having lunch with most days.

"Yes," Christina said, moving her sweater to reveal her own badge. "Since Friday afternoon."

Holly was glad that her new friend had spoken highly of her. But if she were going to join a club, it would be the literary magazine Mr. Baci had mentioned.

"Neat. Um, well, thank you for putting in a good word for me, Christina. I mean, I would love to join the club, but I'm still getting used to the school. Can I think about it?"

"If you need to," Christina said. "But please let us know right away. SOS looks very good on your resume. We are looking for new recruits all the time."

"Recruits, huh?" said Holly. She did not like the militaristic, cultish sound of the word. "I have to run to class. But I will let you know."

જી જી

Holly asked Victor to drive around Fort Greene Park slowly. The leaves on the trees were changing, igniting the parks into bursts of orange, red, yellow.

"I love autumn," she said.

"I know that. You told me yesterday and the day before."

"I'm sorry, Victor. It's a special time of year for me. You know?"

"I know."

"I should write a poem about it."

"You should."

Because the morning drive took a little longer than usual, Holly arrived late. Rushing to class, she saw Christina from behind, standing in the hallway. Her first instinct was to go say hi, but then she realized Christina might ask her again about the SOS squad. She had asked every other day that week.

She liked Christina, but she had decided that the SOS was not for her. She worried that if she didn't join, it might hurt any friendship they had.

She would talk to her, but later. She took the stairwell on the opposite side of the hall.

The rest of the day went well. The classes she looked forward to most were English and Social Studies. Holly liked her Social Studies teacher, Mr. Friedman, immediately on the first day of class. *5'10" and 170 pounds, tinted glasses, bushy beard, round head of curly hair.* Like Mr. Baci, he was passionate about his subject. And there was something about him that she could best describe as "groovy."

He had just finished talking to Daniel, the boy who wore several polo shirts and who always seemed to be scribbling something in a notebook.

"Right on, Daniel," Mr. Friedman said. "That's exactly what Franklin was getting at."

Mr. Friedman wore gray bell-bottom slacks, a brown pullover, enormous lapels and tinted glasses. He leaned, hands in his pockets, against his desk at the front of the room.

"Now imagine you're a colonist and everything is far out," he said. "By that I mean, you're in this place where you get to express your beliefs, without punishment, you know?"

Suddenly, Mr. Friedman pushed away from the desk and began moving through the aisles. He turned once, twice, in something that looked like a pirouette, and then stepped back and forth, one foot at a time, twice. "You have this dynamite new land of opportunity, where you can make your future. Then what brings it down is that the Man, and by the Man I mean the king, and he really starts to really stick it to you, tax you to the max, you know? What's his bag, man, am I right? And all of a sudden 'opportunity' doesn't seem very groovy because you might as well be living in feudal times."

"Today," he said, "we are going to discuss why and under what conditions the American colonists felt they could overthrow their corrupt governing system and establish a new one."

He clapped his hands, took two steps back, went up to the board and pivoted to face it. After writing an outline of the lessons, he pivoted, clapped again and took a step to the left and then a step to the right. Holly smiled.

"So," he said, "let me ask you this: What caused the increase in parliamentary legislation after the French and Indian War?"

Oh, Holly knew that one. She raised her hand up high.

12

ABJECT

Xander had begun to notice a disturbing trend. Holly had been answering almost every question and, of course, correctly. And, of course, she was fast becoming the teacher's pet in several classes.

This trend of Holly's answer-hogging continued in Social Studies with the dandelion-headed Mr. Friedman. Sitting in front of him (the trick of the alphabet again), she was hogging the teacher, as if this were her class alone. Xander could not stand that the teacher was so visibly impressed.

"I'm glad to see someone has done the reading," he said, clearly impatient with the rest of the class. He was hoping to goad them into his Socratic ideal of participation.

Xander did not want to bend to his will, but what incensed him even more was letting Holly get all the glory. He would break his own long-held rule against speaking *voluntarily* in class and show the foolish teacher that he too had done the reading.

Mr. Friedman loved to move up and down the aisles in a jittery, kinetic fashion, a step forward, a step back, a sudden move sideways. It was very unnerving. Xander preferred when teachers stayed put at the front of the class. *They should stay close to the blackboard,* he thought. *Everything beyond the desk is ours.*

Friedman was revving up to a question. He asked one every 2.3 minutes. Xander decided he would answer it. To deflate the teacher's impatient goading and to show Holly she was not the only one who understood the subtleties of American Social Studies. Xander was ready to pounce.

But Mr. Friedman was going on and on, swaying his hips, stepping back and forth. *Was there a question in the offing?* Xander was surprised at how hard his heart was beating in his chest. He felt knotted up, hot, flatulent. *What is taking so long?*

"So," Mr. Friedman finally said, "let me ask this. What philosopher stated that all individuals possessed certain 'natural rights,' such as 'life, liberty and the pursuit of property?'"

Hah, easy! Xander knew this one. His hand shot up, and Mr. Friedman, apparently shocked by the act, stood still. Then he nodded his cottony head toward Xander.

"JohnLocke," said Xander, pronouncing the two words as one in the nervous, stuttering half-whisper of some tiny creature. *What was that?* He had never sounded like that before in his life.

"Right on! Correct. . . . Xander, right?"

Hah! Yes!

Holly's hand had remained unlaunched, her shoulder hadn't even stirred.

There, now you see who knows what!

"So, what did Locke mean by that and why was it important to our country?" Mr. Friedman looked at him in anticipation.

Xander froze. His stomach churned. Sweat—actual sweat—began to pour down his face. He had never anticipated a follow-up question. He couldn't even remember the original question any more. And he didn't want to ask the teacher to repeat it, lest his voice sound again like a mouse squeak.

"Xander?"

Holly's hand was up. With an eyebrow lift as acknowledgment from Friedman (as if the two had already formed their own secret language), she said, "Locke was saying that it was the government's job to secure 'life, liberty and the pursuit of property' for its people. This idea was later adopted by Thomas Jefferson into the Declaration of Independence, although Jefferson used 'happiness' instead of 'property.'"

"Very good, Holly, very good, as always," said Friedman, as he rolled his fists one over the other and made his way back to the front of the class. "And you can say these ideas help justify the American Revolution. Without them, there would be no . . . "

Mr. Friedman went on and on. But Xander was lost now, lost in a swamp of his own sweat, buried deep under his chair, drowning on the other side of the universe.

13

PROFLIGATE

Little light filtered through the high, grimy, gated windows of metal shop. A series of fluorescent fixtures didn't help much. The room smelled of dust and oil and was filled with machinery that looked well worn, as did the shop teacher, Mr. Feeny. 5'9", *early 60s, habitual smoker (judging by the yellow on his fingers).* He was trying to hide both with hair dye and a sporty Van Dyke beard, which showed white at the edges.

Most of the students were gathered around Mr. Feeny. He was holding up Kerri Rivera's tool bit, which had snapped in half. He took out a new tool bit blank, a shiny, parallelepiped piece of steel and began to demonstrate how to use the grinding wheel to turn the blank into a perfect cutting tool for the lathe.

"Point the tool left at 30°, then angle the back end down 10°. You see? You see? Then start grinding until the new face touches both long sides of the work piece. . . ."

Holly took copious notes because she didn't feel she was doing well in this class at all. Apparently, not many of the students were. This was the fourth time Mr. Feeny had given this demonstration.

When he finished, he held up the bit. "Do not fall behind," he said. "You should have all had your own tool bits two weeks ago. Most of you should be up to the tool-and-dye sets, but only a couple of you have even started. How are you going to get the rest of the semester's projects done on time?"

Dejected but determined, Holly went back in line to use one of the grinding wheels. The machine whirred in front of her. She held her brand-new bit and hesitated. This would be her tenth try. She had turned several into nubs and one into a toothpick. She didn't want to have to return to the GO store for yet another ten bits.

Just as she moved forward, she saw movement from the back of the shop, an area darker than the rest of the room, filled with unused and unidentifiable machinery. It was that boy who called himself "Dragon." He had been taking this class, but on a very intermittent basis, it seemed. He hadn't been around the first week of school and just seemed to drift in and out of the other classes he had with Holly.

She watched him slink in, hugging the walls and staying in the shadows. When he caught her watching him, he bravely if foolishly walked across an open space of the shop to come over to her.

"Having trouble with the tool bit?" he said.

"Not at all. I was trying to remember what Mr. Feeny told us to do."

"Everyone screws up their first bits. Trust me, this is the third time I've taken this class. Here."

He took the brand-new bit from her fingers and put it in the lathe clamp. "Keep an eye out for Feeny."

"How did you get in?"

"An unused back door. Lock's been broken for years."

"You're not wearing your apron," Holly said. All the students were required to wear denim aprons that they personalized and kept on hooks at the front of class. The teacher had already yelled at one girl that day for not wearing hers.

"It's way over there on the other side of Feeny," Dragon said.

Holly noticed then that he was sweating, and though he seemed confident with the grinding wheel, he moved nervously.

She heard a metal ping.

"Damn," he said. "Broke it."

"Oh no."

"Don't worry. Just take one of these."

From his back pocket, he pulled out several perfectly shaped bits.

"I can't do that. I'm supposed to make my own."

"These were all made by students—last year—and they passed Feeny's inspection. If you don't have an approved bit, your whole semester gets fouled up."

"Thank you, but I want to be able to do it by myself."

"Don't be stupid. I—"

A very loud alarm cut him off.

KNELL

Xander had had enough of the Teutonic Mr. Kugler and his mindless craft. *Patternmaking!*

After spending weeks drawing the pattern of pawls, the class had moved to making pawl patterns out of wood. Some of the more advanced students, as if being advanced in Patternmaking was something to be proud of, had already completed the task, winning the shop teacher's meager approval, and moved on to doing patterns for T-square heads.

Alas, Xander lingered with the pawl. Time after time, Xander had handed over his crafted pawl, only to be assured by Kaiser Kugler, inspecting it with his woodworking ruler, that the angle of Xander's beveled edge was 42 or 46 or 45.3 degrees, but not the absolutely correct 45!

Why would any high school anywhere offer such a ridiculous class where such ridiculous accuracy was needed? Was he planning on being a carpenter? Or was the administration, aware that not all of them could be astronauts and engineers and physicists of renown, steering them toward unimaginative but dependable blue-collar careers? That would not do for Xander. He had higher ambitions. There would come a time when he would never work again with his hands. They would be soft as margarine, being used only to turn the pages of comic books and pulp novels, languidly.

In front of the standing drill, Daniel Calara also looked flummoxed. He sighed and said, "Gaze upon the shadow, find your true name."

"Yes, whatever that means," Xander said. He checked his watch, only to realize for the five hundredth time since that summer that it wasn't there. He pointed at his wrist to Daniel, who showed him his watch.

Thirty minutes of class time remained. A lifetime. Xander decided that a long, leisurely washing of those hands was due. Not to mention how frazzled his intestines felt since his defeat in Social Studies the day before. They could use some succor.

As Xander went to ask Mr. Kugler for the hall pass, Daniel said, "All the luck you've had, oh."

Xander shook his head in wonder, frustration and stupefaction.

In the bathroom, he immediately went into a stall, shut the door, and pulled a paperback out of his back pocket. He knew exactly how much time he wanted to take and knew how to time himself perfectly: he could read almost forty pages in twenty-five minutes.

When he was done, he took seven and a half minutes to wash his hands. He had no desire to rush back to class. He had no wish to decipher Daniel's inane aphorisms, or whatever they were. He would dawdle for another three minutes.

But then an alarm sounded. Very loud and very attention-getting.

A voice came on over the loudspeakers: "Attention. Attention. All students are to remain in their classrooms. Repeat, all students are to remain in their classrooms until further notice."

What was this? Trapped in classrooms? What was this about?

Xander had no qualms about remaining in place. But he was quite done and quite bored with the bathroom. He went to dry his hands but found the towel dispenser was empty. *By all that is holy!* He had no choice but to use toilet paper. *Double curses!*

The toilet paper stuck to his hands, and he attempted to flick and pick the wet papers off his fingers as he opened the bathroom door and walked slowly back to the classroom. He had to get this mush of paper off. *What would the other students think, the fools? What could they think?* The obvious conclusion would be that his hands were wet and that he needed to dry them! The toilet paper just by being toilet paper would be funny to them. No, he didn't want to help them laugh at him. He didn't want them to think about him at all.

He stood by a large garbage can in the hallway and removed the toilet paper piece by piece. As he took off one piece, sometimes another would stay. He pushed each piece he released into the swinging mouth of the garbage can. The third time he did this, he noticed something red on his fingers. The fourth time, he realized it was blood. He looked at his hands. No cuts? How could there possibly be? He looked at the garbage can. The flap he had been pushing open was smeared with blood. *Did some basketball jock get a nosebleed from living so close to the ceiling?* Now he would have to wash his hands again. He could only imagine what the students would say.

"Stop! Hold it right there! Don't move a muscle, pal."

He looked up and down the hall. Not ten feet away was a police officer with his gun drawn and pointed at him.

Xander's temporarily gratified intestines shivered again.

CONSENSUS

Minutes ago, Holly had been in metal shop, concentrating on not breaking her tool bit on a lathe. Then a security guard had walked briskly into the shop and, without even stopping to tell Mr. Feeny why he was there, walked up to her and said, "Holly, your mother wants to make sure you're safe."

Instantly, she knew what the loud alarms and the warning to stay in class had been for. In the hallway was a police officer she recognized, Wojciehowicz, and she knew that she was right.

"Hello, Wojo," she said. "What's going on?"

"Hey there, Holly. Your mom, uh, she just wants to make sure you're safe."

"From what?"

Wojo led her to another floor, and she could see police and security gathered in front of a teacher's office. He stopped her down the hall from the commotion.

"Just wait here," Wojo said. "Your mother'll be out in a minute."

Holly stood by herself in the hallway, watching the office doorway, trying to imagine what was happening. Since her mother was there, that meant a homicide had been committed. On school grounds.

People were rushing in and out of the office. There was Principal Schnitger in a daze. She clutched her stomach with one hand and covered her mouth with the other. The head of security was there, too (Licata was his name), complaining about the mess he would have to clean up.

This only intrigued Holly more. She took a step closer to the door. No one was paying attention to her.

Step by step, before she knew it, she was at the door. People pushed past her. And then she was inside the office. All too busy doing their jobs, no one bothered to ask why she was there.

At a desk at one end of a room, a body was slumped forward on the desk. The nameplate on the desk read: "Mr. Friedman." Her Social Studies teacher.

Holly looked at the body, focused on it. Then she looked around, concentrating on what was in the office, behind the desk, on the wall. Mr. Friedman had three degrees: Social Studies, English, Education. There were some trophies, one for bowling, one with the figure of a man and woman on top. He loved sports, but baseball in particular, it seemed, the Yankees even more particularly. He had a family, a wife, three daughters.

"Holly?" Her mother, who had been standing by the desk, grabbed her by the arm and pulled her into the hallway.

"Wojo! Where the hell is Wojo?"

Wojo ran over. "Sorry, Lieutenant."

"What the hell did I ask you to do? She shouldn't see that kind of stuff. She's just a child."

"He was killed from behind," Holly said. "By someone he knew. And it doesn't seem like robbery, if that's what you're thinking."

Holly's mother stopped talking and looked at her. "Holly, I'm sorry. I called you out of class in a panic. You shouldn't've seen that. Can I get you some water? Wojo, get her some water!"

"There's only fountains, boss."

"Find a cup!"

Holly said, "You can tell by the blood splatter all over the papers he was grading. His marker pen is still right next to his hand, by the way, so it happened fast."

"What are you talking about?"

"So if he let the person walk behind him, he probably knew him. And those trophies, I bet they could be sold for money, or drugs, so why are they still there? Does he still have his wallet?"

"Holly! Stop! Please. Let me do my job. I'll get you home. I mean, Victor will. Wojo!"

"But I still have class."

"This is more important."

"And you're going to take a long time, Mom. I know. It's okay. I don't mind staying."

"Wojo, go get Victor, her driver. He should be outside somewhere. Hop to it."

As Wojo ran off, Holly's mother looked at her as if she were a stranger. Holly felt a bit stunned herself, like the time she was hit in the face with the volleyball. It was her own fault. She had put her mother in an awkward position, having to protect her and carry out an investigation at the same time.

At that moment, two police officers walked up, holding a student tightly by the arms.

"Lieutenant. We got a live one," said one of the officers. His name was Yemana. Married last year, baby on the way.

The student was squirming—they were holding him tightly—but he didn't hang his head in shame. His head was up.

"Neanderthals!" the boy said.

It was Xander Herrera, the tall, grunting boy from her English, Math and Social Studies classes. The heavyset one with the thick glasses and the bad skin.

Officer Yemana held up a box cutter, using two fingers and a bloody handkerchief. "He was tossing this into a garbage can."

Xander looked scared, guilty. She noticed for the first time that he had braces. She looked down and saw his hands. They were stained with blood.

She didn't know why she had to say it, but she did. The words came out of her mouth before she could think again.

"That's him, Mom," Holly said. "He did it. He's your killer."

16

CALUMNY

Xander didn't understand. Why was he being manhandled? At first, he thought the police officer was trying to be helpful—unlikely as that sounded—thinking Xander had cut himself. But then he grabbed Xander's arm with a hand whose strength made Xander wonder if the man were bionic. Then another officer showed up out of nowhere—also possibly bionic—and Xander was picked up—in the air!— and taken into what looked like a teacher's office.

Standing at the door was the principal, and that caveman-in-loafers head of security for the school: Mr. Licata. And Holly Hernandez. What in the world was she doing here?

She was pointing at him. That was rude. It took him a second to register what she was saying. *Did what? Killed whom?*

It took him another few seconds to realize there was someone in the office slumped over at the desk. A body. A dead body.

"Is that Mr. Friedman?" Xander said. "Great Caesar's ghost, is he dead?" His voice was pitching high again. Was puberty suddenly regressing?

"Like you don't know," Mr. Licata said.

Xander felt them all staring at him. Then he understood. They thought he had killed Mr. Friedman, the peripatetic Social Studies teacher. Mr. Friedman, who was slumped there, no longer alive. There was blood all over his desk. A real corpse. A genuine dead body. Xander was not reacting the way he would have liked. He would have liked not to be struggling to withhold tears. He would have liked not to start breathing in sharp, asthmatic huffs.

A woman in a suit stepped up to him and identified herself as Detective Hernandez. She looked like a movie star version of a detective. Xander immediately disliked her because she made him feel like something small and filthy, floating in a toilet under her hawkish gaze. The woman turned to Principal Schnitger and said, "Is there a private place we can talk?"

The cyborg officers took him by the arms and led him out of the office. As they turned him, Holly took a step toward him. "Xander."

"Fie!" Xander said.

He knew who the originator of his situation was. He knew who had caused this humiliation. "I hate you," he said, not caring about the wheeze in his voice. "From the pit of my soul, I hate you."

They led him to an empty classroom and made him sit in the front row. The officer in the suit, Detective Hernandez (who, Xander quickly sussed out from their similar looks as well as their looks at each other, was Holly's mother), had told him to stay there and "Cool out" for a little while. A silent police officer was also ordered to remain with him. Apparently, one of his duties was to stare at Xander.

The bell rang for the final period of the day, and it felt odd not to be in class. Time passed. The officer continued to stare.

This would be quickly resolved, Xander believed. It had to be. He would be exonerated and he would be home in time for Abuela's pork chops.

Time passed.

Some time later, Detective Hernandez walked in. Behind her, quickly slipping in through the closing door like a germ getting past quarantine, was Licata. Why on Earth was Licata, a loathsome peon, allowed to be there?

"Listen, Xander, we just want to talk for a few minutes," the detective said, "see if you can clear some things up for us."

She handed Xander a handkerchief. Xander took it, wiped his face, blew his nose.

Licata knuckle-dragged himself to the chair next to Xander and squeezed his outsize body into it. He had a large red leather-bound book, with a rubber band as a bookmark.

"This one," Licata said, "this one I been watching. From day one. Day. One. He's a troublemaker. Always involved in some monkey business. Mr. Roger, the security chief over at his junior high school, he's a friend of mine, called me up to warn me, to tell me to watch out for this one." Licata opened his red book and tapped hard on the page. "Now, I have a witness says this one was the stinker who glued all the door locks on the third floor west on the first day of school. First. Day. We had to replace each and every one of those locks. You know how much that cost? Three. Thousand. Dollars. That's parts and manual labor. Three thousand dollars." Licata turned to look at Xander. "What do you say to that, huh, four eyes?"

Detective Hernandez interrupted this intellectual line of interrogation. "Mr., ah, what was your name again, sorry?"

"Licata. Frank Licata. Head of security. We just met, like, ten minutes ago."

"Thank you, Frank. Could I just speak with Mr. Herrera first? Could you maybe leave us alone for a minute?"

Licata's bulk slouched in his chair as if he found the entire world unjust and cruel. "I'm head of the security. Whatever goes on with security in this building is my business."

"I get you," Hernandez said, and then she turned to Xander. "I'm going to have to take you to the precinct, so we can talk there."

Where Mr. Licata is not the head of security. Xander understood.

"That's cute," Licata said. "Real cute."

"But I was just walking down the hall," Xander said. "This is ludicrous."

"'Ludicrous' it may be, but I'm afraid I have no choice," Detective Hernandez said. "What's your telephone number at home?"

"We don't have a telephone."

"What do you do in case of emergencies?"

"We don't have emergencies."

Licata laughed. "Sure looks like an emergency now."

"We'll send a car."

Xander struggled to speak. "My grandmother will be at home. But she doesn't speak English. My mother will be, *might* be home."

☙ ❧

The hallways were empty. He was led down the hall to the elevator, then outside and to a squad car. Xander was put in the backseat by himself. The officers in the front ignored him and talked about how they were surprised that pirates were able to beat some kind of bird. What a ridiculous discussion.

The police precinct building they pulled up to looked like a fortress, Romanesque Revival, a mix of red brick and brownstone, with arched windows and a central tower with an extra, narrower round tower rising from it for extra machismo. They took Xander to an office upstairs. Waiting for them was a detective in a stained, three-piece brown suit, stained brown tie and stained yellow shirt. His cheeks were the color of raw pork. Detective Hernandez introduced him as Detective McCluskey.

McCluskey ignored Xander and said to Holly's mom, "You're a sight for sore eyes, Merce. That's a fancy suit, but I guess the best looking cop in the precinct has to look the part."

"Sure. Thanks, McCluskey. I have to question Mr. Herrera."

"Why don't I take over? I got the gist of the case. Why don't you clock out? Your pretty face looks all in. I'll take over from here."

"That's okay. I can do it."

"And there's that pile of paperwork you need to get done sitting on your desk."

"But I thought you said . . . Sure, I'll get right to it."

Hernandez sat down across from Xander and looked him in the eyes, which made him uncomfortable. The glimpse he got of her face, besides the beauty, was that she looked bushed, beat. She sighed and told Xander he'd be in safe hands, not to worry. Then she got up and left him alone with McCluskey.

The detective lit a cigarette and didn't even look at Xander.

"You want?"

Xander said nothing.

"Good. Keep your lungs clean."

The door opened and Xander's grandmother was led in. Xander was elated to see her. But that meant his mother had not been home. Would his grandmother understand everything that was going on?

"Hoe-la, Seniora Herrera," Detective McCluskey said.

"Her last name is Perez," said Xander.

"Oh? Okay. Seniora Perez then. Grazias por . . . uh . . ." He looked uncomfortable and went back to the door and opened it. "Hernandez! Come back here!"

Someone somewhere yelled, "She took off."

McCluskey yelled back: "What about Rodriguez?

"Out sick!"

"Don't we have anyone that can speak Spanish?"

Someone else yelled, "No speeka de English," and there was laughter.

McCluskey turned back in, looking embarrassed. He stood between Xander and his grandmother.

"Sorry, kid, that was the extent of my Spanish. I'm afraid you're going to have to explain to your grandmother what's going on."

"Me?"

Finally, the detective sat down and Abuela looked at Xander, her big, glaucoma-ready eyes behind Coke-bottle glasses. She was short and broad and older than the mountains, but she was the strongest person in the galaxy, as far as Xander was concerned.

"Abuela," he said.

She said, *"Niño,"* and held him. Xander let go of the tears he had been holding back for hours.

"Your grandmother has waived your right to an attorney. Do you know what that means?"

"Of course. But she doesn't."

"Well, she's the adult, and she's in charge of you, so you're not an adult, so you don't get to be in charge. Okay, so let's get started."

Xander was overwhelmed. He had no experience with the criminal justice system and had never investigated it at length.

"Xander, you were caught red-handed. Literally, with the murder weapon, well, the *likely* murder weapon in your hand. We gotta wait for test results, but it don't look good. That's what I mean by red-handed. You see what I mean? Because there was blood on them. See what I mean? I'm talking to you, Xander. I'd like a response."

"I see what you mean. Clever. Blood is red. Red-handed. The very definition of clever."

"Don't sass me, son. I'm being nice. I don't have to be nice. I had a long day in court today, and I just had time to get home, take a nap, shower and get in here to help my partner Hernandez out."

"Thank you for showering."

"What is that? Is that sass? What did I just tell you about that?"

Xander looked at the ceiling.

"Jesus Christ," McCluskey said. "We know you didn't rob him. He still had his wallet on him, forty bucks on him. Teachers ain't known for being big rollers anyway. So that's not why you did it. But listen to this: A witness said that an hour before all this, Mr. Friedman humiliated you in front of the entire class."

"Holly Hernandez."

"Holly Hernandez, yes, and they don't come more reliable than that little girl. Now your record shows you have a history of delinquency. It shows you got a poor attitude, but I can see that for myself. It also says you're smart as a whip, and you were salutarian."

"Salutatorian."

"Yeah. That. In junior high."

"I should have been valedictorian. I was cheated."

"Is that so? Because this record says you were suspected of cheating several times but never caught."

"When people expect nothing of you, and you surprise them, they always doubt you."

"What is that, a fortune cookie? You're a smart kid, I'll give you that. So why don't you tell me what happened, son? I'm only here to help you out."

"The box cutter was already in the trash. I didn't put it there. Your evidence is circumstantial."

"C'mon, son. A man's head was almost taken clean off. There's enough suspicion on you to make you worth investigating. Why don't you tell me everything again? From the top."

McCluskey questioned Xander for four more hours. Then he got up and said, "We're going to take your grandmother home now. You're going to have the pleasure of being our guest overnight, son."

Xander's grandmother cried when he translated for her. She kept asking, "Why?" in Spanish over and over.

They took Xander back downstairs to a holding cell with two other teenagers. They were sleeping, but they still looked surly. They were sleeping in surlily. They both smelled like skunk. Directly adjacent were cells packed with adult males.

What humiliation. What degradation. But the lowest point had been having to explain to his grandmother what he was accused of and then what Miranda rights were. She had gone home, looking exhausted and deeply sad.

He bent over, putting his head between his legs, prepared to hyperventilate and dive into a deep bottomless pit of despair.

"Looks like fresh meat."

"He's going to pee his pants. Five dollars says he gonna pee his pants."

"You ain't got five dollars."

Xander looked up. The men in the next cell were looking and pointing at him.

"Not on me now, no."

"He's gonna cry. Look at his face. He's gonna cry."

Then, rising above the cacophony of the primitives, came a roar.

"Leave the kid alone!"

"What, is he your punk?"

"Hell, no, he's under my protection. Everybody back off."

Xander immediately recognized the speaker. It was the mugger who had taken his watch. His face was bruised, but he wore the same long coat and hat.

"Hey, kid, remember me? I remember you. You hard to forget. Don't let these fools bother you."

"They weren't."

"That's the spirit. What are you doing in here, kid? I thought I told you to stay out of trouble."

"Misfortune seems to be my burden."

"Nah, nah. You a good kid. I'm not going to let you get into any more trouble."

"Are you still in possession of my watch?"

"Watch? What watch? Oh! That one. That watch didn't work for nothing. What are you in for?"

"They say I dispatched my teacher."

"Dispatched? What, like to go pick up somebody?"

"Murdered."

"Murdered? Damn! She give you a bad grade or something?"

"No, no. Someone else did the deed, not me. They sliced his throat. My displaying that kind of violence is preposterous. That is not my modus operandi."

"Say what? Modus what?"

"Operandi. The way I would do things."

"You mean 'M. O.' Hah. Like you got an M. O. You know what, kid? I'm going to call you 'Jawbreaker.'"

"What?"

"On account of the way you talk. The stuff that comes out of your mouth makes my jaw hurt just thinking about saying it."

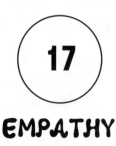

17

EMPATHY

There would be gossip at first, of course, theories about what was going on at school. And then when the news about Mr. Friedman's murder came out, the other students would wonder why she had been called out of class. *What was so special about her?*

Wojo walked her back to get her books. He was a decent cop and wore a decent toupee. He escorted her to the car, where Victor was waiting.

"I heard there was trouble," Victor said.

"There was trouble, all right. Horrible, sad trouble."

"Want to talk about it?"

"Not at the moment, if that's okay?"

"That's all right by me, Ms. Holly. I'll be right here if you want to talk. What do you kids say? If you want to *rap* about it. Right here, at the front of the car, so you know where to find me."

She didn't want to talk. When they got to the family's brownstone, Bandit was there to greet her at the door and followed her as she ran upstairs to her Palace of Solitude.

Being there usually made her feel better, but it wasn't doing any good that afternoon. She put on her favorite records, Janis Ian, Carole King, Gordon Lightfoot, Cat

Stevens, Harry Chapin, Joan Baez, but they couldn't cheer her up. Then she tried the Beatles and the Partridge Family and Tony Orlando and Dawn. Nothing. She tried concentrating on homework, but it didn't work. She couldn't get Xander and the murder off her mind.

Bandit put his head on her lap and whimpered.

"I'm such a creep," she told her faithful Doberman. "He looked scared . . . so scared. I'm so sorry I hurt him. I couldn't stop my stupid mouth, Bandit. With Mom there and all her men staring at me, I was trapped. I needed a way out of there. I needed time to think."

Holly looked up at the star maps on her ceiling and tapped her pencil against her knee. "Of course, I know Xander isn't the killer. Mom always tells me to follow my instincts, and my instincts say he's innocent. Just look at his face. Behind those Coke-bottle glasses and braces, there is shyness and kindness in that face, I'm sure of it. I've seen killers' eyes, you know, Bandit? I studied them at length! Xander just doesn't have those cold, blank eyes. Well, he could just be a near-sighted, shy killer. But, no, no, he's also very smart. At least two times, in English and Social Studies, I saw his graded papers in the teachers' hands before they were handed back to him: He gets As and A+s. No, Bandit, I don't think he would be dumb enough to kill someone in the middle of the day, when he had been recently embarrassed by the victim in class, when he had no alibi, and then be found in the hallway wiping his hands. And poor Mr. Friedman's death was messy. And Xander's clothes, while not spotless, had no bloodstains on them."

Bandit whimpered again, and Holly sighed. "Yes," she said, "it's pretty stingy evidence, isn't it? The criminal mind is not always logical."

She flipped over on the bed. "On the other hand, Xander had been badly embarrassed by Mr. Friedman. People have committed worse crimes for less." She knew that from her copies of *Crimes and Punishment: A Pictorial Encyclopedia of Aberrant Behavior.* "And he had been outside of his classroom for almost forty minutes. That's more than enough time to dispatch Mr. Friedman. His office was down the hall from the bathroom."

Bandit got up, moved in a circle and sat down to face Holly.

"My word," she said. "Why am I worried? Mom can solve this. *Is* going to solve this. She's probably solved it already. I bet some bad guy snuck into the school looking for money. That's the most likely possibility. Of course, that's it. I'll talk to Xander on Monday and apologize for being such a loser. Maybe I should bring him a gift or something, to show I'm sincere. Maybe he can forgive me. Maybe we could actually be friends. What kind of gift do you think he would like?"

Bandit cocked his head and whimpered.

Later, Holly lay half-asleep on her bed, one arm around Bandit and the other around Cha-Ka, the Pakuni Teddy Bear from Another Dimension. She heard her mother's car pull in the driveway. It was eight o'clock, much earlier than she usually got home. She hadn't been home this early in months.

Holly put on her pink robe and ran downstairs. Her mother was in the kitchen, still wearing her work clothes, looking in the refrigerator.

"Mom, what happened?"

"Well, it was a sad end to a long week, but I'm glad it's over with. I'm really sorry you saw what you saw." She pulled out some leftover food and sat down at the kitchen counter. She looked exhausted.

"Mr. Friedman still had his wallet on him, didn't he?"

"As a matter of fact, he did."

"So it likely wasn't robbery. I knew it! Mom, what happened to Xander? Is he okay now?"

"Let me think. He should still be over at the precinct unless. . . ."

"Oh no. Unless he didn't make bail?"

"Well, yes, sweetheart, it's a pretty serious crime, and his family has no money. I doubt he can make bail."

"So he's still at the jailhouse?"

With a mouth full of food, she looked at her watch and said, "Actually, since it's Friday night, and everything's pretty much shut down, they'll probably send him to Spofford for the weekend."

"Spofford? In the Bronx? Why? I thought you were just going to interrogate him at school. The evidence is circumstantial."

"Funny, that's what Xander said. I was going to question him at the school in a comfortable atmosphere. But it took a while to get to him, and then your school's head of security, Licata, he came in and started beating his chest like a gorilla. I didn't want him disrupting the interrogation. So I had to take Xander to the station. Then I remembered all this paperwork I had to do, so I let McCluskey take over."

"McCluskey! Not him." Holly felt a coldness running through her body. She thought she might become violently sick.

"McCluskey's . . . old-fashioned, but he's my senior."

"But why is Xander in prison?"

"He's not in *prison* prison. Spofford is a correctional facility for juvenile offenders. It's no Disneyland but it's not prison."

"Mom, I've read about that place. It's horrible. Why send him there?"

"He's a juvenile. And with the governor's new Crime Package Bill, juvenile offenders get it just as harsh as adults."

"But, Mom, what if I was wrong? What if he's not guilty at all?"

Finally, her mother stopped eating. "Holly, first of all, I don't like discussing this case with you. I don't want you to have nightmares. Second, while I was surprised when you said he was guilty, it's not why we had to question him. He's a solid suspect."

"But, it's clear that Xander didn't do it. Why would he kill Mr. Friedman, then go the bathroom, then go into the hallway to dump the box cutter? He's smart. He's too smart for that."

"We don't know that he went to the bathroom. He could have just been walking that way."

"There was toilet paper stuck to his left sneaker."

"Was there? I didn't see that. Listen, he could've got that some other time he went to the bathroom."

"That's a pretty stuck piece of toilet paper."

"Is that sarcasm, Holly? That is not what I need at the moment. And you'd be surprised how long toilet paper can stick to your shoe."

"Sorry, Mom. But he had no blood on him besides what was on his hand."

"Mr. Friedman was attacked from behind. So it's possible Xander didn't get too splattered. Or he cleaned up."

Holly found herself yelling: "But he wasn't wet! He didn't have time to dry!"

"Holly! You keep your voice down. There is nothing to be done until he confesses, the evidence clears him, or we find another suspect. But your friend is the only one with a clear motive. He's a bad egg, you know? I've seen his school rap sheet. Nothing major, but he has a long history of rubbing people the wrong way."

"You're convicting him already!"

"Holly, are you talking back to me?"

Holly couldn't quite tell what the look on her mother's face meant. Was it anger? Surprise? She had never seen that look on her face before. And then it suddenly softened.

"Okay," she said. "Tell me something: Is this Xander boy a friend of yours?"

"Yes . . . kind of . . . yes!"

"Listen, let me make a phone call."

Her mother went into the library and shut the door. Ten minutes later, she emerged.

Holly jumped up.

"Here's what I know," her mother said. "Your friend has been transferred to Spofford. There's nothing I can do about that. But I have a pal at the crime lab—you know Bart Fox. He's going to speed up the lab work on the box cutter. That's the best I can do, Holly."

Holly hugged her mother. "Thank you. I know I ask too much."

"No, baby, no. I'm just . . . I'm just glad I could do something for my super-smart daughter."

Her mother hugged her until she said it was time for her to work on her case files.

18

COGNOMINATE

What's going on? Xander thought, trying to parse the looks on the guards' faces. *Am I to be freed?* He didn't dare to hope.

Their bionic arms were taking Xander and the skunky teens out of the cell.

"We're finding you overnight accommodations some-where's else," one of the officers said.

At that moment, the man who mugged him, who had dubbed him "Jawbreaker" for no sane reason whatsoever, shouted at the guards. "Wait up, wait up, wait up," he said, pressing his face to the bars. "Let me say something to him."

One of the officers and the mugger exchanged extreme-ly vulgar language, but the matter was quickly settled, and the mugger was allowed to say his peace.

"Jawbreaker," he said, "they're gonna take you to Spof-ford."

"In the Bronx? Why would I ever want to go to the Bronx?"

"I know. It's a bad place, kid. A *mean* place. Listen. I can't go with you. But when you get there, soon as you can, you find my cousin Little Jesus. He's there now. Matter of fact, he's there most of the time."

"'Little Jesus?' You're joking."

"That's what they call him. Tell him Sammy Aviles sent you. That's me. Tell him. . . . Come closer, kid, I won't bite. . . ." Sammy whispered something to Xander. Then, in a normal voice, he said, "Jesusito will watch out for you. Take care, Jaw-breaker! *¡Vaya con Dios!*"

Xander and the two skunk boys were put in a van and driven up the expressway, through Queens, and across the Triborough Bridge. A large sign next to the highway read, "Welcome to the Bronx." Across those letters someone had spray-painted, "Burn Baby Burn."

This was the first time Xander had ever been to the Bronx. From all that he had heard and read, he was surprised that it was not engulfed in flames, steel girders melting, charred bodies decorating the landscape. Instead, it had buildings just like Brooklyn, and a lot more highways crisscrossing through them. He had never in his life had any desire to visit the Bronx, and now he was being forced to. He was sure the experience would be memorable and noteworthy and not in a good way.

The van stopped at a complex whose soullessness shocked Xander. It consisted of squat, white brick buildings surrounded by a fence with razor wire curled all along the top. It wasn't that it looked menacing. It was that it looked plain, municipal. Like a public school.

The inside of the place, however, felt very much like a prison. Guards, cells, CCTV. The smell of cigarettes and sweat and urine and dirty socks and other things Xander couldn't—and was sure he didn't want to—identify. And there were boys everywhere, some no more than blank-faced children, others well acquainted with shaving. They all looked bad. This was the worst of the worst, people he would walk across the street and around a block to avoid. And now he had been added to their mix. What did that say about him?

Xander was given a monastic-looking room with plain walls, the reek of urine, and a flat surface that he guessed was for sleeping. It looked more like a slab for a corpse. A brooding young man with a halo of orange hair sat on the other slab in the room.

The halo stared at Xander and said, "Look at this. Fresh fish."

Xander said nothing and sat down on the cot.

"Man, you is ugly. I gotta run tell everyone how ugly you is." The young man got up and left the cell.

Within seconds, boys came to the door and peeked in. Some walked by. Some lingered and stared. Some said mean things, stupid things, and words Xander couldn't understand. Then more and more of them lingered there, staring and taunting, until they filled the doorway and blocked any escape.

Was there no authority here? Was there no one who could cease this chaos?

Xander's roommate squeezed back in through the phalanx at the door and said, "Told you. I told you. He's way ugly. And he's a big fish, too."

They started chanting something that sounded like "Chin check," the meaning of which Xander was unable to fathom. He did, however, begin to understand that he was in danger.

He said, trying to conquer that nervous voice whisper that had been plaguing him of late, "I want to speak to Little Jesus."

"Little Jesus' all the way on the other side of the building," said his orange-headed roommate. "He can't help you, fish."

"Stand him up," someone said from the doorway.

"Stand him up and knock him down," someone else said.

"You hear that, fish? You better stand up or I'll make you stand," his roommate said.

"Hold up! Hold it up!" A very short and skinny teenager squeezed through the crush at the door. He said to the orange head, "Trey, we don't want to mess with Little Jesus. Not this week. This cat could be blood."

So his name was "Trey." Xander would still call him "Clyde" in his head.

"Damn," Trey/Clyde said. "I was all ready to go."

The short and skinny teenager grabbed Xander and pulled him up. "C'mon, fish. Get up."

Xander was walked out of the cell and down several halls and up a floor. Again, it seemed as though the guards were wax figures who were there only for decoration.

He was taken to a cell that was double the size of the others and had a console television set in the corner, as well as a full-sized refrigerator. There was a haze of smoke in the room and there was that skunky smell again.

A dark-haired teenager with a baby face and, incongruously, a bushy mustache, reclined on a recliner.

"Who you, fish?" he said.

"I am an acquaintance of your cousin, Sammy Aviles." Xander was happy the quake in his voice had settled. Perhaps he experienced such humiliation, had reached such low depths, that he had become acclimated.

"Sammy, huh? A lot of people know my cousin is Sammy. What are you trying to pull, bro?"

"Can we talk in private?"

There were about a dozen other people lined along the walls of the room. Some appeared to be sleeping.

"This is as private as it gets in here, bro," said the reclining teen.

"I need to tell you something, something Sammy said to tell you." Xander took a step forward, and the dozing figures in the room suddenly woke up and stepped in front of Little Jesus, standing like bowling pins.

"Say, man," he said, "clear a space. I can't even see the fish."

They stepped aside, and Little Jesus said, "Come here. Talk to me. If you try anything, you'll leave the room without your feet."

Xander thought this was an incredibly absurd yet shockingly original threat. He moved in closer and leaned over Little Jesus and quietly sang the theme song from *Scooby-Doo, Where Are You?*

Suddenly, Little Jesus jumped out of his recliner. "This cat is all right. He has our full protection. Everybody got that?"

Xander towered over him. Little Jesus was little.

"And we need to find him a new room. Marco, go find him a new room."

He turned to Xander. "What's your name, fish, so I don't have to keep calling you 'fish?'"

Xander was about to tell him his real name. But instead he said, "Jawbreaker. Your cousin called me 'Jawbreaker.'"

"Right on! Say, how do you know my cousin?"

"He mugged me."

"That's Sammy. He makes friends everywhere."

STUPENDOUS

On Sundays, Holly usually enjoyed sleeping late, buried under her blankets, lullabied by Bandit's vigorous snoring. Until the smell of Marta's cooking breakfast woke her up.

She had not been able to sleep well the past two nights, so she was awake when her mother knocked on her door at eight in the morning. Bandit immediately uncurled himself from the foot of her bed and jumped off.

"Holly?"

"Yes, Mom."

Her mother wore her at-home outfit, Holly's favorite outfit for her. Because the red velour pajama pants and old police academy T-shirt meant she wouldn't be going to work for the rest of the day.

"Good morning, sweetheart. I've got good news. Your friend Xander has been released."

"That's terrific! Did the lab tests clear him?"

"Yes, the blood on the box cutter doesn't match Mr. Friedman's blood. Whose blood and whose box cutter is a whole other mystery. In any case, Xander is free."

Holly jumped out of bed and hugged her mother. "Oh, this is wonderful. Wonderful!"

"Just remember to thank Bart at the lab next time you see him."

"Yes, Mom, of course. And thank you."

"I was just doing the right thing. That's the most important thing. Okay?"

"Okay, Mom. Thank you, again."

"But here's the thing," she said, putting on her serious face. "Some of those things you said, about the murderer being someone Friedman knew, about the . . . splatter. Those were pretty good guesses."

"Well, it wasn't so much a guess. It seemed obvious. He still had money in his wallet, right?"

"Right. But wait. Nothing's for certain yet. Thing is, I think it's best that I don't discuss this case with you anymore."

For some reason, Holly felt disappointed. "But why not?"

"Well, a few things. Xander is your friend, and that makes this personal. If it turns out he somehow is still involved, I don't want you to get upset. Do you understand, honey?"

She had more questions, but she could tell her mother felt bad and so she left it alone. "I understand."

When her mother closed the door, Holly danced around her room. She put on her stereo to listen to her old Bay City Rollers LP—the first she ever owned—because she felt like dancing.

Xander was free! Xander was free!

20

LIONIZE

Early that morning, the guards had come to Xander's cell.

"You're discharged," one of them said.

Xander turned slowly. He picked up his glasses and slowly cleaned them on his T-shirt. "Discharged? Do you mean to say I can leave this dungeon and go home?"

Xander didn't want to be transferred to some other prison, on some isolated island surrounded by sharks. He wanted them to clearly state what they meant.

"Yeah," the guard said. "Get your stuff."

Xander stretched and yawned. "What happened?"

"You've been cleared. That's all I know. C'mon, c'mon, get up already before I leave you here."

Xander smiled at him, showing off his braces. "I am moving as fast as I can to get out of here."

Out into the main hall, Xander walked, chin high, chest out, slowly toward the exit doors. As he walked toward them, he heard his name.

"Jawbreaker!" It was Little Jesus, waving from an upper tier. "Congratulations! See you on the outside, bro!"

Xander waved to him.

"Anytime you're back in my house," Little Jesus yelled, "you come see me."

"I don't plan to come back."

"That's what they all say."

As he turned, he heard Little Jesus begin a chant.

"Jawbreaker! Jawbreaker! Jawbreaker!"

First one, then another, then another voice joined in.

"Jawbreaker! Jawbreaker! Jawbreaker!"

The guard turned to him and said, "Looks like you made some friends."

Xander said, "That's me. I make friends everywhere."

ZEALOUS

Holly knew that her job was not finished, that she had more to do. Mr. Friedman had been a good teacher, and his death made no sense to her. Holly knew what her mother had been trying to say, that she shouldn't know about the investigation because it was personal, but Holly owed Xander a debt.

Her mother had hinted that Xander was still a suspect. He was the only one with motive and opportunity, so far. Mr. Friedman *had* humiliated him, and Xander had been out of the classroom. She would need to clear Xander's name for good. To do that, to solve this mystery, she would have to take on the role of detective. And she had to do it without asking her mother for help or her mother finding out. *What a pickle!*

"It looks like we're on the case, Bandit," she told her Doberman. He barked and sat up.

She went to her desk and from a drawer took out a brand new pink spiral bound notebook. Bandit took his usual sentry post on the floor beside her.

In the absence of any obvious suspects, her investigation would have to focus on the Social Studies teacher. She wrote down everything she knew about Mr. Friedman. Then she listed all the questions she could think of.

Wife and children?
Colleagues?
Friends?
Enemies?
Was he in any trouble? Financial? Personal? Professional?
Anything of value missing?
Knew his killer?
Stranger?

Also, security was "good not great" at the school. There were at least six entrances and not all of them were guarded. So, someone might've entered the building and escaped just as easily. She thought of Dragon sneaking around the hallways without a pass. She bet that he knew more than a little about ways to get around the school unnoticed. Maybe she would ask him about it.

And if Mr. Friedman did indeed know his killer, as the position of the body suggested, and that person had not snuck into the school, then that could mean the killer was on the staff or a teacher or even a student. Now, *that* would be interesting. But her instinct was telling her it was an adult. It was not scientific at all to rely on instinct, so she wouldn't dismiss the idea of a student killer. But she would first concentrate on looking at the adults.

She considered giving Xander a call. Then she remembered what her mother had mentioned about him: He didn't have a phone at home. She would have to see him at school tomorrow, and they would talk . . . because they would have something to talk about . . . and everything would be okay. She would solve the case, and *everything would be okay.*

22

PERTINACIOUS

When Xander came through the door of his apartment late that Sunday morning, his grandmother hugged him fiercely. She pulled him down to her bosom and wrapped her arm around his head in a move akin to a wrestler's, a warm and tender wrestler who smelled of *culantro* and garlic and powder.

His mother, watching them from where she sat in the kitchen, said, "Welcome home, Mr. Jailbird. Look at that. I guess it looks like you're no better than anybody else, huh? Blood is thicker than water."

She laughed to herself and kept on laughing for no reason for a while. Xander was happy to note that, because she had finished eating, she left quickly.

Xander's grandmother fixed him a heaping plate of rice and beans and pork chops and *maduros* and a big glass of milk. She said nothing to him while he ate. She sat next to him in silence and did her *mundillo*.

Afterward, he thanked her and then went to the basement, two flights down.

Xander had been playing down there ever since he was a little boy. It was dark, dank, dangerously crowded with spiders, none of which bothered him.

He liked to think of it as his base of operations, his lair, his Hall of Xander.

The ceiling was low and the walls were lined with shelves, boxes and broken appliances. Xander also stored paperbacks, comic books, old textbooks, family pictures. In one corner was a large iron desk that long ago must have been squeezed through the small basement door in the sidewalk in front of the building and down the concrete steps. Xander cleared off the surface of the desk and pulled a stool out from under it.

So, Holly Hernandez had humiliated him. She had had him imprisoned in a miserable hell for approximately thirty-six hours and forty-seven minutes. The police knew him now, plus the principal, the security chief and the teachers at the school would look at him differently. He would be treated differently, not ignored, as he preferred, but watched and studied. And judged. Like a science project. Like a petty criminal. Like an animal.

It was all her fault.

He would find a way to get back at her.

But how? Glue her locker closed. *Too easy.* Outsmart her in class. *Perhaps, perhaps.*

It was then that he had a eureka moment: *If he could find the true killer of Mr. Friedman, he would not only clear his own name, but also make Holly Hernandez look like a fool.*

He would begin plotting his investigation immediately, that is . . . after checking to see if Abuela had one more pork chop.

෨ ෩

On the bus to school the next morning, Xander looked again at the new section of his loose-leaf binder he had made the night before. He had written down all that he knew and all that he had observed about Mr. Friedman.

At Flatbush Tech, walking among his fellow students, Xander made sure to look closely at every face, to see if any face screamed, "Killer!" The suspect could be anyone in the building, of course. Or, perhaps a stranger who had broken in. But this seemed unlikely to Xander. The police had immediately focused on him as a suspect. If they had suspected or heard of a break-in, that would not have been the case. The murderer could of course be a staff member, a janitor or even a security guard. That too was unlikely. What would be the motive? Why would a teacher mix with the staff? He wouldn't. So why would one of them want to kill him? Xander eliminated staff, but if he ran out of suspects, he would come back to them.

It could also be another teacher. Xander thought this unlikely as well. They were all weak-limbed intellectuals. They had no passion or violence in them. They were concerned only with their reputations, their salaries, the next day's lesson plan, the piles of papers on their desks. He would only come back to them once he had combed through his main suspect pool: The students.

Xander knew that a student was perfectly capable of committing such a horrific crime. After what he had witnessed at Spofford, he knew youth was no barrier to violence. In them was the passion, in them was the violence. Only a student would have the nerve to undo a teacher.

What could the motive be?

It hadn't been money. During his inquisition, Detective McCluskey had said, "At least you're not a thief. He still had his wallet and money on him." So the murderer was not a mugger.

Mr. Friedman did have a nasty habit of calling on students who did not want to be called on. And of asking annoying follow-up questions. Was that enough? Perhaps, for some psychopath of a student. There were none in his class. He needed a wider pool. He would have to get a list of all of Friedman's students, present and past. But how?

There was someone speaking behind him. He turned and saw it was Daniel.

"He told me I'd never, ever need fear."

"What?"

"That this valuable tree would always be here."

Xander became confounded. He began, "I . . ." and then realized his train of thought had been interrupted and said nothing.

They proceeded to class, passing by Mr. Friedman's office. Its door was closed, probably locked. Xander looked at Daniel, and another brilliant idea occurred to him.

23

ALACRITY

"Well, you look like the cat that got the mouse," Victor said, watching Holly in the rearview mirror.

"I'm not sure that's the way that expression works, but I'll take it."

"You're smiling. Things must be going good."

"They are. I have a mission. A goal. A case!"

"Uh oh. Should I ask?"

"Not yet. But I do have a favor to ask of you, Victor."

"What's that, Ms. Holly?"

"Please don't wait for me all day here. When I'm in class, I think about you out here, working on the crossword all day. Aren't there things you'd rather be doing?"

"Your mother wants me here to wait for you. And that's what I do."

"Don't you have any hobbies? What would you be doing if you didn't have to be here?"

"I can't say."

"C'mon."

"I really shouldn't say."

"C'mon, Victor, I won't tell."

"Well, okay. I'd be at the racetrack, playing the ponies."

"Ooh, I've never been to the racetrack. If I didn't have important things to do, I'd say we should go! It would be fascinating!"

"Ms. Holly!"

Just after homeroom, Holly saw Xander stomping down the hall. He walked quickly, past all the other students and, she noticed, he was going out of his way to step in the four-square lane. His body leaned forward slightly and he kept his head slightly forward as well. He was headed right toward her. She wanted to say something to him. She needed to apologize.

Holly stopped directly in his path and waited, but Xander walked around her without even acknowledging her existence. She turned and watched as he continued to stalk down the hall. What could she have said, anyway? What would have made what she did all right?

Well, she had to do something. She had to show him somehow that she was sorry.

She was more determined than ever to prove he was innocent.

Holly ran up the stairs to gym class. She changed quickly into her blue uniform and joined the girls on the crowded floor. Soon, a cacophony of rubber soles squeaking on maple filled the space.

Holly was playing volleyball again and had just returned a ball, bouncing it off her forearms, when the image of Mr. Friedman's office popped back into her head. She saw the whole scene again. Just then, she heard a rush of air and then a loud smack and a hollow ring.

One of the girls helped her up and said, "Wow, you really need a lookout."

"Pardon?"

It was Brandy Vega. She and her hair towered over Holly. "Your head's always in the clouds?" she said as she tossed the volleyball she was holding back to one of the players.

"Kind of," Holly said. "Thanks for that."

"You're in my shop class," Brandy said.

"Yes, and Math and Social Studies."

"Shop is my worst class. I have no idea what I'm doing." Holly smiled. "That makes two of us."

"I wanted to ask you. . . . Your mother is a detective, right? I love police. I watch all the cop shows."

"Oh, so do I."

"Is she going to find out who offed Mr. Friedman?"

"Um, yes. But—"

"I knew it!" Brandy turned and called out, "Sharona! Sharona! Sharona!" Then she led Holly to a corner of the gym, where the two other girls from the locker room were not doing anything athletic whatsoever. The coaches usually made any idle girls move, but Holly had noticed that Coach DiGeronimo and Assistant Coach Gorney often let these girls be.

"What? What? What?" said a girl with bobbed hair.

"Wait . . . " Holly said.

"Holly, this is Sharona."

She was boyish. *Olive skinned. Hazel eyes. Contact lenses.* "Hi," Holly said.

"Her mother is the detective," Brandy said. "Told you."

"I saw her on the news. It's so cool she's a detective. Does she have a gun? Of course, she has a gun, right?"

"Hi," the third girl said. "I'm Beth." *African-American. Freckles. Round face.* "I see your nose is still on."

"Yeah," Holly said.

"Can you tell us more about the case? We're all fascinated. A murder, right here in our school. It's the most interesting thing that's happened all year."

"I can't. I shouldn't."

Brandy said, "Does your mom know about Coach DiGeronimo having a fight with Mr. Friedman? I bet she didn't know."

Holly's eyebrows flew up. "Actually, I don't know if she knows that. When was this?"

"About two weeks ago," Sharona said. "It was in the hallway. Was it the first floor? Had to be the first floor, duh."

"It was right before homeroom."

Brandy shook her head. "It was right after homeroom, right by the trophy case in the entrance. We was thinking about sneaking out for a smoke, and there she was in her *I Love Lucy* hair yelling, and he was yelling back. They didn't care who was watching."

"Did you hear what it was about?" Holly said.

"I wasn't that close. Sorry."

"It was about money. Wasn't it about money?"

"Personal money?" Holly said. "School money?"

Brandy said, "The coach said something like, 'torpedoed my budget.' Something like that. Budget was definitely part of it."

"What did Mr. Friedman say?"

"He was saying 'Sorry' a lot, right?" Sharona said. "Yeah. 'Sorry. Sorry. Sorry.' He was very apologetic."

"So she was the one showing the anger?" Holly said.

"Not just her," Beth said. "After a while he got mad, too."

"Did they get into an altercation, you know, a physical fight?"

"If you call a lot of finger-wagging 'an altercation,'" Brandy said, wagging her finger.

"My word. You're right. That could still be something. I'll have, uh, I mean, my mother will have to check it out."

"So, does your mother carry a gun?"

"Does she have a badge? She must have a badge."

Holly felt a presence and turned to find Assistant Coach Gorney standing cross-armed behind her. "Hernandez, what is this, a coffee klatch? All right, all you girls, let's go. Gym is not the time to exercise your mouths." She clapped her hands loudly at them as they dispersed. "Let's go!"

Brandy and her girls mumbled, "Okay."

Holly rejoined the volleyball game. She played as best as she could, but in her mind spun the words "torpedoed my budget."

24

DISCOMFIT

On his Saturday afternoon in Spofford, Xander had won thirty packs of cigarettes playing acey-deucey with Little Jesus' gang. One of them, Sifredo, wanted to earn some of the cigarettes back, especially since Xander said he wasn't going to smoke any of them.

(He had smoked a cigarette *once*—half a puff—and threw up an exquisite dinner of fried chicken and mashed potatoes and French fries. *Never again!*)

"During the game, you said you were here because of breaking and entering," Xander said.

"That's right. So?"

"I want you to teach me how to pick a lock."

"Seriously?"

"Is five packs serious enough?"

"I'll be right back."

It turned out Sifredo had a large notebook filled mostly with crude graffiti, but in between the endless parade of tags and exaggerated body parts were detailed drawings of locks and step-by-step instructions.

"I was planning on writing a textbook," Sifredo said.

"They could use you at Flatbush Tech. It is a technical skill, after all."

Crouched in front of Mr. Friedman's office while Daniel stood watch, Xander recalled what Sifredo had taught him.

The lock was a standard five-pin tumbler lock, an old one, but the keyhole and springs were in good shape. So no one had busted into this office to kill Mr. Friedman. They either had a key, were invited in or they did the same thing Xander was doing.

Using a homemade pick and tension wrench (read: bent paper clips), Xander worked to determine the correct amount of torque needed to open the lock.

As Sifredo had said, "It takes some kind of feel. And more than a little bit of natural talent."

Sweat dripped down Xander's face. It was taking longer than he had predicted. He glanced at Daniel, who looked more nervous than he felt.

Daniel stood in the middle of the hallway behind Xander. He wore two white polo shirts, two T-shirts and a bright orange clip-on tie. On his chest was an SOS badge.

Xander had convinced Daniel to join the SOS. It was, Xander had surmised, the best way to not get caught, to have a lookout cover, to have a partner of sorts, while he accessed Mr. Friedman's office. It was a good thing the initiation period was so quick and they didn't ask for much. Apparently, Daniel's grades were very good. *Who would have guessed?*

Finally, the tumblers clicked and the door opened. Xander signaled to Daniel that he was in and then closed the door behind him.

Autumn rain clicked against the chicken-wire windows.

There were three desks, several file cabinets, two bookcases stuffed with papers, clothes, boxes. Xander went to the desk with Mr. Friedman's nameplate on it. The desk blotter was missing. No doubt it had gotten stained with

Mr. Friedman's blood and had been removed. Xander checked the desk drawers and found sneakers, a sweatshirt, a towel in one drawer. In the other, more pencils and pens than anyone could use in a lifetime. In another, he found what he was looking for: a Delaney book.

The worn book was stuffed with notes and memos. It seemed to go back three, four, five years. Each page spread covered a class Friedman had taught, each student denoted by a small Delaney card, a Lilliputian encyclopedia of student information. Friedman had made each student write down his or her name, homeroom, address and parent's first name. The cards were arranged to correspond to where each student sat. On the back of each card was a tiny calendar with slashes over dates to indicate absences. On the front, under the addresses and test and homework grades, Friedman had used several grade boxes for notes about each student. "Hopeless." "Bright." "Lice?" "Trouble."

Seeing this, Xander quickly looked for his card. In Friedman's obnoxiously neat scrawl it said, "Potential."

Xander then peeked at Holly Hernandez's. It said, "A jewel."

Xander harrumphed and squeezed the Delaney book in between the paperbacks and large college-ruled notebook in his briefcase. As he did, he spotted a date book resting under it. He decided to take that as well.

When he went to the door, he heard voices. He lay himself down and peeked under the door. He recognized Daniel's blue Pumas. He also saw two other sets of feet there, both in shoes. Not security. Teachers?

Xander strained to listen to the conversation.

" . . . you doing here . . . should be in class . . . "

Young voices. Robot-like. As Xander predicted, a member of the SOS, the school's Nazi Youth, had come to check on Daniel and, as Xander had hoped, Daniel was keeping them at bay.

He could hear Daniel stuttering, trying to reply. " . . . He wants to eat your brains . . . "

"What do you mean? I do not want to eat your brains. I just think you should get to class. This is not your shift. As a SOS officer, you must . . . "

If they caught Xander in the office, he would get in very big trouble. Expulsion. Even arrest for breaking and entering. Even worse, it might give the police a reason to suspect him again. He couldn't let them catch him. But he couldn't exactly fly out of the window.

His fate was entirely in Daniel's hands.

"He wants to eat your friends. . . ," he heard Daniel say.

"I do not know what you mean. Please get back to your designated floor for this period before . . . "

Xander watched Daniel's feet turn and move away. The SOS drones followed him. *Good! The coast was clear.*

Xander quickly opened the door and scooted out of the office. He had leads he could follow, a Delaney book full of suspects.

He now had what he needed to get his revenge on Holly Hernandez.

25

GARRULOUS

When the bell rang, the rest of the students in Holly's homeroom class rushed out in a frenzy of talking, giggling, shrieking. Holly stayed behind in the now eerily quiet room. Quiet except for Mr. Albertson, her homeroom teacher, busy stacking together papers on his desk. *Early 60s and gray-white furry beard, wild white hair.* He wore the same baggy, wrinkled, stained white shirt and baggy, wrinkled, stained black pants every day. He always seemed preoccupied, so much so that Holly felt bad about bothering him. But he was the best place to start.

"Mr. Albertson, I have a question."

"What is it, my dear?" he said, not looking up, shoving papers into his briefcase and then sighing and slowly taking them out again to search for something.

"I know you're busy, so please pardon my intrusion," she said.

"No need, no need. A teacher's work is never done, young lady." He looked through the papers and pulled out several sheets. "Never done."

"I think I understand, Mr. Albertson. So, I'm working on an essay about a high school's organization and operations."

He didn't look up. "For which class?"

"English."

"English?" he said, his head bent down almost in his desk drawer, searching for something. "That's an unusual topic for English."

"That's exactly why I picked it. And I know that teachers at schools like this one are put on committees."

"Well, they ask us, and some of us do it. Some of us don't, since we don't get paid extra . . . and anyway, we're too busy tutoring students after hours and on weekends in order to pay rent."

"That's too bad. Teachers should definitely be paid extra for their time."

"You don't have to convince me." He had finished going through all the drawers on one side of his desk and was now going through the other.

"Is there a finance committee that makes that decision, not to pay the teachers, I mean."

"No, that's not what they do." He had begun looking through his own pockets. "It has to do with the union and the city, my dear. It's very complicated."

"Who chairs the school's finance committee? Does it change from year to year?"

Mr. Albertson pulled out a new piece of chalk from the suit jacket he had draped over his chair. He held it up and looked at it as if was a priceless artifact, an ivory idol. "Mr. Weinberg, the Economics teachers, he chairs that committee every year. He loves it." Mr. Albertson stopped. He turned from the chalk and looked directly at Holly. "Why do you want to know this again? Who's your English teacher?"

"Is that what you were looking for?" she said. "Chalk? But there's a lot of chalk on the board behind you."

"I'm aware of that, my dear, but those are broken and stunted. They are not brand new and unbroken like this one. For teachers, it is a *rara avis,* such a piece of chalk, not something to be taken for granted."

"Oh, I better get to class before I'm late. Thank you, Mr. Albertson."

"Of course, of course, my dear. Good luck with your book report!"

Mr. Weinberg was willing to talk for a few minutes after class. *5'7", mid-fifties. Gray and black curls like a tossed salad. Yellow, button-down shirt, bow tie. Slight limp in left leg. Possibly a veteran.*

"I have a tuna sandwich that I'm not particularly anxious to get to," he said. "What's your question, Holly?"

"Thank you, Mr. Weinberg. I'm very curious about economics."

He looked very surprised, and happily so. "Are you really?"

"Especially as they pertain to education."

Weinberg laughed. "That's very funny. It always seems as if educational institutions have no budgets."

"Even Flatbush Tech?"

"Even Flatbush Tech. Don't feel bad. It's still a great school. But its best days are behind it. I fear what the future is going to bring."

"Is it because of money?"

"More than that. But it all comes down to money. It seems that when politicians are trying to balance budgets, the first thing they cut is education. The country will pay the price for it in the long run, you mark my words. Sorry. I'm lecturing. Old teacher's habit. Did you have a particular question?"

Holly smiled. She liked Mr. Weinberg. He found a way to take a subject that wasn't very exciting and teach it in a fascinating way. "I was wondering how money is apportioned among the departments. Is that all determined by the principal?"

"Hardly. There are committees set up to handle that, to make sure all departments are treated fairly."

"Who sits on these committees?"

"Ahhh, well, yes, the main finance committee is chaired by the vice principal and manned by the head of each department."

"Are all of them men?"

"Well, no. Actually, now that you say that. They are. Except for Phys Ed. That's co-chaired by Mr. Jacobetti and Coach DiGeronimo."

"Everything is decided by committee?"

"Ahhh, yes, with the vice principal as the deciding vote if there's a tie."

"So the vice principal has a lot of power?"

"Well, yes and no. Sometimes the group agrees and a lot of times it doesn't, but ties are rare. For example, just last year Mr. Berger was out sick for a few months, so Mr. Friedman was put in charge and. . . . Wait a second. You're not really interested in economics at all, are you, Holly?"

Holly gave him her best innocent smile. "I am. But now that you mention it, was there any trouble in last year's committee? The one run by Mr. Friedman? I heard some people weren't happy with the cuts."

Mr. Weinberg smiled at her. "There's always trouble. There are always cuts. But more than that, I can't tell you."

"Even if it could help find Mr. Friedman's killer?"

"Aha! I was wondering what you were really up to."

Holly shrugged and smiled shyly.

"So you think a teacher is responsible? Uh . . . I was going to say that was crazy, but I've met a lot more teachers than you have, and now I'm thinking maybe it's not so crazy. Anyway, I thought that kid did it. The one with the thick glasses and the bad attitude."

"Xander Herrera is innocent. He was cleared this weekend."

"Was he?"

"There's still a killer on the loose, Mr. Weinberg."

"That's awful. And scary."

"Can you tell me anything else about the people on the committee? How do they get along?"

"As much as I'd like to avoid that tuna sandwich for as long as possible, I'm afraid I can't, and shouldn't, say anything else."

26

PARIAH

The school cafeteria's food was execrable but adequate. It was often overcooked, underflavored, unidentifiable. Because of Xander's family's income, he was eligible for free lunch and thus was given a packet of tickets to get his meals. For the first weeks, he had been happy to let the Tech chefs' lukewarm and greasy vittles sate his hunger. Then he decided that the lunchroom, a den of noise and social interaction and cologne, made even that meager repast unsavory. So he had taken to selling each ticket to Daniel for a dollar and spending his time in the library. Besides, this left room in his belly for his grandmother's far superior cooking.

The Flatbush Tech library was a huge room lined with deep wooden bookshelves.

Xander took his favorite seat, far in the back of the room, and got out his notebook and Mr. Friedman's Delaney book. Keeping careful watch for the one librarian the school had, he made notes of every student who had been given low grades in Social Studies. Of course, there could be some, like him, who were offended by grades in the 80s. They would be his second wave of inquiry. For now, he would concentrate on the poorest performers.

There were more than fifty, quite a number. Although, overall, Mr. Friedman seemed like a fair grader. There were plenty of 95s along with 85s and 75s, and only a few 65s. Xander would start with those.

He made a list of their names and addresses. Meanwhile, his stomach growled. He ignored it.

He put the Delaney book away and took out the date book. It contained little useful information. Meetings—and there were a lot of them—were marked simply as "Meeting, 3 pm" and the like. That was no help, and Xander pitied the man for having to sit in one meeting after another. It sounded like hellish drudgery. There were some birthdays, a dentist's appointment, not much else.

"Arranging your calendar?"

Xander looked up. Mr. Gladstone, the librarian, stood next to him. He had a bushy mustache and an addiction to sweater vests. How had he snuck up on Xander so quietly? *Was the man secretly a ninja?*

Xander mumbled.

"What was that?"

"I said, 'Yes, I am.'"

"That's a very nice date book."

"A present."

"Very nice."

"Did you finish that *Frankenstein* paperback?"

"Yes."

"I haven't seen it back on our shelves. That's a special copy you have."

"Yes."

"Please return it before it's due. Late fees, you know."

"Yes."

"Very well. I'll leave you to it."

Xander resisted harrumphing and turned to the next page of the book. At the top of the page it read, "Talk to Steve" and "4 p.m." It was dated two weeks before the murder. It wasn't much to go on, but it stood out from all the other entries. It had to have some significance.

He leafed through the book and found two other references to this Steve. "Lunch—Steve" on April 28 of that year. And then the same on June 1.

Xander drummed his fingers on the table until he heard Mr. Gladstone clear his throat. Fine. He was about to begin his math homework, when he decided to cross-reference his first list to search for this "Steve."

It took just a few minutes. There were seventeen Steves. Who knew Steve was such a popular name! Xander looked closer and found that three of them were in Mr. Friedman's class the previous semester, in the spring, and had done badly or failed. And one was in that semester and also in the present semester. He had failed (53! F!) and was retaking the class. His attendance this semester had been shoddy.

Xander made a list of their names on a new page, putting a star next to the repeater. His stomach growled again. He ignored it.

He smiled when the bell for the next class sounded. The hunt was on.

27

EXACERBATE

There was a strong smell of dirty socks. Mixed in were the smells of damp towels, stale sweat (like boiled potatoes), floor cleaner. Holly knocked on the open door of the Girls' Gym office. On the wall were several posters of female athletes and one on correct posture.

After talking to Mr. Weinberg, Holly felt she had no choice but to talk to Coach DiGeronimo face to face.

Sitting at the front desk was Assistant Coach Gorney. She was drinking tea from a black mug with the name "STEPHANIE" on it, and she appeared to be totaling up something with one of those fancy thin calculators. Her ponytail bounced as she punched the buttons on the calculator like they had insulted her.

Holly said, "Uh, hello! I'm here to see Coach DiGeronimo."

"What do you want?"

"I need to talk to the coach."

"You can talk to me. I'm the assistant coach."

"I know that."

"Oh, do you?"

"But it's for a class. And I need to talk to the head coach. I'm doing a report."

"What difference does it make? We do the same thing. She's just been here longer than I have, that's all. What class is it for?"

"Social Studies. I'm very fascinated by the world of sports and would love to know more about athletics and maybe even be a gym teacher one day."

"That's funny. You don't even like playing volleyball, and everybody likes to play volleyball. It's the easiest game in the world."

"I like volleyball," Holly said. "I'm just not very good at it. Is Coach DiGeronimo not in?"

"She's in the can. The ladies' room. Who knows how long she's going to be? Why don't you ask me your questions? I know all about sports and athletic careers. Just make it fast. I have about five minutes before I gotta hit the head myself."

"Oh. Well, um . . . "

Just then, someone tall gently nudged Holly out of the doorway. Coach DiGeronimo.

"Holly, right?" the coach said, looking down at her. She had the healthy glow of an athlete, or it could have been her make-up. It made her smile seem welcoming and genuinely friendly.

"Yeah," said the assistant coach. "This girl says she wants to interview you about sports and athletic careers for her Social Studies class. I told her she could interview me, but I guess I'm not good enough for her."

"It's not that," Holly said. "I just thought it would be best if I talk to the *head* coach."

"That's okay, Holly," Coach DiGeronimo said. "Why don't we go into my office?"

Holly followed her into an inner office. The assistant coach, Stephanie, went back to assaulting the calculator.

Once inside, Holly said, "Actually, this is pretty personal. Do you mind if we close the door?"

"Oh, now I get it," the coach said. She got up and closed the door and then pulled some pamphlets from a file cabinet and laid them on the desk like playing cards. "So what is it? Problem with a boy? Hygiene?" She picked up one of the pamphlets, titled "Sex and the New You," and aimed it at Holly.

"No, no, nothing like that," Holly said. "I'll be honest with you and get to the point. I wanted to find out why you were arguing with Mr. Friedman about the budget in the hallway. A lot of people saw you."

Coach DiGeronimo's smile stayed friendly for a few more seconds. But then she cocked her head to the side, and her face lost any emotion. "So, what is this? You're playing policewoman here? Is that what you're doing? Curiosity killed the cat."

"But satisfaction brought it back," said Holly, completing the quote.

At this, Coach DiGeronimo smiled again. "So what is this all about?"

"I'll be honest with you. A friend of mine was accused of the crime. I want to clear his name and find out the truth."

"Now that makes sense. Sort of. But I appreciate your honesty, young lady. Not that you have any right to know my business. Just to satisfy your curiosity, Mr. Friedman and I argued all the time. We were like brother and sister. Loved each other and hated each other. So while we weren't acting exactly like adults that morning in the hallway, that afternoon we acted like mature adults and apologized to each other over cheesecake at Junior's. That's what colleagues do when they decide to let bygones be bygones. He even went back to the committee and came up with a compromise that allowed me to finally buy a new volleyball net, the same one you've been playing with this term."

"So you have no motive for . . . wanting to see him harmed?"

"Geez, no! I loved Mr. Friedman as a friend and a colleague. He was a decent and honorable man, and he was alive, you know what I mean? Alive in a way a lot of people never get to be."

"I think I understand."

"I don't think you do, but one day you will. And not that I need to tell you, but I was out that day at a meet with the track team. We won. You can certainly check that. If that is all, Holly, thank you very much for stopping by and please make sure to participate more in gym class."

Holly got up. She felt shameful and silly. But as she turned to go, she found she had one more question. "Coach DiGeronimo, what do you think happened to him? Why would someone kill him?"

The coach looked sad suddenly. Then she said, "I don't know, Holly. He was a good guy. I have to tell you, this isn't the safest school. This place is going downhill. The week before school started, someone attacked the guidance counselor in her own office."

"I didn't know that."

"Don't spread it around. You watch out for yourself, okay?"

28

PAUCITY

Xander went alone to the payphone in the main lobby. He had been wondering what a "Steve Christakos" would look like. Names were such odd things, and in Brooklyn they were even odder. "Steve Christakos" seemed Greek in origin, but he could be Polish or Asian or Puerto Rican or Indian or Irish or Italian or Martian.

Martian! Wouldn't that be fantastic?

What did a name mean anyway? Xander's own name was officially "Alexander," of course, a name he admired. *A name of kings!* It felt far too conventional for him, however. So at the age of nine he declared that he wanted to be known as "Xander." Since then, at the start of every semester, he handed every teacher on his schedule a short, typed letter stating his preferred *nom de guerre*.

He waited in the lobby as part of his plan. He had called the school secretary and claimed to be Steve Christakos' father. He said that he needed to pick up his son because of a family emergency. Could they call his son down and have him meet him in the lobby of the front entrance by Dekalb Avenue in 15 minutes, at 1 p.m.? Yes, yes, of course they could. Thank you so much!

At 1:05, Xander took a casual stroll by the lobby of the front entrance, and there he saw the student who must be Steve Christakos sitting on a bench, looking like he was about to cry his eyes out with worry.

Xander made a mental note of his features. Curly hair, face blighted by the bright red horrors of acne and his sad scrunching didn't make him look any better. Xander was forced to sympathize. His own skin had been betraying him recently, much to his dread.

The next day Xander found Christakos easily in the crowd of students in the cafeteria. He took a seat behind him. He had kept his lunch ticket for the day and endeavored to enjoy a grilled cheese sandwich that had clearly not been grilled, but was rather two pieces of dry bread with a slice of orange gelatinous material in between that had been assembled by a cruel machine and gently warmed until it fossilized.

Christakos was accompanied by three other students, and Xander could hear their conversation very well. They were argumentative, annoying and apparently all they cared about in the world was music.

Xander wasn't sure what he was looking for. Certainly not for Steve Christakos to casually mention that he had killed Mr. Friedman between discussions of Black Sabbath and Blue Oyster Cult. He hoped to get a sense of his character, to see if Christakos was capable of murder. But he and his cohorts only seemed concerned with one subject.

"I can't believe this! I can't believe you like Donna Summer!"

"I said I liked *her*, not her music!"

"What's the difference? Disco sucks!"

"All's I'm saying is that she's kind of hot. Of course, disco sucks. I don't like disco. Why would I like disco?"

This discussion continued for some time. Finally, Xander heard something of interest.

Christakos said, "Hey, was that one of you guys that pranked me yesterday?"

"Pranked you?"

"What prank?"

"Somebody called the school and said he was my dad. He said there was this family emergency. They told me to go down to meet him and I sat there for like a half hour."

"That's messed up."

"I didn't do it, but I wish I had thought of that."

"That's not funny. I thought something happened to my mother or my big sister," Christakos said.

Then one of his cronies said, "My sister was playing disco music the whole weekend. The Bee Gees! Can you believe it?"

They were back to music again. Would the cultural battle between disco and rock ever be settled to their satisfaction? According to this lot, disco heralded nothing less than the end of civilization.

Xander wished he could *will* the subject of Mr. Friedman into their conversation, just to gauge how Christakos reacted. To catch the conscience of the Christakos! Now, they were on to Van Halen. One said Van Halen's last LP was "totally rockin'" and that the band would be "rockin' forever." Another objected, saying nothing could surpass Queen. Another said they were fools if they didn't worship Led Zeppelin. But they all agreed that anything was better than disco music, anything.

This was getting Xander nowhere. He would keep an eye on Christakos, but it was time to move on to the next Steve.

He was finishing his sandwich and milk and looking forward to going to the library for solitude (as much as could
be gotten in a high school), when he felt someone slam his
back with a giant palm.

"Jawbreaker!"

Hearing the nickname again froze his viscera. He turned.
The face that had spoken his name was not familiar. He was
very tall, with unkempt curly hair and a thick mustache that
made him look too old to be in high school.

"You don't know me. But I know you, bro."

"And you are?"

He laughed, a big grown man laugh. "My name's Juanito. I'm a junior here. You-know-who told me to look out for
you. You need anything, you let me know. See ya on the flip
side!"

Juanito patted him on the back with the slab of beef he
called a hand and walked away. Xander stayed in the lunchroom and looked at the rest of his sandwich for a long time.

29

WILY

Footwork. Her mother once said that was the only way a good investigation worked. You followed every lead, and if you came to a dead end, then you worked your way back and followed the next lead. You developed a theory and you tested it, adjusting it when necessary, then tested it again, until it broke or it held. Shortcuts were for lazy people. Your case had to be solid.

Holly felt the information about the guidance counselor being attacked might have nothing to do with the death of Mr. Friedman. Two acts of violence in such a short span of time, however, was too much of a coincidence not to investigate.

The guidance counselor's name was Linda Barkley. Holly recognized the woman's button nose and chubby cheeks from the first day of school. She sat almost hidden behind a small mountain of paper in an office that could have fit in Victor's Cadillac. On the walls were promotional posters for colleges and notices for scholarships. She had that picture of the kitten hanging from a branch that read, "Hang In There, Baby!" There were lots of kitten pictures, many Smiley faces, a small dancing trophy inscribed with "3rd Place" and at least three calendars.

Her desk was cluttered with paper, too, all the way up to a coffee maker at the end. Holly guessed it was there because there was nowhere else to put it. A bookshelf by the window was overflowing with brochures and dead or dying plants.

"I always say it's never too early to start thinking about your future," Barkley said. Her face was half hidden behind stacks of paper. "So I'm very glad you decided to pay me a visit today. Very glad."

No ring. Possibly divorced. Two kids and a dog in the pictures on her desk. When she had stood up to welcome Holly, Holly noted she didn't use antiperspirant.

"I think it's important to think about the future and where you're headed in life," Holly said. "I'm so glad you had an appointment open today."

"Well, to be frank, to be honest, it's early in the school year, and unfortunately many students don't start thinking about their next step until the spring."

"That is unfortunate," Holly said. "Students need to think ahead."

"Oh, yes." They should. We have so many resources available to them. So many. Look at this." Barkley pointed to a pile of paper on top of her file cabinet. "Scholarship opportunities. Hundreds of them. Thousands. Nobody fills these out. Nobody. They collect dust. I can't believe it."

"That's too bad. Students should be lining out the door to get those forms."

"Yes! You said it. I don't know why they're not. These are supposed to be bright kids. Bright!"

Holly nodded and kept her eyes on Ms. Barkley's eyes. "I noticed your office is a little out of the way. You're down the hall away from anything else, near one of the back exits."

"Well, it is out of the way, isn't it? What can you do? We're here. We're not hiding. People can find us."

"You're right. It takes no effort," Holly said. "Doesn't it get a little scary here? Being this out of the way?"

Barkley shrugged. "I don't know. A little? Actually, yes. A bit. Quite a bit. But it's a great space. A great space. But, well, things have happened."

"Oh my, really? What kind of things? Not something bad?"

"Yes, well, yes," Ms. Barkley said, looking past Holly and into the hallway. Then she lowered her voice. "I shouldn't tell you this. I really shouldn't." She peeked at the hallway again. "Just a month ago. Has it been just a month? Feels like yesterday. Well, a few weeks ago, I had my back to the door. I was watering the spider plant and my little fern who I call 'Vern.' So I didn't see this person come in. My back was to the door, like I said. He grabbed me by the neck, like he was going to choke me, and then all of a sudden he pushes me to the floor. I could have broken my head. Died! But I was lucky. I landed on a pile of SAT prep manuals, that pile right there."

"My word. Did they catch the person? Please say it wasn't a student. Do you think it was?"

"A student?" Ms. Barkley said, and then it seemed like she was thinking it over. "A student? No. Oh, no. Well, I'd like to say, 'No,' but I don't really know. I really don't. I didn't get to see his face at all."

"Of course, he was behind you. How did you know it was a 'he?'"

"Well, from the floor I turned and saw this person at the doorway, looking left and right, you know, to see if anyone was coming. He had a ski mask on, and sweatpants and a sweatshirt."

"So you didn't see skin or hair color? How about height?"

"Nothing. I was focused on the ski mask. It had snowflakes on it, of all things. Snowflakes!"

"You must have been so frightened."

"I was. I was!"

"Did he have a gun or a knife?"

"I didn't see, not at all. He had both hands around my neck. Strong hands, I tell you."

"And he didn't threaten you or say anything?"

"No, my purse was right here, on the front of the desk. When I was on the floor, he could've taken it. But he didn't. I don't know why."

"I see," Holly said. "It's so good you weren't seriously hurt."

"I tell you, Holly, it was the experience. . . it was just unnerving."

"I can imagine, yes."

"Oh my god, the memories. Well, enough about that. You don't want to hear about that. Let's get back to you, Holly. What kind of career are you thinking about? Where do you see yourself in the future? What is Holly doing in 1990? You have to think about these things."

"Wow. I'm not sure. I was curious about majoring in Arts and Science here, then maybe moving on to physics or biology in college. I love the sciences. I'd love to be a scientist."

"Nice! Nice!"

"Or I thought I could become an English major. I really love literature."

Barkley's face scrunched up. "Ooh, let me stop you right there. You want to make some money, don't you? You want to be able to pay bills? Here, look at this brochure."

30

SEMAPHORE

The trick with the school secretary had worked with Steve Christakos, but Xander knew he couldn't use it a second time. (He knew this because he had tried it. The same secretary heard him speak and then said, "Okay, who is this *really*?") He would have to find Steve Gomes another way.

He went to the Lost and Found office and handed the security person there a wooden T-square. On it he had written the name "Steve Gomes" in magic marker.

Xander surmised that Steve Gomes was at least a junior, since he had failed Social Studies and was retaking it. Perhaps he was still taking Technical Drawing as well, or even majoring in Architecture. In any case, he must have been in possession of a T-square at one point, and even if he still had the very first one he'd bought, he might be curious about one suddenly appearing with his name on it.

"Hello, miss. I found this in the bathroom," he said, which was the truth. He had used his little bathroom trick again, lifting the T-square from some unsuspecting lower-classman.

Xander was leisurely making his way back to class when he heard "Steve Gomes" being paged over the PA system.

He went back to the administration floor and tried to seem lost as he paced the hallway.

In a few minutes, someone who looked to be about the age of a junior showed up. He had a round face, a round afro and a varsity jacket.

Hola, Steve Gomes.

Xander waited outside the southwest entrance at the end of that school day. Then he waited outside the northwest the next day. On the third day he spotted Steve walking out of the northeast entrance.

He followed him along Dekalb Avenue. It was easy to follow undetected because hundreds of students were moving in the same direction. They were all headed for the Flatbush Avenue subway station.

Gomes walked down into the station and Xander followed. Gomes joined the horde of students who flashed subway passes to enter through the metal doors and not the turnstile. Xander only had his bus pass, which was supposed to be used only for the bus. But who was there to stop him? Someone was talking to the token booth clerk, blocking her view. And there were no transit officers around. Xander flashed his bus pass and walked in.

Gomes met two other Flatbush Tech students on the D train platform bound for Manhattan. Perhaps Gomes was part of a gang, and these were his fellow gang members. When the train arrived, Xander got in the car next to theirs. At every stop, he peeked out the door to see if they were detraining.

Alas, at West 4th they got out. Xander followed them to a movie theater that was immediately outside of the subway station. The movie named on the marquee was *Zombi 2*.

Intriguing.

Xander had just enough to pay for a ticket and an absolutely essential container of popcorn. Movies, he believed, were worthless without popcorn. He had not indulged himself in a movie in months. Spending the money for the movie meant, of course, that his monthly quota of comic books would be decreased. Fair enough. This was about justice!

Steve Gomes was the kind of guy who would go see a horror movie after school instead of doing homework or taking a part-time job. What did this tell Xander? Anything? Anything at all? Xander concluded that this told him absolutely nothing. Yes, the movie was spectacularly gory and violent. Could enjoying this kind of fare mean one is capable of murder? Perhaps. Perhaps not. Still, Xander found himself enjoying the movie very much. Did that say anything about him?

What he did not enjoy was Steve Gomes and his buddies roughhousing during the feature. Rather than sit quietly and pay attention, they laughed, they yelled, they made disgusting noises. They mooned each other and the screen. Xander couldn't hear the dialogue for a significant portion of time! This was no gang. This was a pack of simian-brained fools.

After the movie, the fools went into a nearby pizzeria. It was tiny. There was no way Xander could go in without being noticed.

Besides, it was getting late and he needed to get home. He didn't want Abuela to worry. She had always been almost overbearing with her worrying, and it had gotten worse since his imprisonment at the Devil's Island of Spofford.

He went back into the subway station and remembered that he did not have a token. He figured he'd just use his bus pass again. The token booth clerk was again preoccupied with a long line of commuters. Xander flashed his pass and opened the door.

"Let's see that pass."

Xander turned. *Uniformed police! Two of them! Where had they come from?*

An officer with a florid mustache grabbed the pass from Xander's hand. They must have been just beyond the gate, behind a passel of passengers. Xander hadn't seen them at all.

"This is a bus pass," the officer said. He seemed bored. As did the cop with him, who looked like he'd rather be shooting something. "You know you're not supposed to use it here, right? Come here."

They roughly turned him around and pushed him against the wall. The officer took out a pad and clicked a pen.

Xander's intestines turned ice cold. He would receive a ticket. Which he would have to pay. Would his humiliation never end?

Just then there was a scream and commotion. Someone was jumping the turnstile in an Olympic-level arc and then running down toward the platform.

"He took my purse! Stop him!" It was a very loud yell from a very short lady. "Stop that little crook!"

The officers turned and gave chase immediately. "You stay here," the mustachioed cop said to Xander. In the vacuum of authority, they had left behind his bus pass. It fluttered in the air and down to the dirty station floor.

Xander didn't hesitate. He snatched up the pass and went back upstairs and out onto the street. He walked as fast as he could, checking behind him for blocks, just in case those cops came chasing after him, in case they sent out an ABP.

In time, he found another subway station. He fished in his pockets and found enough chump change to pay for a token. He was not tempted at all to use his bus pass again. He had had enough intrigue for one day.

QUIXOTIC

Holly sat in the lunchroom, waiting in her usual spot by the window. Christina might join her, she might not. Ever since she joined SOS, Christina seemed to have less time to talk and was rarely around for lunch.

Still, Holly was eager to dive into the seven tater tots on her plate. She had a particular weakness for tater tots. That, and for Twizzlers and any Twizzler-like candy. One time she had eaten an entire pound of them. What they did to her intestines taught her more about discipline than a thousand warnings from Marta. So while she could have eaten a pound of tater tots, she knew it was best to enjoy them in small doses. *Slowly.*

As she was in mid-scarf, Sharona, Beth and Brandy descended on her. They were in the midst of a conversation that did not stop as they sat down around her.

" . . . Estrada is so cute," Sharona said. "I think he's cute. Isn't he cute?"

"Oh no," Beth said. "Larry Wilcox is cuter."

"I don't know what you're talking about. Wilcox is totally cuter," Brandy said. "Are you still watching *Charlie's Angels?*"

"I love their outfits," Sharona said. "And the hair!"

Getting on one knee, squinting an eye and aiming her finger like a gun, Beth said, "Hold it right there!"

"What do you think, Holly?"

Holly tapped her chin with her finger, then shook her head. "I tried to watch that show, but it seemed very fake. There are no real mysteries to figure out."

"So what shows do you watch?"

"I like *The Rockford Files, Barnaby Jones, Hawaii Five-O.* Typical stuff."

"*The Rockford* what?" Sharona said.

"I would love to watch *Kate Loves a Mystery,*" Holly told them, "but it's on too late. I'd watch *Barney Miller,* but it's too much like going to my dad's job."

Suddenly, the chatter stopped. Holly realized the girls were looking at someone standing right behind her.

Holly turned. It was Christina. Holly immediately noticed that Christina's Farrah-feathered hairstyle was gone. Her hair now hung straight down.

"Hello, Holly," she said.

"Hi, Christina. How's it going? Do you know Beth, Sharona and Brandy?"

"I haven't asked in a while. I didn't want to bother you. I mean, I was wondering if you were still thinking about joining SOS."

"Oh." Holly had never gotten back to Christina about that. She felt horrible.

"The SOS?" Beth said.

"Oh my god, not the SOS," Sharona said.

"You don't want to do that, Holly," Brandy said. "Trust me. Not the SOS."

"Um." Holly felt trapped.

"Don't listen to them."

"Weirdos."

"School pigs."

"Nerds."

"Hey, Holly." A new voice cut through the noise. Holly looked over and there was Dragon. "Can I talk to you?"

"Oh my, yes," she said. "Let's talk over there."

She gave Christina a sheepish smile and heard the girls giggling behind her. "I'll be back."

"No, you won't," Brandy said, and there was more giggling.

Holly started walking quickly toward the exit. "Thank you, Dragon. I was going to ask you, are you related to the Captain and Tennille's Captain?"

"No!"

"Well, he's Daryl Dragon, so I thought maybe."

"I'm not."

"I see. So what's your real name, anyway?"

"You don't want to know. It's so boring."

"'So Boring' is your name now? Hello, Mr. Boring. Or should I be informal and call you 'So?'"

"No, it's Steve, which is so boring. That's what I meant."

"No. I knew that. Never mind. I want to thank you again for helping me with the drill bit."

They stood on the sixth-floor landing. Students were beginning to fill up the stairwell around them.

"But you didn't take it," he said.

"I appreciate the intention."

"Sure. Just doing my manly duty."

"Well, I wouldn't say 'manly.' A lot of the girls in the class got their bits done perfectly, so testosterone isn't a necessary factor. I finally finished mine this week. Now I can catch up to the rest of the class."

"But isn't it manly work? Working with tools and machines."

"Not at all. Why would having a different set of pipes— as my uncle José would say—give anyone any special skill at anything?"

Dragon—*Steve*—looked puzzled.

"I wanted to ask you something," she said.

Holly saw something in his eyes, something a little dangerous, a little interesting. She understood where his mind might be going. She had heard that boys fall in love fast, faster than a traffic light changed. She didn't have the patience for that kind of silliness. It could hurt their friendship. And her investigation.

She said, "That secret doorway routine of yours really intrigued me. I was wondering . . . how many of those are in the school?"

"Lots. I'd say at least ten. That I know about. There's probably more."

"Can you show them to me?"

He smiled. "Sure. Yeah! How about now?"

"How about after school?"

"Aw, that's no fun. Besides, I got something to do after school today. How about now? Now is good."

Holly shook her head. "Sorry, I've got to go to class."

"Class?! Are you a goody two shoes?" Steve said. "Don't you like breaking rules? Don't be a sheep."

"Well, I'm no sheep," Holly said. "I break rules all the time. I break them when I want to break them. And sneaking in and out of the school is enough rule-breaking, wouldn't you say? Let's not push it."

"I was just asking."

"Good. Then how about we break rules after school tomorrow?"

32

QUAINT

Mr. Lynch, the new Social Studies teacher, looked older than the Constitution. He wore a tie and a tweed jacket with elbow pads and spoke in a drawl so slow it took decades for him to end a thought. He was discussing the downfall of the Roman Empire, with the promise of bringing it back to a question asked twenty-five minutes earlier about what chapter the class should study next.

The rear door of the room opened and in walked one of those athlete types. He stood poised above a seat at the back of the class.

"Excuse me, young man," Mr. Lynch said. "Your name is?" The new teacher had not moved from his spot in front of the classroom. He had not moved at all since the class had begun. He did bend down just slightly to where he had a list of student names.

Most of the class was still focused forward, but Xander saw that Holly had craned her head around to look at the latecomer. Perhaps the Perky Wonder had an attraction to jocks?

"Dra—, er, Steve, Steve Gaffney," the student said.

A light bulb exploded in Xander's head. *Of course!* Gaffney hadn't been to class in days, maybe weeks. He always arrived late, if ever, and never asked or answered questions (not that that was a bad thing). No wonder he was so hard to find. This had to be the Steve he was looking for.

Mr. Lynch made a note on his sheet. "Have a seat, Mr. Gaffney."

After that, the lecture proceeded at its usual tectonic pace.

Several decades later, at the end of class when the bell rang, Mr. Lynch finally said, "Chapter twenty-eight." Xander got up to follow Steve.

Just then Holly Hernandez squeezed in front of him and walked up to Steve in the hallway. Xander went past them and turned a corner, coming to a stop immediately past it. He kept his ears wide open.

He heard Holly say something to Steve but couldn't quite hear it among the general student chatter.

Then: Steve clearly said, "Outside. Southwest exit."

Xander walked past, pretending he had a million other better things to be thinking about than a secret rendezvous between Holly Hernandez and her paramour.

Xander lingered in the hallway for Steve. He wanted to keep an eye on him for the rest of the day. He was looking for anything suspicious. A return to the scene of the crime. A peek inside his locker revealing the murder weapon. *Something, anything. A clue!*

Luckily enough, they were both scheduled for gym next period. Xander spotted him in the locker room and then saw him again on the track.

The school's track was located at a mezzanine level above the gym floor, circling around the room. You had to reach it through a separate staircase. Xander liked to go up there whenever he had gym. Not to jog or do anything that would make him sweat. *What an unbearable thought.* No, he liked to walk casually around and around. He found he could make the period pass reasonably comfortably in less than ten complete cycles.

The oval-shaped track was set into a rectangle of walls, so each corner of the level had remaining non-track space. These spaces sloped slightly, but students could sit there to rest or just hang out. That's what Steve was doing: laying back, reading a book.

Gym teachers rarely came up to the second level to check on students' running techniques, and Xander himself had finished several books in that same corner. He walked slowly past Steve to get a look at the cover. He couldn't see it.

He walked slowly past again. Nothing.

The next time, he decided he wouldn't look because he didn't want to be noticed. So he tried to go by casually. As he did, Steve raised the book in the air so that the cover was easy to read: *Elric of Melniboné.*

Xander was impressed, though. He had expected Steve to be reading *Frog and Toad Are Friends. Elric of Melniboné* required intelligence and sophistication.

Did that make Steve more or less likely to be Mr. Friedman's killer?

At 2:25 pm, Xander was across the street from the southwest exit. He took a position behind a tree in front of one of the brownstones.

He spotted Holly first. He ducked back behind the tree and willed himself to be invisible and/or thinner. It had never really worked before, but there was always a chance that this one time it might.

A minute later, Steve Gaffney showed, strolling out from the southwest exit. He greeted Holly. No smooches or the like. Perhaps their relationship had not advanced to whatever base that was purported to be.

They both looked around cautiously. Xander concentrated on the words "invisible" and "thin" in an effort to will himself into an undetectable, unseen, indiscernible state. He would have been more grateful if the sycamore had been a few decades older.

Xander peeked out. Holly and Gaffney were taking the stairs down into the back alley of the school. Why go down there? Unless it was for an assignation. That would be an odd choice. They would no doubt be going up the ramp on the other side, which Xander had a good view of. Time went by and they didn't reappear.

More time. No Holly or Steve.

Xander risked leaving his blind and tiptoed across the street, as if they would hear his feet. He tentatively peeked through the gate around the ramp.

No one. There was no one. Where had they gone?

They hadn't come back up the stairs and they hadn't gone up the ramp.

The only way to go was the closed rear exit doors. Xander knew for a fact those were kept locked. He had cruel assurance that those were kept locked.

He tiptoed down the steps. The door was indeed locked.

By the Ageless Vishanti! They disappeared!

33

ARCANE

They were in a little-used hallway that led out through steel doors to the back alley. The door had been securely locked, and like a magician Steve asked Holly to check the handles to assure her that they were.

He took a quick check around, then pulled a short metal tool from his pocket. It looked like a can opener with a hooked point at the end. He placed it behind the cylinder, yanked and out popped the cylinder. He then placed the hooked part of the tool into the space and turned it. It opened.

"What is that thing? It looks like a can opener."

"Don't be too impressed. This got made in metal shop. But not by me. It was handed down to me by a . . . by a friend. It doesn't look like much, but it can open just about any door. As you can see."

Inside the entryway, it smelled of metal and cigarettes. Holly said, "Should we be quiet?"

"Down here, I don't think so. Security never comes down here. Only the janitors are around, and they don't care what we do. Sometimes I hang out here and have a cigarette with them."

"I must say, you don't seem particularly worried about truancy."

"There are more important things to worry about. C'mon, let's get into the auditorium. It's super cool. It's right through here."

Steve led them down a narrow, cinder-block hallway.

"This way goes behind the stage," he said, pointing around like a genuine tour guide. "And then it swings around to the dressing rooms."

They came to another steel door, this one much older than the exit door.

"I don't need a special key with this one. Watch." Steve grasped the handle and pulled up, going on his tippy toes. The door came open easily.

"That doesn't seem very secure."

"It's not. The opening for the door is not square, so the door's never really secure. It just needs a little help and it comes right open."

"Very impressive."

"That's nothing," he said. "Wait till you see door number three."

They walked out of the dim hall and into the dark backstage of the auditorium. He reached for her hand.

"Don't be scared," he said.

"Why would I be scared?"

"Because it's dark."

Holly carried a flashlight in her purse, she always did. "There's nothing to be scared of in the dark," she said. "There's nothing there that wasn't in the light."

Steve shrugged. "I guess that's a good way to look at it. Just be careful. Okay, right through here. Another few feet. Ready to see it?"

"Yes, of course."

He opened a door and suddenly the air and the sound changed. Holly had seen the auditorium on the first day of the class. It had looked impressive from the seats. Now, from backstage, the auditorium was remarkable on a whole new level. The gigantic space was like a cavern, dimly lit by the windows set high in the walls on both sides. Holly and Steve stood center stage, framed by enormous velvet curtains. Every sound they made echoed in the vastness.

"This is absolutely lovely," she said. "And a little eerie."

"Eerie? Why?"

"This huge space was built to be filled by people, by noise. But now it's empty and quiet."

"It's empty, but it's still alive. That's exactly what I like about it, why I like coming here. It's like a great beast that's, you know, resting."

"What do you do here? Do you pretend that you're Hamlet? Or Julius Caesar?"

"Why? Would that be weird?"

"Um, no, not at all. Do you? How about poetry? Do you recite poetry?"

He seemed embarrassed, and Holly was almost ashamed herself for asking him.

"I do," he said. "I love Robert Browning a lot."

"He wrote a lot of dramatic monologues, so I can see why. They would be so much fun to perform in this space. Are you going to be an Arts and Science major?"

"Hah, no, I'm already technically a *senior* senior, although I'm a junior on paper. But Arts and Science, no way. I went Engineering Science."

"Huh," Holly said. "I don't know you very well, but that seems . . . out of character. You seem to love the arts. Why else would you come to a place like this to recite?"

"Oh, that's only because my stepfather's been drilling literature into my head for years. I hate the arts now. But I like things like this, finding out secret passageways, you know, how things work underneath, things that nobody else sees."

"Okay. So, did you figure these all out? Or did a 'friend' show you?"

"That's a secret I'll never tell. I'm good at keeping secrets. I am. Say, we should go to the architectural room."

"What's in there?"

"The Architecture majors get to build a house from scratch. It's the coolest thing."

"Super. Let's go!"

"Okay. But first we have to go through to the pool. It should be empty at this time of day. Should be."

As they moved away from the stage and into another narrow cinder-block hallway, Holly had the feeling that they were being followed. She thought it was just paranoia, until she heard footsteps, heavy, plopping ones, but still faint. Steve hadn't seemed to notice it. When she looked back, it was too dim to see anything.

When she looked ahead, she saw that it was pitch black. As the darkness surrounded her, she glanced back again. If it were a security guard, and he had seen them, he would have confronted them. It could be a teacher or staffer, but why would they be back here? It was more likely another student wandering around in the school's bowels for fun and kicks.

Or . . . Or . . .

Could it be Mr. Friedman's killer?

No, she was overthinking things. She was just being paranoid.

Whoever had killed Mr. Friedman probably knew his or her way around the school. Maybe that was exactly how he or she had gotten away, through a secret passageway or tunnel like this.

Then Holly had a thought that made goosebumps rise at the back of her neck: *What if Steve were the killer?*

She was more surprised than scared by the idea. She ticked off the reasons for her suspicion.

1. He knew how to sneak around the school.
2. He seemed to dislike the authority of the school.
3. He had been left back a grade or two, so he might have a grudge against a teacher, against Mr. Friedman.

But if Steve was the killer, then who was following them and why?

Holly decided she had to continue, to find out as much as she could and, she hoped, survive long enough to eliminate Steve from the suspect list.

Soon she could only hear Steve's footsteps in front of her. When they had turned another corner, she could see nothing behind her. The only light was a thin line of brightness shaped like a door ahead. As they got closer, Holly was sure she heard heavy, almost labored breathing coming not from Steve in front of her but at a distance behind. She mentally prepared herself to confront their follower.

Then she smelled it: chlorine. Thickly chemical. The air was moist and warm.

Steve was at the door now. She could just see his outline in the dark.

He said, "For this one I like to use a bump key."

Steve inserted a toothless key into the lock, then he reached for a brick on the floor that seemed to have been left there just for this purpose.

With a quick whack, the door lock opened. Bright light replaced darkness, and just before they entered a small room behind the pool, Holly turned back to see two glowing points in the darkness. Reflections, likely off a pair of glasses. Tall. The points of light seemed to become aware they could be seen and so slid off to the side in darkness. Something about that movement. The glasses. The height. Could it be who she thought it was? What would he be doing following them?

"You okay?" Steve said.

"Yes," Holly said. "I'm fine." She closed the door slowly and silently.

ABSTRUSE

Xander bent down and took a good look at the lock on the door. It was not sophisticated. A simple pin-by-pin job. Elementary school level. He took his kit from his backpack and made quick work of the lock.

As Xander stepped inside, a janitor was giving him a deadpan look.

"You lost?" the janitor said.

"Um . . . No," Xander said. "Just have to use the bathroom."

He had found most people didn't ask too many questions if you pretended a sense of urgency over something universal.

"Sure. Up and to the right."

The janitor didn't seem to care that Xander had broken in. Xander was not crazy that someone had witnessed his breaking and entering. If this somehow got back to Principal Schnitger or that grimy security person or the police, he would be right back in a hellhole of trouble. Still, he was on a mission. The possibility of success was more important than the fear of defeat.

He went down a narrow hallway and found an old door. He looked behind him. The janitor was gone.

This lock was even easier to pick.

Xander went through the door and heard voices. Voices that were clearly trying to be hushed.

He was in the backstage of the auditorium. *Fascinating!* What fun he could have back here in the shadows. What tricks could be played.

He moved slowly, not wanting to make a sound, following the hushed voices. As he got closer, he recognized one as Holly's. *Voila!* Then he heard Steve the Athlete talking.

"A secret I'll never tell. I'm good at keeping secrets. I am."

Steve the Athlete seemed strangely adamant about that point.

"I didn't say you weren't," Xander heard Holly say.

They sat on the edge of the stage. Xander stood behind the heavy stage curtains and wished he had something he could sit on while watching. Just as he thought this, to his surprise, he felt vaguely unsavory about what he was doing, about being a voyeur. It didn't seem quite right. Just the same, he wanted to know what they were saying.

Then Xander realized something. *Oh my stars and garters.* He had been stalking Steve the Athlete in order to figure out his connection to Mr. Friedman. *What if Steve the Athlete is the one who killed Mr. Friedman? Was Holly planning to make him confess with her investigative wiles?* She would be a fool if that was true.

She would also be in danger.

What was Xander to do? He wanted to embarrass Holly, not wipe her off the planet. Should he run out to the middle of the stage and *J'accuse* Steve the Athlete while telling Holly to run? They would laugh at him.

Well, then, should he just wait until Steve the Athlete pulled out a knife and eviscerated Holly?

Perhaps a situation would present itself in which he could save Holly's life. *What larks!* Then she would surely bow to his greater genius!

As he struggled to decide, Holly and Steve got up and began moving toward stage right.

He followed them at a good distance, keeping Holly's huge head and Steve's obscenely athletic back in sight.

They went down another narrow corridor and took a left and then a right. He followed. The hallway grew dimmer until there was no light at all. Xander couldn't see them ahead. He heard a door open and click shut.

Xander found himself in complete darkness. He fumbled for his kit again, but the pitch blackness made it hard to get a sense of which part of his bag he was shoving his hand into.

He found it! While pulling the kit out, his hands brushed against something rough, making him drop the kit into the pitch blackness. He began to feel around on the ground. It felt damp, dirty, disgusting. It seemed like the janitor needed a good talking-to.

Xander got on his hands and knees. The tension wrench couldn't've have gone very far. Was he sitting on it? He felt around some more. *Ye gods! What disgusting thing was that?* He couldn't identify it. His imagination flew in many directions. *The indignity!*

35

TORPID

"Are you sure no one is here?"

"Yeah," Steve said, "today's usually basketball practice, but they're over playing at St. Francis Prep."

"Oh. That's my uncle's alma mater. He wanted me to go there."

"So, why didn't you?"

"A lack of empirical evidence."

"Okay. Um, but it would have been better than this old place."

"I don't know. I like this place. The Gothic architecture, the beautiful worn, wooden desks, the fireplaces in the library. And it has a foundry! What other school has a foundry? How cool is that?"

"I guess."

"You don't seem to find the school charming at all."

She couldn't see Steve's face, but he sounded more sad than bitter when he said, "I've just been here too long, I guess."

Here was a good chance for Holly to ask Steve if he had ever been in Mr. Friedman's class, to see if he had a motive. They had entered through an old door that led into a small storage room filled with exercise mats and volleyball nets.

The room was just off the pool. They walked through the humidity. She was about to ask Steve a question when her feet flew out from under her.

She found herself hovering over the sloshing pool. Steve had caught her in time.

"Slippery tiles," he said.

"Thanks."

They pushed through a heavy door, and it clanged shut behind them. Holly gazed at rows of gray metal lockers.

"I can't believe I'm in the boys' locker room. I was very curious about it."

"You were? Why?"

"To compare it to the girls'. Overall, this is pretty disgusting."

"I bet it's a lot worse than the girls' locker room," Steve said.

"Actually, the girls' locker room is much, much worse."

He didn't seem to know what to say after that, which was good because just then she heard someone entering the locker room.

They ducked into one of the shower rooms, narrowly avoiding stepping into a soapy puddle of water. Steve and Holly turned to each other with index fingers held in front of their mouths. Holly added a "Doy" shrug. In the shower room, any noise would be magnified. They ducked behind the wall.

Someone was moving around, jiggling keys and muttering.

Steve slid into a corner in what looked like a six-year-old's attempt to be invisible. He closed his eyes and put his hands over his face.

Holly pulled his hands away and mouthed, "We should leave."

Steve energetically shook his head. He mouthed something that was either "They'll catch us" or "That's ketchup."

Holly found that she was excited by the situation. It was ridiculous. There was nothing technically illegal going on, no destruction of property or anything untoward, although she knew it wouldn't be seen that way. The main reason she didn't want to be caught in the boys' locker room, of all places, was that if her mother found out where she was and what she was doing and who she was doing it with, she might shoot someone.

She heard something metallic snap, and then something heavy and metallic hit the floor. *What in the world was that?*

They had to get out of there. She took a look at Steve and, careful on the slippery tiles, moved silently out of the shower.

In order to get to the pool and the storage room, they would have to pass an open space in the locker room. She peeked around the corner of a locker to see who might be around. She immediately drew her head back. It was Licata, the head of security. He was carrying an enormous set of bolt cutters and a large garbage bag. Now she knew what the metallic sounds were. He was snapping off locks. Signs were posted all over the locker rooms stating, "Locks on lockers left overnight will be removed and contents discarded."

While she stood there, she heard Licata grunt as he snapped another lock. She risked another peek.

Licata was rooting through a pair of gym shorts—*disgusting!*—that he had no doubt gotten from a locker.

"What have we here?" he said to himself.

In his hand was a small bottle of liquor. Licata opened it and smelled it. Then he took a sip. "Rotgut," he said, took a second sip, then a third and then tossed it into the garbage bag.

She heard him move to another lock.

How many students had left their locks on? This could take forever. They would have to make a break for it. Running back to the pool was their best option. If they could hold the heavy door and stop it from making noise. And if they didn't slip and splash into the pool.

They might run into Xander, of course. She was sure it was him who was following behind them. What could he say? He wasn't where he should be either.

She tiptoed back to where Steve was and signaled for him to get up. He shook his head and mouthed, "If we stay here, he'll go away eventually." Or it could have been: "If we stay here, it'll snow even-stevens."

Another grunt from the locker room, another lock hit the floor.

This could take forever. They were trapped.

Suddenly, they heard a splash. A very big splash.

Licata yelled, "What the hell?"

Holly heard steps, heard the heavy door swing open. She grabbed Steve and they tiptoed to the shower room entrance. They froze in place. Licata's body was half in and half out of the door.

"What the hell are you doing? You're not supposed to be here."

Poor Xander, she thought.

She led Steve to the other side of the lockers and then out the door and into the hallway. They raced to the stairs, then slowed down, trying not to look suspicious in case they came across anyone.

When they reached the northwest exit, Steve stopped and said, "Hey. Sorry we didn't make it to the Architecture room."

"Next time."

"Sure. Next time, definitely. So, you want to get some-thing to eat? I got a car. Hey, we could go to Coney Island."

Holly smiled at the idea of Coney Island. But she said, "You have a driver's license already?"

"Learner's permit."

"Impressive. But, actually, it's pretty late," Holly said. "I need to get home."

"Okay." Steve hung back as she moved toward the exit.

"Aren't you leaving?"

"I'm not really in any hurry to get home. See you on the flip side, I guess."

He ran off, and just as he disappeared around a corner, Holly remembered that she forgot to ask him about Mr. Friedman. *Oh what a spaz I am!*

Outside, it was darker than she expected. A block from school, Holly saw Victor smoking outside the car.

"I'm pretty sure I told you I could get home by myself today," she said.

He opened the car door for her. "What was that, Ms. Holly?" he said. "I got trouble hearing."

"You waited for me this whole time?"

"Almost."

"Ah, so how were the ponies today? Were they kind?"

"They were not, Ms. Holly. They were not."

In the car, she wondered what was going to happen to Xander. Why had he been lurking around the school? And what about Steve? Why was he in no hurry to get home? For someone who didn't show up to class a lot, who said he didn't like the school much, he sure seemed to like spending time there.

36

RECALCITRANT

The pool water was surprisingly warm. But not very deep. Not where Xander had slipped and fallen. He was grateful that, by dint of his super quick thinking, he had tossed his briefcase to the side and it had not gotten damaged. He was not worried about the pleather briefcase itself, but in there he had two Mack Bolan paperbacks he had recently purchased as well as Mr. Friedman's Delaney book. He didn't want to lose any of them.

Xander had run from the pool door when he realized 1) that Licata was going to take a very long time to finish with the locks, and 2) that he had to use the bathroom. At least he had taken care of that, now that he was in the water.

Licata came over to the edge of the pool, red-faced, ranting, ridiculous. As Xander climbed up a ladder out of the pool, Licata continued to scream right in his face.

Something happened then as he heard and smelled Licata. Something made Xander's fear leave him even as he stood there, dripping wet with his underwear riding up on him.

"You're going to get into so much trouble," Licata yelled.

"Are you going to snitch on me?" Xander picked up his briefcase casually. Water spun and dripped off his curls. His sneakers were soaked.

"Yeah, dimwit. What did you expect?"

"Right now you'll snitch on me? This minute?"

"Yeah! The principal's in her office. I'll march you right over to her. So what, big brain?"

"Very well, then. Let us go, then, you and I. I'll tell them all about how depressed I've been, and how I tried to commit suicide by drowning."

"In the shallow end, genius?"

"I wanted to make it easier to be fished out, since I just wanted attention."

"That's rich."

"A few weeks of counseling, then a little notation on my file. I'll be treated kindly and with deep sympathy."

"You can get expelled for sneaking around after school hours. Expelled. You know what that means, knucklehead?"

"I don't think I will."

Xander had been running away from the pool door when he slipped. He had been watching Licata move from locker to locker through a small window in the door.

"I think the powers that be will be more interested in why you smell like you gargled with a distillery."

That did it. Licata looked horrified. He raised his hand to his mouth, breathed and smelled. "Sweet Jeezus."

"Let's agree to let our indiscretions go unrecorded, shall we?"

"Why, you little dirtbag."

"Good night, Mr. Licata. I better be getting home before I catch cold. Enjoy your evening."

As he walked through the locker room, Xander looked for Holly and Steve. Where had they gone? He had seen her peeking at Licata. They must have slipped out.

Very well, he thought. *Like Clarice says, "There's always tomorrow."*

He left wet footprints behind as he squish-squish-squished out of the locker room.

37

TRENCHANT

At home that night, Holly took a look at her pink case-book and made more notes. Despite her momentary bout of paranoia, she felt that Steve was not the killer, although there was more to his story than he was telling. What bothered her more was Xander. What had he been doing there? Did he like to explore FTHS after school, too, or had he indeed been following them? Could she be wrong about his innocence? No, it didn't make any logical sense. Xander was up to something.

She made more notes and was in bed by nine. When she couldn't sleep, she picked up a book by Agatha Christie and stayed up until eleven.

In the morning, a knock on her bedroom door woke her from a fuzzy, mystery-filled sleep.

"Holly? It's Mom. Can I come in?"

She looked at the clock. It was five a.m. She wasn't supposed to wake up for half an hour. "Yes," she said groggily.

"Good morning, Holly. Listen, I hate to start your day like this, but I wanted to tell you in person before I have to rush out. I'm already late."

"Tell me what, Mom?"

"A Ms. Barkley, the guidance counselor from your school, is dead. She was murdered."

"My word! How?"

Holly sat up in bed. She had just talked to her a week ago—not that she would reveal that to her mother. She would ask her why and, no matter what story she might make up, she would realize Holly was investigating Mr. Friedman's murder on her own. She hated not telling her mother everything. It bothered Holly immensely. At the same time, she knew she had to do this.

Now, someone else had been killed. Holly hadn't known Ms. Barkley that well. She had seemed like a genuinely good person.

"I just wanted to let you know, so you wouldn't be surprised when you heard about it at school."

"Can you tell me how she was killed? Was she stabbed?"

"Holly!"

"You might as well tell me, Mom. Whatever it is, it's only going to be much more horrific in my imagination."

She crossed her arms. "Holly, I thought you told me a long time ago that you weren't interested in police work."

"I'm not. Let's just say I have a passing interest. I read that talking about your work helps clear the mind, helps you see things you might not see otherwise."

"I never thought about it that way. Is that really true?"

"It's true! So, how was she killed?"

"Hmm. Okay, she was strangled."

"Oh my." She thought again of Ms. Barkley. She must have been horribly frightened, fighting to breathe while someone took her life away. "Can I see crime scene photos?"

"Holly!"

"Where was she found?"

"In her car. About a block from your school."

Holly immediately thought of Steve. Where had he gone to after she left?

"Do they have a time of death?" she said, worried about the answer.

"Had to have happened before 3 p.m. She was seen leaving for the day at 2:45. Then a secretary said she saw her sitting in her car at about 3:15. She said it looked like she was resting her head. Then the owner of the house she was parked in front of knocked on the window, and when she didn't respond, she knew . . . she knew to call us."

"Mom, do you think this is at all related to Mr. Friedman's murder?"

"I don't know. It's certainly possible. The incidents are more than a month apart and the M.O. is slightly different. One attack was during school hours, one was after. One involved a sharp object, the other a scarf."

"So there was a scarf found on the scene?"

"Yes. Around her neck. Looks like it belonged to her. That's one of the things I have to check on this morning."

"So, a weapon of opportunity. Maybe whatever was used to kill Mr. Friedman was also on the scene before the killer arrived. If we could figure out what's missing, we would know what to look for."

"That weapon is probably long gone."

"You know, Ms. Barkley was attacked in her office just before the start of the semester. Do you think they could be related?"

"Hey, how did you . . . ? A passing interest, huh? Well, her office is on the first floor, near an exit door that doesn't close properly. It looks like a botched robbery, that's all. But you're right. Maybe we should take a look at that again."

If she had any suspicions about Steve, they were gone. She had been with him, traversing the secret passageways in and out of the school at that time. And Xander. This could clear Xander as well, *should*.

"One more thing, Mom! Can I ask, do you know where Xander was?"

"We asked him late last night. Do you know what he said? He said to ask your security head, Mr. Licata. So we did. Licata said they were playing chess in his office."

What? How could that be? She had seen Licata herself in the locker room. After his drinking, he might not have been in any condition to talk to authorities.

"I know. Hard to believe that Licata plays chess, let alone with a student I could have sworn he hated."

"Don't you think it's suspicious?"

"It's fishy, but I don't think it has any bearing on this case. Still, I'm keeping an eye on those two."

During the day, Holly watched out for Xander. She still hadn't had a chance to talk to him and say how sorry she felt about accusing him. She also wanted to ask him some questions for her investigation.

When she caught up with him, he was more surly than usual, if that was possible. He refused to look up at her when she spoke to him. Which she guess was better than getting the stink eye. And then he stormed off.

In Chemistry, students were allowed to sit wherever they wanted. She'd seen Xander in his usual seat in the back, hunched in the corner. She had avoided eye contact with him and took her usual seat in the front row.

"Don't trust atoms," Mr. Styczynski, her Chemistry teacher, said. *Late thirties, pockmarked face, sandy hair, lab coat.* "They make up everything!"

Mr. Styczynski tried hard to make a tough subject amusing.

"I was reading a book about helium this weekend," he said casually. "I just couldn't put it down."

Holly was too distracted to be amused. She kept thinking that the murders had to be connected. Why was Ms. Barkley attacked twice? Maybe it hadn't been a botched robbery so much as a botched murder attempt.

Mr. Styczynski must have noticed Holly's lack of focus. He stood in front of her seat, gave her a gentle smile and said, "Holly, ask me if I know any jokes about sodium?"

Slightly mortified, she said, "Mr. Styczynski, do you know any jokes about sodium?"

"Na! . . . All right. Let's get to acids!" And then he went back to the board.

38

BRAZEN

After two weeks of relative punctuality, the B61 bus had been late, very late, and this made Xander more incensed than he had been when he woke up. He gave the back of the driver's head a particularly stern look as he de-bussed.

When he got to school, he plowed through the students in the hallway. He used his significant height and width to push his smaller, shorter, slower fellows out of the way. He had no patience for their turtle-footedness today.

Daniel appeared by his side, wearing three polo shirts—one red, one white, one blue—and began to walk with him, struggling to keep up.

"There you are," Xander said. "They descended upon me last night. The police, they came to my house and rang the bell at 10 o'clock at night. I was asleep. Very much asleep. Blissfully asleep. Not only was I humiliated, but I also failed to get my regular eight hours of sleep. Eight hours of sleep are absolutely essential to the daily development of the human brain, especially at my young age. I abhor getting even one minute less than eight hours. And weekend naps do not count in making up the loss."

"No-Neck Bradley was a burly, burly man with a curly curly beard," Daniel said.

"And then they took me to their medieval precinct and grilled me for hours, asking me inane questions about a guidance counselor I never had a reason to meet. Who is this Linda Barkley? Have you ever heard of her? I haven't."

"And they called him No-Neck for no reason at all."

"Exactly! They kept asking me the same questions. Holly Hernandez's mother, that's who. She and her cheap gunsel, McCluskey. I'm sure that man is up to his gin blossoms in corruption and the blood of the falsely accused."

Daniel came to a stop in front of their French class, but Xander did not. He kept walking ahead and left Daniel behind. *À bientôt!*

Xander had no interest in French at the moment. He decided he needed to think in peace, at his own pace, in his special place. So he went instead to his sanctum sanctorum: the library.

As he went in, he nodded at Mr. Gladstone, who eyed him with suspicion. He knew Xander was not supposed to be there during fifth period. Xander had to give him credit because the librarian left him alone to stew at his favorite back table, almost completely hidden behind shelves.

The police had asked Xander about his whereabouts at 3 p.m. Of course, he could not tell them that he was in pursuit of Holly and Steve at that point, venturing deep into the entrails of FTHS.

Their questions also meant that Steve could not have killed the guidance counselor.

Although they had not said so, Xander was convinced that the murder of Linda Barkley and the murder of Mr. Friedman were connected. And if Steve was innocent of Barkley's murder, it was likely he was innocent of Mr. Friedman's murder.

Unless Steve were part of some Satanic murder cult in the school. As exciting as it sounded, it did not seem terribly probable. Steve had talked about poetry, not about dripping candles, pentagrams or human sacrifices. That was a pity. It would have made him more interesting.

Very well. Xander needed to find out the truth. He needed more leads. He needed more information, and he knew exactly where to look: Mr. Friedman's office.

He needed to sneak in there again.

REQUIEM

Mr. Baci always looked serious, with the dark circles under his eyes and his intense stare. To Holly, he seemed incapable of cracking a smile. He was particularly manic, even melancholy today. His dirty-looking hair swung back and forth as he wrote some brief notes on the board. He wore a dark brown turtleneck sweater and mustard-colored corduroy pants. He had worn pretty much the same outfit every day since the beginning of the term, but the coolness of the mid-October day finally made his outfit appropriate.

When he turned around, he brushed his long, thin beard and stared out the windows.

"All right, I'm going to say something," he said. "The principal would probably have a conniption, because I'm about to go into a sensitive subject without warning. I think that would be ridiculous because life doesn't warn you, life won't ever warn you, and it's better to learn now how to handle it when you're young, so you won't grow up to be defenseless."

Then he shrugged. "I guess I just did warn you, indirectly, so never mind. I won't be here tomorrow because I'm going to a funeral of someone very close to me, someone who was on the staff, someone who meant a great deal to me. The thing is, man, this isn't the only funeral I've had to go to recently. Many of you probably knew Larry Friedman, the Social Studies teacher. Larry Friedman and I were, if not the best of friends, colleagues for a long time, and our families had been close. He died recently too and in a very awful manner, as unfortunately did Linda Barkley, who was the school guidance counselor. Some of you may have met her."

Holly noted that his voice became strained, and she wondered if those were tears that were changing the look of his eyes. He turned and picked up the class textbook from his desk. "Linda was a lovely woman and a great friend of mine. So I'd like to read you something, because it is important to remember that death is a big part of life. It's certainly a big part of literature. This is from 'In Memoriam A. H. H,' by Alfred, Lord Tennyson, and it's written to remember a dear friend of his, Arthur Henry Hallam."

He read several stanzas, and then ended with one that was familiar to Holly:

I hold it true, whate'er befall;
I feel it, when I sorrow most;
'Tis better to have loved and lost
Than never to have loved at all.

After he stopped, he went back to looking out the windows, not even seeming to see anything, just looking. No one else moved, and the students were silent. Holly couldn't even hear Xander's usual sighs of frustration that she often heard from behind her in this class (and every other one she shared with Xander).

The power of poetry, of language to evoke emotions, to communicate feelings and ideas between people across distance and time stunned Holly again. The excerpt Mr. Baci read had been one of the poems she turned to after her father was killed. She had found it in her dad's collection of books, in a book of poetry that he had obviously read through many times. Holly bit her lip to stifle her tears.

"Well," Mr. Baci finally said, "let's get back to our regularly scheduled lesson, shall we?"

He started writing on the board and then said, "One more thing. We're having our first meeting for the school literary magazine, *Horizons*, right after school. Holly, you've asked me about it more than a few times, so I expect you to be there."

Holly had no intention of missing it.

At the end of the school day, Holly made her way to the *Horizons* magazine meeting. The semester's first meeting was set to take place in the print shop in the basement.

The hallway was empty and the lighting, as always, was dim, but it seemed especially so now that fall was in the atmosphere. It also smelled heavily of metal and ink.

The door of the shop was open. No one had arrived yet. Several massive, platen printing presses, of black cast iron and giant, oiled cogs and wheels, sat silently in the room. On every inch of the walls were examples of the shop's output: invitations and placards, report cards and diplomas. There were several cabinets and shelves filled with tiny type blocks. Several caged overhead bulbs gave the room only meager light.

There was a large, long table tucked into a corner. Mr. Baci had said that the magazine staff would meet in print shop once a month. They could look through typefaces and clip art in order to get ideas for the design of the issue.

Holly sat down at the table, facing the door. She was surprised that no one was there, not even the shop teacher. Surely, this equipment was valuable and not meant to be left unguarded.

She got out her loose-leaf notebook and turned to a new section she had created in anticipation of the meeting. She had already written down ideas for themes for the next several issues. She even had an idea for a poem, and she already had a title for it: "Arresting Silence."

Holly thought about the poem Mr. Baci had read. It was about love between friends. Of course, a superficial interpretation might say it was just about a broken love affair. What about that? What was Mr. Baci's connection to Ms. Barkley? Perhaps they were more than friends. What of Mr. Friedman? Her mother's police file, which she had left on the dining room table—something that happened quite often since her mother brought so much work home—said that Mr. Friedman was divorced and his ex-wife had moved to Europe. She knew Ms. Barkley had pictures with children, but no significant other. But she knew nothing about Mr. Baci. Had he been in love with Ms. Barkley? At the same time that Mr. Friedman was? Could the connection between the murders be a love triangle? It certainly made for a good motive.

If that was true, then Holly was alone in a dark basement room waiting for a murderer.

Her nostrils flared. She closed her loose leaf and picked it up to put it away, when she heard, "Hey, Holly. I'm not surprised you're on time."

It was Mr. Baci. He stood in the doorway, holding a cup of coffee. The doorway was, as far as she knew, the only way out. Steve's tour of the school had taken them nowhere near this room.

Where were the other students? Why weren't they here?

Just then, she had scary thought: What if Mr. Baci were the killer? What better way to get another victim?

She may just have walked into a trap.

40

DECORUM

In the hallway outside of Mr. Friedman's office, Daniel stood vigilantly in the same spot he had assumed before. At the office door, Xander diligently turned and worked the lock. The door had been sealed with police tape for weeks. Now the tape hung indigently to the side of the door. Xander got through the lock much more quickly this time. He was getting better.

Once in the room, he was ecstatic to see that Mr. Friedman's things, out of laziness or sentimentality, had not been moved.

He went quickly to the desk. He replaced the Delaney book and the date book where he had found them. He had already memorized or copied over all the information he felt was relevant.

"Now," he whispered to himself, "what else do you have to tell me?"

The desk was the same as before. There was nothing new on it, in it or under it. He turned to the wall behind the desk. Schedules. An unmarked bank calendar from 1976. On the windowsill was a trophy, about six inches high. There was something odd about it. Ah, it had been moved recently. He could tell by the lack of dust just around it.

He picked it up to read the tiny script at its base: "2nd Place Mission Venus Disco Champs 1978." How sad to win "2nd place." Why bother having a trophy at all? Why bother celebrating one's lack of achievement, one's mediocrity?

Bah! Perhaps the police had moved it when they searched the office.

As he placed it back, he thought of Holly Hernandez and her mother, the detective, and his mind started spinning with ideas. There it was! An idea too delicious not to execute.

Xander took the trophy from off the shelf and, knowing there was little room in his packed briefcase, tucked it into his pants, under his untucked shirt. He was scanning the walls for any other clues, when someone said, "Can I help you?"

Xander froze and turned slowly around. It was a teacher he had seen once before. A bald man who wore a pullover stretched far over his paunch. Bob was his name.

Xander said the first thing he could think, something irreparably inane: "Uh . . . Mr. Friedman?"

"No, not Mr. Friedman," Bob said. "Haven't you heard?"

"Yes," Xander said, trying to recover, trying to stop a squeak rising in his voice. "I know." He then looked at the floor in an attempt to appear in mourning.

"How did you get in here?"

"The door was open," Xander said. Why hadn't Daniel warned him? He was going to have to give his incoherent associate a good talking to about the proper way to be a lookout.

"It was?" the teacher said. "The police didn't want us to use this, but I have all my papers here, so I have no choice. Still, I thought I had closed it. My mind has been slipping lately. Must be this new medication I'm on. Makes me loopy. I was away with this." The teacher pointed to a cast on his leg. "It was just so sad, how he went. But, sorry, why are you here?"

The teacher's meandering talk had given Xander ample time to come up with an excuse. "I had handed him a report that I wrote myself. It wasn't an assignment. It was something I wanted him to read.'

"Really?" the teacher lifted his glasses and rubbed his eyeballs. "Tell me about it."

"It was an essay about how the Antichrist had returned and the end of the world was coming."

"Oh."

"I gave it to Mr. Friedman to look over. I was hoping to have it published."

"You were?"

"Yes, but I gave him my only copy. I know I should have made a copy but I thought he would give it back to me."

"I'm afraid I can't let you go through his files. You didn't go through his files, did you?"

"Oh, no. I wouldn't do that."

"I'm sorry, son. I'll make a note to ask the dean about it. Then I'll find the paper for you, if it's here."

"That would be . . . very nice."

"Sure. What's your name so I know what to look for?"

Xander's intestines began to rebel in anxiety. He had already been incorrectly connected to the murder. He didn't want his name being brought up again. They would conclude he was a murderer wishing to get rid of evidence.

"Bob," someone said, "You were told not to come in here. The police haven't finished their work."

Principal Schnitger entered the office looking at Bob, and then she saw Xander standing there, looking at the floor. "What are you doing here, young man?"

"I must have left the door open," Bob said.

She ignored him and kept her eagle eyes on Xander. "Unlikely," she said.

INTROSPECTION

"Did you like today's poem?" Mr. Baci said, looking at her with his dark-circled eyes. "It's a bit cliché, but I've always enjoyed Tennyson."

"Tennyson is terrific," Holly said, then wondered if she sounded stupid saying it.

Mr. Baci nodded, his long hair flopping. "Tell me something. How did you get into poetry? You don't have to go deep, I just want to see where you're at."

Dad, she thought. *It was because of my dad.*

"Shakespeare," Holly said, "I read all of Shakespeare's plays and sonnets by the time I was in fifth grade." It sounded like bragging, which she didn't like to do, but it was true.

Mr. Baci was not moving from the door. He kept his hand gripped firmly on his coffee cup. If he was the killer, his M.O. was to go for the neck, to attack from behind. She was sitting behind a large table. How would he do it? Would he ask her to stand up, come over and take a look at the printing press? Something like that?

"Funny, my, uh, stepson," he said, "I read through all of Shakespeare with him, when he was a kid, nine years old. We did *The Iliad,* Homer, *Beowulf,* a lot of the stuff we're doing in class. He loved it then. At least it seemed like he did. I can't say he cares for it anymore."

He looked even sadder than usual now. Holly wasn't sure what was going on.

"That's too bad," she said, and then before she could stop herself, she said, "My father. . . he was the one who taught me to love poetry. We read Shakespeare together, too. We would act out all the parts from the plays." She was nervous talking. *Oh no!* He would see that she was scared.

"That's terrific." He leaned against the doorframe and turned his head to look out. Was he making sure no one was coming? "Do you have a favorite poem?"

She answered automatically with the true answer. "'Evening Solace' by Charlotte Brontë. 'The human heart has hidden treasures, In secret kept, in silence sealed; — / The thoughts, the hopes, the dreams, the pleasures, / Whose charms were broken if revealed.'"

"Oh, that's a great one."

"Sorry, we're late."

At that moment, four students burst into the room, brushing past Mr. Baci and going straight for the table where Holly sat. They mumbled apologies while taking out notebooks and pens. They introduced themselves, and instantly Holly felt safer. And sure in the fact that Mr. Baci was not the killer. Although he seemed to know quite a lot about Ms. Barkley and Mr. Friedman. Perhaps they were just close colleagues. She thought about the questions she should ask him. Then she remembered his voice as he read Tennyson in class that day, and she decided not to ask him anything.

"Okay," Mr. Baci said. "Let's get started."

ADVERSITY

Principal Schnitger's purple eyeglasses seemed as large as plates, and she kept pushing them back up her nose as she listened to Daniel.

"You make an eloquent point, Mr. Calara," Principal Schnitger said when he finished. "Specialized schools like this one are getting in enough trouble. People think we're elite, and they think that means prejudiced and unfair. No one thinks about what's fair to the smart kids, the brilliant kids. Now every year, we have to lower our standards to make people feel better. But that doesn't change the matter at hand."

Principal Schnitger sat at her desk, her long, straight hair pulled back. Xander could smell her coffee breath from way across her large wooden desk. Her office was lined with dark wood and several large shelves full of dusty-looking, atlas-sized books. On the walls were portraits of previous Flatbush Tech presidents, all men in suits, looking colonial, critical, constipated.

Daniel and Xander sat in large leather chairs that seemed to swallow them the more Principal Schnitger spoke. It was particularly uncomfortable for Xander because he was sitting on the trophy, which he had managed to move to the back of his pants.

The principal sighed deeply, as if she were physically pained. "I don't know what to do, I really don't. This is a conundrum, it really is. Xander, you have been having an interesting year, and it looks like you're someone to whom trouble is not unfamiliar. Meanwhile, Mr. Calara has a spotless record, and he appears to be someone to whom trouble has always been a stranger."

Xander took a chance to break from the twin eyes of Mordor to look over at Daniel. The kid looked catatonic, like this was the first time he'd ever been caught for doing anything wrong. Maybe it was.

"Xander, almost all of your teachers have said that despite rarely, if ever, participating in class, you are one of the most brilliant students they have had the pleasure to teach at Flatbush Tech. You turn in well-written, insightful reports; you pass every test with flying colors. I just hate to see you losing your potential this way. And, Daniel, you're also doing very well in your classes, especially in French, and you've recently joined the SOS squad, which will look very good on your resume. Why you would jeopardize all that to play lookout while Xander breaks into a teacher's office is beyond me. Was this just for kicks and thrills, can you tell me that?"

Daniel said nothing. His gaze was now firmly affixed on his sneakers, which floated above the floor.

"Xander, was that it? Did you break into Mr. Friedman's old office out of some morbid curiosity? I for one don't think you had anything to do with what happened to Larry, uh, to Mr. Friedman. So I'm not going to report this to the police. But I'm afraid I have to do something to show you two that this is a place of learning, not the setting of a Hardy Boys adventure."

Xander and Daniel sat in silence, awaiting the ineluctable verdict.

"I have no choice but to suspend you both for a week," she said. "You will still be responsible for all your homework for that week, and you'll bring it all in when you get back. Daniel, I've already called your parents, and your mother will be here to pick you up. Xander, I have this letter for you to bring home. It's in English and Spanish. With this time away, maybe you two will think seriously about how you want to shape your lives. If you want to do something serious and help the world, or if you just want to add to its population of lazy, self-absorbed rule breakers."

Xander and Daniel walked out of the office like zombies. They shuffled down the hall, past one of the SOS squad who watched their feet closely as they went by.

Finally, Xander could not longer contain himself. He said to Daniel, "What happened? Why didn't you signal me that the teacher was coming? I told you about this. I had a plan."

Daniel said, "Surging now through the open sea."

Xander barked back, "What? Why can't you talk like a normal person? Conversing with you is like trying to read tea leaves."

"Look upon the shadow. All the luck you've had, oh."

Xander stopped in place. The horde of students moved around them. "Shadow? You've certainly been shadowing me. Like a puppy. Do you think you're a poet of some sort? Because that would be very sad, pathetic even."

"Find your true name."

"Great Rao!"

"Say the word of the unbinding."

"Is English your second language? Is that what this is about? Before you say anymore indecipherable nonsense, please allow me to go about the rest of my day in peace."

Daniel began sobbing as Xander turned and stormed off down the stairs and out of the building.

43

DIVERGENT

As she was leaving Math, Holly spotted Steve out of the corner of her eye. There he was, wading through the crowd of students, way on the other side of the floor. She hadn't seen him in weeks. She felt she had to talk to him.

"Steve!"

He half turned, then quickly made for the stairwell.

She stepped in his direction, but was blocked by an SOS who said, "Three squares, please."

"You have to be kidding me," she said, stepping back onto the prescribed tile.

She made it to the stairwell, looked down and then up. There he was.

She squeezed through the thick line of students moving up the stairs on their way to class. They had three minutes of freedom, and probably wanted to make the most of it, but they didn't want to be late either.

Both she and Steve were slowly inching up the stairs. Higher up, the students thinned out, and she was only a floor behind him. He ducked into the eighth-floor entrance. The school foundry was on that floor and not much else. She would catch him!

But by the time she got to the entrance on the eighth floor, it was too late. He must have slipped through one of the many secret passages he knew. He was gone.

Later that night, as Holly was trying (and failing) to get to sleep, she thought of Mr. Friedman and what he must have been thinking before he died. She tried to think about logical things, that the attack must have been quick and that he probably did not feel threatened before it happened. Instead, she kept thinking about his last thoughts, how he must have felt betrayed, and how sad it must be to feel your life ending and not have time to say anything to the people you loved.

Her thoughts were interrupted by the sound of her mother's voice downstairs.

She ran down to say goodnight and was surprised to see Commissioner Maguire there as well. She decided it was best not to be noticed and slipped back up the stairs. She tip-toed back to her room.

Knowing her mother, Holly figured she had been working late. Sometimes after work, she went to the local police bar, Mr. Cuffington's, and maybe the commissioner was there, and they came here to discuss something private about police work. *Maybe they'll discuss the murders at school!*

The previous winter, Holly had discovered that if she lay down near the vent in the floor of her room, she could hear any conversation that took place in the dining room.

First, she heard glasses clinking and then her mother's voice. She sounded tired, even sad.

" . . . can't find any connection between the victims. I'm at my wit's end."

"Say, any chance these two were in some sort of secret relationship?" the Commissioner said. "Maybe he was dizzy with this dame, the guidance counselor? Workplace romance, if you know what I mean."

"Well, Friedman had been dating the coach for a while is all we know. But Barkley was not dating at the moment."

Holly's eyebrows flew up. *Friedman was dating Coach DiGeronimo? That's news!*

"Don't you worry, Merce. You'll catch a break and crack the case wide open. You're a great cop."

"Thank you, Commissioner. I just hate to think of Holly being in a place like that. Two murders already."

"I wouldn't worry. I'm sure she's completely secure. And so is your promotion now."

"Thank you. I can't tell you how glad I am to hear that."

Then the commissioner said, "Say, what's a fellow got to do to get one more nightcap around here?"

"Actually, Commissioner, it's a bit late, and I better turn in."

"I told you. You can call me Bob after hours, and these are after hours."

Holly wasn't sure what made her do it, what made her pop up to her feet, run out of her room to the landing and say what she said. The look on her mother's face told her it was the right thing to do.

"Mom! I'm glad you're here."

"Holly!"

Holly cradled her lower belly with both hands and put her best sick face on. "I feel awful, Mom. I'm so glad you're home. I feel just terrible."

The commissioner's face went from smiling to sunken. He mumbled something and then quickly left.

Holly's mother looked at her and, with what looked like tears in her eyes, said, "Thank you. You should get some sleep now."

"I'm actually not feeling bad."

"I know, Holly."

Her mother turned away and went into the living room without turning the light on.

44

CONFLAGRATION

The New York Public Library (not the one with the lion statues), on 45th Street and Madison Avenue in Manhattan, was a quiet place to work. And do research. Xander knew he should have been completing his geometry homework or working on his essay for Mr. Baci. Instead he sat at a table piled with all the D encyclopedias. He'd known disco was popular, but now he was learning a lot more. When he wanted to learn about something, he wanted to learn everything about it. Certainly, he was procrastinating about doing homework, but curious to see if the trophy he had found in Mr. Friedman's office actually meant anything significant.

According to sources, the term "discotheque" was used in Europe in the 1940s to describe a club where no live music was played. The style of music now known as "disco" was an amalgam of Blues, Rock, Soul and Funk, the result being what one magazine called "infectiously danceable musical style." Modern disco dancing could be traced back to inner cities in the late 1960s and early 1970s, when urban Latin, black, gay and hippie communities popularized the music. Xander wondered why people would be named after a dead language, and he wasn't sure what "gay" meant, since he thought everyone who danced was supposed to be happy. Disco progressed exponentially in popularity, becoming the subject of big hit movies, such as *Saturday Night Fever* and *Thank God It's Friday.* The *Daily News* called it the "soundtrack of the Me Generation."

Then a backlash occurred. Earlier that year, July 1979, the Chicago White Sox hosted "Disco Destruction Night." A case of disco albums was blown up in between games of a doubleheader. Afterward, the thuggish sports fans rioted in glee, destroying part of the stadium and causing the cancellation of the second game. An editorial in *The Village Voice* noted, "The message of hate is clear. The animosity against disco is not about music it all. It's straight-up prejudice against the people who created and enjoy this kind music. The 'Disco Sucks' crowd wants to stomp out anything that doesn't come from them and comes from others."

Xander took many notes. He found some references about discotheques in the city, including Mission Venus. It was in the microfiche files for *The Village Voice* that he hit a goldmine.

In the winter of 1978, there had been a disco dance contest at a place called Mission Venus, which piqued Xander's interest because it was apparently named after the 1960s science fiction TV show. "Disco Champions Declared" headlined a brief article, which was dominated by pictures of the event. In one corner, posing near the champions, was a smiling Mr. Friedman. He stood behind a couple and a man in a bright silk shirt. The caption read: "Denny Shabat crowns the King and Queen of Disco 1978, Hector and Marie Chevres. The first place winners get $500 for showing off their boogie shoes." They held aloft a tall award, with two dancing figures on top, a larger version of the award Xander had smuggled into his pants. A woman stood next to Friedman, but her face had been cropped out of the photo.

So, Friedman had come in second place in a dance contest with some woman. If he had won, then there might be a motive for murder from the runners-up. Second place just wasn't worth killing for. Although it was intriguing to find out something so personal about a teacher, it seemed like a dead-end lead.

Xander returned the microfiche and went back to finally tackle his homework. At the next table was Daniel. He had stuff for Geometry homework out but he was scribbling into a spiral notebook.

Xander went up to the table and said, "You see, it's not so bad being suspended. You get to roam around the city whenever. You're not even doing homework. What is this?"

Daniel abruptly closed his notebook, got up, put his other books and 45-degree drafting triangle into his book sack and walked away without saying a word.

"Daniel?" Xander was flummoxed. *How dare that kid?* "Daniel! Wait!" he said, doing his best to keep up with him. "I have another mission for you!"

45

CONFLUENCE

Holly's life as some sort of a teen detective at Flatbush Tech had come to an end. She dutifully went to classes. At home she walked Bandit, did her homework, listened to records. She polished her poem for the *Horizons* literary magazine.

For more than a week she'd been behaving like a regular student. Her investigation had come to a dead end. Really, who did she think she was? It wasn't her job, was it?

In Gym class, she tried her best with volleyball.

Still, all this practicality was no comfort. The case was on her mind. All the time.

She had been watching Coach DiGeronimo. The coach had an alibi for Mr. Friedman's murder, but Holly was sure she knew something more about what had happened to the Social Studies teacher. Still, Holly couldn't think of any way to approach the coach about it. She hadn't exactly been friendly the first time around.

Then there was Steve. She hadn't seen him since he escaped onto the eighth floor. Perhaps he had quit school altogether. How could he possibly pass any classes now? Did he want to be a *senior* senior senior?

Holly also had been thinking about Xander Herrera. She hadn't seen him in any of their classes together, and while Xander hadn't been the most vocal student in class, he had usually been present on a regular basis. She wondered if something had happened to him.

Later that day, Holly spotted Daniel watching her from across a stream of students. She remembered meeting him in the elevator during the first week of school. She had seen him and Xander together many times. Her impression was that they were friends, although she could imagine Xander making that difficult for anyone.

Daniel was eating a candy bar and, when he saw her see him, he zigzagged like a frog in her direction and stopped right in front of her.

"Daniel," she said.

He looked up and gave her the biggest, warmest smile. His lips were covered with chocolate.

"Hello again," she said.

"I see you on the train in your new blue jeans," he said.

"What? That's very sweet. But these aren't new and they're not blue jeans. I also didn't ride the subway recently."

"I see you reading a book, I don't know what it means."

"Wait. Is that the ELO song?"

"I have a nice place, I try to keep it clean. Why won't you come over?"

"Yes! I love ELO."

Daniel smiled widely. His face blushed bright red.

"Wait, do you know what's happened to Xander? I haven't seen him in school in a while. Do you know where he is?"

Daniel nodded fiercely and said, "I am alone. The lonely guy. I have my books. I read them all."

"That's Harry Nilsson now, right?"

Daniel smiled. Beautiful crooked teeth.

"So he's in the library? Of course. Thank you, Daniel!"

Holly glided into the library. Mr. Gladstone nodded as she entered. She nodded back. She didn't want to alert Xander to her presence. Not that he had anywhere to run to now. She had him trapped.

The Flatbush Tech library was a beautiful room on the fifth floor of the building. It was lovingly lined with ornate, dark wood shelves. Wooden carrels and long tables were tucked here and there for students to use.

Holly spotted Xander alone at a table in the back. Of course. There were books piled all around him, and he seemed to be making lists of something.

Without a word, she took the chair opposite him.

He said, "I knew it was you. I could smell you before you came over."

She smirked. "I'm going to take that as a compliment."

He grunted.

"Okay. Xander, listen, I wanted to talk to you. I want to be friends. I've been trying to make friends at school. I made friends with this girl named Christina, and she was really sweet and now she doesn't talk to me anymore. I have these other three friends . . . and now they don't seem to like me either, though I'm not sure why. I thought we could be friends, but I'm afraid you hate me, too. And I can understand why, but I've been trying to talk to you to explain. Sorry, I'm blathering too much and not coming to a point. Even saying 'blathering too much' is blathering. Oh my! The thing is, I never had a chance to talk to you about Mr. Friedman and what I said and how I got you in trouble and what happened to you. I know you were sent to Spofford. I know it must have been horrible. I'm sorry, truly sorry, sorrier than I can ever express. I can't apologize enough, Xander."

Xander grunted again. He wouldn't look at her.

She nodded. At least he wasn't trying to walk away. "And what's more, I've tried . . . I've been trying to figure out what truly happened to Mr. Friedman, who killed him . . . because I want to clear your name completely, to change the way people look at you . . . and because I really liked Mr. Friedman and I think he deserves justice, and so does Ms. Barkley. I didn't know her that well, but I'm sure she deserves justice too. Everyone does. I know those two murders are connected. They have to be! And I mean, I'm not a police officer, and I know I don't want to be a cop. At least I don't think so. Oh, Xander, I don't know why I'm telling you all this, maybe I had too much soda for lunch, maybe I just wanted you to know I'm still trying to make things right, and . . . and . . . oh, I don't know."

Xander didn't grunt this time. "Look at me," he said. "I know how people look at me. Like I'm a mangy dog from the street, and they're going to treat me like one. That's my luck. Nothing you can do will stop that. I know how they look at me, and I don't care."

"Xander," Holly said, "I'm sorry. Um, honestly, it's not going that well. I've run out of suspects. And the victims, the only connection they have so far is Flatbush Tech. Wait. Are you trying to give me the stink eye? That's not very nice."

Xander was indeed giving her the stink eye. Which was no surprise. Then he did something that completely surprised Holly. He smiled. She could see his braces fully now. It was a warm and cold smile at the same time.

Xander said, "Did you know he was a disco king?" He turned and took something out of his briefcase. He put a small trophy on the table.

"Mission Venus? I've heard of that. Where did you get this?"

"In Mr. Friedman's office. Overlooked by the police. Perhaps your mother would be interested in this evidence."

"Is this supposed to be blood?"

He crossed his arms across his chest. "Maybe. Maybe not. Obviously, the police lab should check."

"It's ketchup."

Xander looked at her, embarrassed. "It might be. It might not."

"If it's supposed to be Mr. Friedman's blood, it's been too long. Blood doesn't stay red. It oxidizes in the air and turns rust brown."

"I knew that."

"And it smells like ketchup. What are you trying to do, Xander?"

"Just trying to be helpful."

Holly tapped her chin with her finger. "It has Mr. Friedman's name on it, and I vaguely remember this being is his office. How did you get it?"

Xander grunted.

"I guess I shouldn't ask. This might actually be an important clue. The trophy, not the ketchup."

"Perhaps. Perhaps, but I'm not the detective," he said. "You are."

46

PELLUCID

Despite Holly sussing out his little prank so horribly quickly, Xander was glad to get the trophy off his person. He had hoped she'd taken it to her mother and wasted the police lab's time for a few days. *Well, let Holly try to carry it around in her pants for a while.*

When he returned home that afternoon, his mother Carmen greeted him from the foldout cot she slept on in the kitchen.

"*Mira quién es. El varón* is home."

"Where is Abuela?" Xander said.

On the table was a glass of milk and a plate of cookies his grandmother always left out for him. Next to these were several empty bottles of beer.

"She's still napping. She doesn't like the fall weather. It gets to her bones. That's what she says."

Carmen was tipsy, and when she was tipsy she became talkative, and not in an interesting way. Xander knew it was more likely that his grandmother had gone to her room to escape his mother's meandering mouth.

He sat at the table and tried to ignore her and enjoy his afternoon snack.

"C'mon," his mother said, sitting up and patting the space next to her. "Sit down. C'mon." She lit a cigarette as Xander sat down. "I want to talk to you."

"My cookies come first."

"Oh my god, this one! Just because you got a few hairs, you think you're a man all of a sudden that can speak to me without respect."

Xander ignored her and took his plate and glass and sat on the cot. He was uncomfortable sitting close to his mom. Carmen was little more than a stranger to him, and he had never been fond of strangers.

"Okay. I get it. You know, I know I haven't been that great a mother," she said. "What can I say? It's not like there's a school for it." She laughed to herself, then she said with all seriousness, "There should be. There should. But I would probably play hooky anyway and miss the most important lessons." She laughed again. "How to hold a baby's head. What to feed him. I didn't know, you know. I had no idea. My mother really helped me out there, I can tell you."

"Uh huh," Xander said.

"For her it came natural. That lady could take care of a rock and it would come out okay. But it's not natural for some people, you know what I mean? For me, I didn't know what to do, and I gotta be honest with you, I didn't want to know. I just didn't have it in me. I know that makes me sound like a horrible person, but I'm not a horrible person, I'm just a person, and not all of us are made to do something. I mean, I was made by God to be a mother with my body, my body can make babies. But in my heart, I couldn't. I didn't want to."

Xander looked her in the eyes, something that was not easy for him to do. "Why. . . why didn't you have an abortion?"

"Well, it wasn't because of your father. He practically came after me with a hanger himself. *Esto y lo otro.* 'I've got too many kids already,' he said. 'I can't support you.' 'Get rid of it. I'll pay you later.' What a piece of work that guy was."

"I don't know. I never met him."

"You're not missing anything. So it was your grandma, of course. She knew I was pregnant before I did. She saw me here one morning, and out of nowhere she says, *'Estás encinta.'* I said, 'No no, no way,' although I never used protection, so, you know, I knew she could be right. And two months later, I saw she was. And she knew what I was thinking. I told her what your father was telling me, and she wasn't having it. *Jesucristo* this! *Jesucristo* that! She told me I had to have that baby. That it would change my life and make me a better person. She said she would help me. And she did. I'll be honest. She did. She came through."

"She's the one who took care of me since I was a baby."

"That's true. It's true."

"She didn't 'help' you. You didn't do anything."

"That's not true. I tried. I wiped your butt a thousand times. You were like a little volcano. But I couldn't take it, I couldn't take none of it. So I cut out."

"You decamped, departed, disappeared."

"I come back when I can, Papi, but you know how it is. I'm still young. I still got my life ahead of me. I can't be anybody's mother, not yet."

Xander said nothing. He stared at his empty glass of milk and the one cookie he had left. He didn't want to eat it anymore, but he ate it anyway.

"So tell me about yourself," Carmen said. "You're in trouble with the law now. Don't tell me you're taking after your father. Not after all I sacrificed. I don't want you to end up no jailbird. You're too smart for that. It would break my heart, Papi."

"I'm never going to be arrested again," he said.

"Good, that's good to know."

"The police are never going to put cuffs on me ever again."

"I'm so proud of you, Papi. I know you're going to go to college and make something of yourself."

"What do you do?" he said.

"What do you mean?" Carmen finished her cigarette and immediately lit up another.

"Where do you go?"

She laughed. "You're asking personal questions. You can't do that, I'm your mother."

"Do you go to discos?"

"Shoot, you kidding me. I go all the time. Studio 54, 1018, Paradise Garage, Mission Venus, Funhouse, Revelation, Gazebo, you name it. I go to them all."

When Xander heard "Mission Venus," he sat up straight. "What do you do at the discos?"

"Dance! What else? Men buy me drinks. Listen, I'm no lady, but I'm no tramp. It's fun. I love it. Getting dressed up and going out. There's nothing better in the world. You like staying home like a hermit. But I gotta go out. I can't stay home. I get bored.

"But I tell you something, they've been changing. Everything costs so much. Plus, the people are different now. You know, I lived in this neighborhood for thirty years, and I've been going to discos since I was nineteen, and I have never been called a 'spic' in my life. This summer, matter of fact it was the week after July 4, I got called 'spic' twice in one week. At two different discos."

The same week as the Chicago stadium event, Xander thought.

"So why is my son so interested in discos all of a sudden?"

Xander got up and went to his briefcase. He took out a newspaper clip he had been carrying. "Do you know this guy in the corner?"

"Oh my god, yeah, that's Larry Dazzle."

"Larry Dazzle? That's Mr. Friedman. This is the guy they said I killed."

"This guy? Oh my god! Someone killed Larry! I didn't know that. Wow. Everyone on the scene knows who he is. He used to win all the dance contests. He was terrific."

"He came in second place for this contest."

"That's weird. He always used to win. Maybe he had a bad night. Oh, wait, now I remember. Oh shoot! Wow."

"What?"

"That dance contest. That friend of mine who died, Hector Chevres. That's who won the contest last year."

"How did your friend die again?"

"Oh, some crazy person pushed him on the L train tracks. So sad."

"Did they catch this person?"

"Nah, the police never catch anybody."

Xander felt the hairs on his arms rising. Two people who participated in a disco contest were killed within months of each other. That was suspicious. This was too much of a coincidence.

This required further investigation.

MULTIFARIOUS

After school, Holly asked Victor to stop at a record store. There were several to choose from on Atlantic Avenue. Victor pulled the car in front of the largest.

"Shopping for music?"

"Yes, my friends tell me it's time I bought new records." She was about to jump out, then she stopped. "Victor, can I ask you a question?"

He looked scared in the rearview mirror, but then smiled. "Sure thing, Ms. Holly."

"Is my mother all right?"

He seemed surprised by the question. "What do you mean?"

"She seems so preoccupied all the time now. And sad."

"Well," he said, "as far as that, I don't think she's gotten over what happened to your dad. I don't think she'll ever get over it. But you have to let her grieve in her own way. You know what I mean?"

Holly felt herself choking up. She felt it was something else that had been bothering her mom. She told Victor about the commissioner's coming over late at night and abruptly leaving.

Victor laughed.

"What's so funny?"

"Man, your mom's got a lot of . . . uh, courage. She does. I don't know if you know how much she has to deal with on a daily basis, not only being a Puerto Rican cop, but also being a lady cop, which may be even tougher. She doesn't have it easy. She has to work real hard for them old boys to take her seriously, harder than everybody else. If they work 100 percent, she's gotta do 200, 300. You understand?"

"I think I do, yes. I wish she would talk to me about it."

"Parents don't like to burden their kids, Ms. Holly. She's lucky she's got you. And don't think she doesn't love you and worry about you all the time."

"That is sweet of you to say," Holly said. She looked out at the busy sidewalk. "Okay, I better get some records."

"What you getting?"

"Have you ever heard of Grace Jones?"

"No."

"Neither have I! But she looks amazing!"

"C'mon, girls, move it, move it, move it!" In Gym the next day, Assistant Coach Gorney was giving them all a hard time. "I'm sick of students who don't have their act together!"

Coach DiGeronimo was out again, for the third day in a row, with a bad cold. In the meantime, the assistant coach kept yelling at them like they were in the army. She did not let them have free time. She wanted them to do drills, to run and do push-ups and sit-ups. It was all very boring and very stressful. What was worse for Holly was that she was not able to talk to Beth or Sharona or Brandy.

"Come on, faster, faster!" Assistant Coach Gorney yelled. "You call that running? I call that napping standing up."

As soon as Xander gave her the trophy, Holly knew the red stain was ketchup. She didn't know what Xander was playing at, why he was trying to make a fool of her. Maybe it was some form of revenge for what he did to her.

In any case, the trophy itself had her thinking. She had taken it out on the drive home, as Victor was describing a particularly close race at Belmont Park, and she looked at it and looked at it. It was familiar. Hours later, as she was finishing up her dinner of chicken marsala, she remembered!

She had gone to her casebook and found her notes about Ms. Barkley's office: "3rd Place trophy—dance." If memory served, the trophy was exactly like the one Xander had given her. She hadn't thought about it much then, but now she knew it had to mean something. She formulated a plan about finding out what. But she would need the help of the girls she hoped she could call friends.

At one point, when the coach lined them up, Holly found herself in between Brandy and Beth. Realizing she wouldn't have much time to speak, she said, "Girls, I really need your help with something."

"Is it a boy?" Brandy said.

"Is it about your hair?" Beth said.

"My hair?" Holly said. "What?!"

"I think we should talk at lunch," Sharona said. "Coach incoming."

"You three!" the assistant coach yelled. "You ain't. I mean, you *aren't* going to break a sweat by yapping your mouths. Give me ten laps!"

"What do you know about disco?"

They were in the lunchroom, not quite enjoying cold grilled cheese, when Holly asked.

"My parents won't let me listen to that," Sharona said. "They say it's the devil's music."

"I thought rock and roll was supposed to be the devil's music," Beth said.

"That is too. Isn't it?" Sharona said. "All music is devil's music, according to my parents."

"Even John Denver?" Holly said.

"I don't know John Denver. Is he good?"

"He's the one who sings about the mountains," Beth said.

Brandy leaned forward conspiratorially. "So tell us why you want to know about disco all of a sudden."

"Disco is kind of dying, isn't it?" Sharona said.

"It's been dead."

"It died last year and no one told it that it was dead," said Brandy, who chuckled to herself.

"To be honest, it's about Mr. Friedman," Holly said. "Mr. Friedman and Ms. Barkley. Well, maybe."

Brandy looked around. "Does that mean you're helping your mother on the case? Is that what this is about?"

"Is that legal?" Sharona said. "It doesn't sound legal."

"Do any of you go to discos?" Holly said. "I know we're young."

"Well, we're not supposed to get in."

"My big sister goes all the time," Brandy said. "Sometimes she takes me. I've been to Studio 54 a few times."

Holly said, "So, thing is, I need to go to a disco."

"Here comes the 'Dancing Queen.'"

"Sure thing. There's one in Brooklyn in Sheepshead Bay that's pretty good."

"No. The one I need to go to is Mission Venus."

CONSPIRE

At lunchtime Xander found himself not going to his usual sanctum sanctorum in the library, but up to the rowdy, noisy lunchroom. It smelled of hot dogs and feet in there, and the mid-autumn sun shining through the barred windows did little to cut the fluorescent gloom that hung over the large space.

He was still plotting his next steps regarding the Friedman Case, as he liked to call it, but decided he did not want to spend the next period contemplating it. He found Daniel at the end of a corner table, sitting by himself. He was writing in his spiral notebook.

"What are you writing in there anyway?"

"I walk the roads, with my thumb out."

"Okay, I won't ask." Xander took the seat across from him. "I was just walking through the lunchroom. How did you do on that Geometry quiz?"

"Poor, hungry or sad I'll never be," said Daniel, smiling, showing him a quiz marked with a circled 100.

"I guessed you would do well," Xander said. "And, uh, I guessed that that teacher must have been hopping along with his cast, and you thought he was going to go one way, but he went another, straight to Mr. Friedman's office."

"Daddy has left me the Silver Tree!"

"Yeah, sure he has." Then Xander saw, under the quiz that Daniel had tugged out, another quiz, for Chemistry. The grade was clear: 54.

"Is that what you got in Chemistry? Are you not retaining the information? There's a big test in two days."

"Sorry and sad faced, he said he was dying."

"Gadzooks!" Xander looked through Daniel's papers at some other equally distressing quiz scores. Here was incontrovertible proof that Daniel was never going to be a chemist. For his part, Xander had somehow mastered the basics of chemistry despite Mr. Styczynski's rather pedestrian sense of humor. He was able to pay attention in class and get good grades. He decided that he needed to help Daniel. It was the honorable thing to do.

"Something must be done. Although there's not enough time to catch you up. We both have Mr. Lynch's report due tomorrow. You could come to study at my house. Wait, I prefer not to have guests at the moment. Or ever, frankly."

"On the bus going back, he patted my head."

"I could go to your house, of course. I don't enjoy traveling out of my usual environs. However, I do have an idea!"

At the end of the school day, Xander didn't have to look far to find the person he was looking for. He had seen him before, across the street from the school, on one of the benches outside of Fort Greene Park. He hung out with what were no doubt his cronies, who looked as if they had skipped school all day, which they very likely had. Normally, Xander kept his head down and avoided any eye contact.

Today, he went directly across the street, ignoring the beeps of the cars.

Juanito spoke before Xander had a chance to say anything. "Say, Jack. Look who's here," he said. "It's Jawbreaker."

49

EQUANIMITY

Holly had never done anything like this before. Of course she had lied to her mother from time to time, little white lies that made her mother smile. This was different. Holly wasn't just lying, that she had washed her hands or brushed her teeth when she hadn't or that there wasn't a freshly baked birthday cake waiting for her mom in the dining room. It wasn't even the lies of omission she had been guilty of ever since she had started this investigation of hers. This was very different.

This was going out. At night. Under false pretenses. What made it worse was that her mother trusted her, so she was easy to lie to.

"Mom, some of the girls from school are having a sleepover next weekend. Can I go?"

"Sure. I'm happy to hear you're making new friends."

"So am I."

"And there won't be any boys there, right?"

"There won't be any boys there!"

That was all it took. She never asked about it again. When Holly reminded her that it was tonight, she said to have fun. Holly felt guilt press on her chest but knew it was the right thing to do. Wasn't it?

Her mother wasn't the only defensive perimeter she had to circumvent.

Victor parked in the narrow street in front of Brandy's house in Richmond Hill. It was a pretty, two-family brick house in the middle of a block of identical houses.

He turned around in his seat and said, "If you want, I'm sure I can find a parking spot and stay around here all night, just in case."

Somehow, it felt worse to lie to Victor. Holly was tempted to tell him the truth but knew she couldn't.

"There's no need," she said. "The girls will make fun of me. And it's just a sleepover."

"It's no big deal. I'll listen to the radio."

"No, please, enjoy the night off."

"I don't mind. It's my job."

"I know. But I'll be fine."

"There won't be any boys there, right?"

"Victor, please. I already have a mom. Thank you."

He looked shocked at what she said. "I'm sorry, Ms. Holly, but I'm here to watch out for you."

Holly couldn't help herself. She felt herself snapping and couldn't stop herself. "Victor. I don't need a driver. I don't need a bodyguard. I am fine. It's been years since what happened . . . to Dad. I know that's why Mom probably hired you. But please . . . go home."

"Yes, Ms. Holly," he said, with obvious reluctance.

"And please don't circle the neighborhood for hours."

"Okay," he said. "I'll pick you up tomorrow morning?"

"Yes! Nine o'clock."

"On the dot!"

Victor nodded. Holly took her sleeping bag and overnight case out of the car. She felt *awful*. She knew he would wait there at the curb until she got in. She knew she should say something but had no idea what to say. She rang the bell.

Brandy and the girls screamed in joy when they opened the door. They were all wearing pajamas or sweatpants.

She met Brandy's parents very quickly and then was rushed downstairs by the girls to a finished basement. Covering the entirety of one of the longer wood-paneled walls were clipped magazine covers of Diana Ross, John Travolta, George Benson, Teddy Pendergrass.

Three sleeping bags were laid out on the shag-carpeted floor, along with half a dozen board games and open bags of chips and cheese-flavored snacks.

Even though the sleepover was a ruse, Holly found herself wishing they could stay there all night playing Monopoly and Clue (her favorite!) and eating sweet and salty snacks. But there was work to be done.

"What about your parents?"

Brandy said, "They're on schedule to go to bed at nine, and when they sleep, they are dead to the world. I've snuck out so many times now, it's not even that much fun anymore."

Loud disco music was playing. Beth asked Holly if she liked Barry White.

Holly said she wished the lyrics were more interesting.

"Lyrics!"

The girls changed from their pajamas and sweatpants into outfits fit for a disco. Brandy put on a purple stretch-jersey polyester wrap dress and sling back sandals. Beth wore tight satin pants, a lovely diaphanous blouse and platform-soled shoes. Sharona wore a light green stretchy, strapless tube, a short skirt and knee-high boots with chunky heels.

Holly had on something she thought was appropriate for the occasion. She wore new bell-bottom blue jeans, a pink argyle sweater over a white blouse and clog mules she had taken from the back of her mother's closet. She hoped she looked sporty enough for the evening.

When she was done, the other girls were looking at her.

"What's wrong?" she said.

"Your hair," Brandy said.

"What about my hair?"

"Let's have some fun with it."

Despite Holly's protests that she had already washed and blow-dried her hair (for an hour!), the girls re-washed it and then teased it out.

When she looked in the mirror, she didn't recognize herself. The hair on top of her head was straight, but cascading down the right side of her face, and the back of her head was a waterfall of brown curls.

"That's . . . cool."

Beth said, "What about those glasses?"

"Hold up!" Brandy said. She went into a wardrobe and came out with a pair of contact lenses. "It's an old set," she said. "My emergency pair."

"But I never . . . ," Holly protested. "Our prescriptions . . . "

"Doesn't matter," Brandy said.

"What about make-up?" Sharona said. "She needs make-up, right?"

"Make-up?" Holly had never really thought about make-up. All she had was strawberry lip gloss.

"Glitter!" Brandy sang.

"Glitter!" Sharona and Beth echoed.

They snuck out the back door and through the narrow alleyway behind Brandy's house. The world swam in Holly's eyes. Not only was she trying to get used to the feeling of two hard and uncomfortable discs sitting on her eyeballs, Brandy's prescription had turned out to be weaker than hers, and everything seemed out of focus. What didn't help was that it was dark out and the streets they walked on were canopied with trees, which filled the night with shadows and jutting roots. Somehow, she made it the two blocks they needed to go without stumbling *too much*. They waited at a corner in the cold autumn night for Beth's older sister, Dawn.

"I hope she's got the heat on this time," Brandy said.

"Fingers crossed," Beth said. "I'm freezing. Where is she?"

"Any second," Sharona said.

Ten minutes later, a red Chevy Nova pulled around the corner and came to an abrupt stop in front of them. "Pile in!" Dawn said. *About twenty-four-years old. Skin smooth and glowing. Glitter, oval face. Wig. Gap-toothed.*

They piled in, and Dawn sped toward Manhattan. Then she came to an abrupt stop one block away. Looking around at them, she said, "Did you girls not do your make-up yet?"

"We did," Beth said.

"Then we have to do it again. You all look like teenagers sneaking into a club. You need more glitter."

Forty minutes later, they were on their way to Manhattan and Mission Venus.

Mission Venus was located in the East 50s. Dawn refused to pay for parking, so she took twenty minutes to find a space ten blocks away from the club.

Holly heard the thumping music a block away. As she got closer, she could just make out the words "Mission

Venus" in plain letters on an old-fashioned movie marquee. Snaking away from the entrance was a long line of people that went around the block.

Dawn said, "Now, you have to act mature. Please do not embarrass me."

"Are you sure we'll be able to get in?" Holly squinted.

"Yeah," Dawn said. "I know the bouncer tonight. Should be no problem. Just don't act like high school girls."

The bouncer—6'4" *and 250 pounds, blurry*—looked like a small, implacable mountain as they walked up to him. Dawn shouted his name, "Edwin!" Then his implacable face broke into a wide smile.

Dawn kissed him on the cheek and he opened the velvet rope without even looking at Holly and the girls.

As they entered, Holly recognized the song playing at high volume by a group called Machine. She was glad she could appreciate the music, but she felt bad that with her fuzzy vision she couldn't fully appreciate the scenery. She was also a bit self-conscious about her new hair and her face glimmering with glitter. As much as she could see of all the adults there, she felt a bit young and childlike. Brandy, Beth and Sharona seemed comfortable, though, so she tried to follow their lead.

Once past the vestibule, the chill of the outside was gone. It was steaming hot inside the disco. The design theme seemed to be variations of purple and orange and red. These blended together in Holly's eyes. Every surface was brightly colored. Every surface (that she could see) seemed to vibrate to the beat of the music.

The place was thick with people, and they had to squeeze through slowly, holding each other's hands. They made their way through a long hallway and into a larger room. At the edge of this was the dance floor, which must

have been a theater auditorium years ago, from the look of
the walls.

Dawn yelled that she was getting a drink. Yelling was
the only way to talk in there. Then she yelled, "You all are
too young to drink, so you're all getting Shirley Temples and
that's it. You're lucky I got you in this far."

Holly yelled, "Thank you, Dawn. Thank you for all your
help."

"Brandy told me what you're doing. Be careful, little
thing. There are serious people in here."

Holly stood near the girls at the edge of the dance floor
and watched the blurry crowd move in sync to the beat of
the music. Some people seemed to be dressed in dramatic
costumes, some seemed barely dressed at all. They all
seemed hypnotized by the music.

"Let's go dance," Brandy yelled.

"Should we? Yes!" Sharona yelled, although she had
already started and was working her way into the crowd.

"No, not me, thanks," Holly yelled. "I've got something
to do first."

Holly could hear Brandy calling after her as she, squinting hard, sunk into the crowd and made her way toward
what looked like a purple stairway at the other end of the
club. She took a step into a hallway on the left, and it was as
if she had popped out of the crowd. There was no one in
the hallway. Farther in, she saw a man who looked to be
guarding a door that opened up to the stairway. *Six-five,
three hundred fifty pounds, red hair.* She couldn't see much
of his face. He might have had shades on, or he had two big
holes in his face.

She got an idea and ran up to him. "You have to help
me," she said. The music wasn't as loud here but she still

found herself yelling. "My friend is in the bathroom and she's really sick."

He didn't seem concerned and didn't look at her. "Tell the janitors," he said in a normal tone of voice.

"But she might die," Holly yelled, then repeated, in a normal tone, "She might die."

"Tell the janitors."

"Okay," she said, seeing that she was getting nowhere. "Look, my friend's not really sick. I have to see Mr. Shabat. It's urgent."

"Mr. Shabat is not a music producer," the guard said, still not looking at her and reciting the words as if he'd said them a million times. "If you want to find a music producer, you could throw a rock on the dance floor and hit a hundred of them."

"I'm not a musician or a singer."

"Mr. Shabat has no connections with choreographers. If . . . "

"I'm not a dancer either. Okay, I have news about a possible raid, and I need to see him right away."

The guard finally turned his head. "Where'd you get this news?"

"Um, Commissioner McGuire's son told me. He's my boyfriend."

He nodded and unlocked the door behind him. "Denny's upstairs. I'll ring you up."

Holly ran up the carpeted steps and came to an old-fashioned door that was covered in leather. There was a doorbell in the wall. Before she could press it, she heard a buzz and the door unlocked.

"Ha, come in."

She stepped in, the door swung closed behind her. To the delight of her ears, Holly realized that she could hear again. None of the music from downstairs reached into the room. In fact, the only sound was the faint volume coming from a large television set playing what sounded like a rerun of *The Honeymooners.*

"You look really familiar," said Denny Shabat. He was sitting in a white leather recliner. He had his shoes off, and it looked like he was drinking cocoa with marshmallows. "Ha, I know you. You're the pretty baby from McGuire's house this summer. You had glasses. But I recognize the cute little cat teeth. Well, welcome to Mission Venus!"

"My name is Holly Hernandez."

"How alliterative. Do you want some cocoa, HH? I just made some."

"No, thanks," she said, although the cocoa did smell good. "Don't you like listening to your own music from the club? It's so quiet in here."

"Ha, that stuff? It's all Bee Gees and Village People *all* the time now. Mass produced like Kentucky Fried Chicken. I miss the old days, before Travolta. Before all the three-piece suits. They just kill the ambience."

"What do you mean? People seem to be enjoying themselves."

"That's all a show. Let me tell you something. When I started, I was spinning records in tiny bars hidden away on dark side streets, and every night people would come in and fill up the little dance floor and dance till the sun came up, and I'm not talking about the bright, shiny people you see on TV. I mean, all the rest of us who have nowhere to go, who aren't living the Great American Dream. In those bars and clubs, honey, we could dance and be ourselves in ways that we could never be anywhere else. Now, what's downstairs, what people think is disco, that's just polyester *meshugas.*"

"Oh. I didn't know. I-I'm sorry to bother you, Mr. Shabat. I need to ask you something about Mr. Friedman. Lawrence Friedman. Maybe you knew him as Larry."

"My bell is not ringing. Are you some kind of undercover detective? Are you really thirty-five or something? Ha! That would be wild."

"He won the second place trophy at your contest last year."

"Our Disco Champion? That was Larry Dazzle. Ha, I guess I never thought that was his real name, but to tell you the truth, I didn't give it any thought. Who you are outside of this place doesn't matter. Who you are here does. You come here to let go, to have fun. Not to bring the worries of the world with you. At least that's the way it used to be."

"Was there anything unusual about that contest? Did anything bad happen?"

"1978 seems so long ago, so last year." He laughed at his own joke. "But wait, it is funny about that contest. Larry Dazzle and his partner won first place, tens from all the judges. Then the strangest thing happened: Larry turned around and took the mic and then said he was giving the award to the couple that came in second. He said the judges were prejudiced against them."

"Oh? Who were they?"

"A Puerto Rican couple. Hector and Marie. They used to come here all the time, although I haven't seen them lately. I hope they're not frequenting that Studio 54 dive. Scratch. Right off the Christmas list. Ha!"

"Do you think the judges were prejudiced?"

"I don't know. Everyone is the same to me. Sure, the kind of people who pack in here have changed. It's gotten . . . weird. But we're all the same *underneath*. That's what I believe."

"But the judges?"

"Look. The record companies pick the judges, not me. I just run the show. Everyone's welcome in my show."

"Do you know where I can reach that couple?"

"Sorry, HH. I have no idea. Here's something else you might find interesting. When Larry gave away the award and the $500, you should have seen the look on the face of his partner. She. Was. Livid."

"She was? Who was she?

"Some intense little thing. Let me think . . . "

At that moment, a red siren mounted into the ceiling lit and began to spin.

"No, not again, not again."

"What is it?"

"A raid, sister! It's a raid."

50

VORACIOUS

"You're in luck," Juanito said, "Styczynski likes to use the same exams from year to year, all based on the Regents. He's too lazy to change them. So I can get you a whole set for the entire semester."

Xander shook his head. "The semester is almost over. Besides, I only require this week's exam. The one he's giving the day after tomorrow."

"Are you sure? You got Geometry or Pre-Cal this semester? I can get those. Buy one, get one free."

"No, just the day after tomorrow's."

"I don't know, Jawbreaker. That's pretty particular. That may need more digging."

"Hardly. I'm in the seventh-period class. No doubt he's giving the same exam earlier in the day. You just need to get the exam from some student in an earlier class and then get it to me before then."

"I hear that. But what about the answers? You need the answers."

"If I have it before lunch, I won't."

"You're pretty cocky. Little Jesus said you were like that. He said you told him that's what makes you 'interesting.' I don't know that I find it interesting. Anyway, I'll get it for you before lunch period, no problem."

"Good." Xander turned away. It was getting cold and he wanted to get home. He had to finish a report, and Abuela was making a fresh pot of *arroz con gandules* and had promised to save him all the *pegao* that was stuck to the pot.

"Wait up. Wait up."

Juanito put a hand on Xander's shoulder, and Xander looked at it as if it were a bug. Juanito pulled his hand away.

"What?" Xander said.

"Jawbreaker, this isn't a one-sided deal. This is business. *I* get you something, now *you* get me something."

"How much do you want? How much will it cost me?"

"Not money, brother. I don't need money from you."

"What then?"

"You know Mr. Licata?"

Xander thought of the lowbrow, law-breaking, liquor-swilling head of security. "Unfortunately."

"Well, he's got something we want, and I need you to get it for me."

WRETCHED

Holly sat on her living room couch, praying her mother would not kill her. Bandit had his head on her lap and whimpered as her mother paced the rug in front of her.

"It's just . . . ," her mother said. "I can't . . . "

During the raid, Denny Shabat had told Holly her best bet was to hide in his clothes closet and hope they didn't search it. "And, believe me, I really hope they don't search it," he said. After the cops left, then she could sneak out, going down the stairs she'd come up and out a side door.

"But what about my friends?" she said.

Denny flicked on security monitors and together they found that the girls were already being rounded up.

"Oh no! It's my fault," she said.

"Don't worry. The worst thing they'll get is a reputation," Shabat told her. "You, pure thing, you don't need a reputation. And me, I have one already. That's why I have to split and face the piper, ha." He locked the door behind him, leaving his cocoa half-finished.

Holly had waited as long as she could. It was stuffy and smelled like too much musky cologne. The worst thing was what was happening to her eyes. They were drying out, and the contacts lenses felt like pieces of broken glass stabbing her pupils. She had to get them out. Maybe Shabat had some eyedrops in his office. In any case, she had to get out before her eyes melted.

She gingerly opened the closet door. At that moment, the office door was kicked in. Two uniformed officers stood there looking at her. They were blurry at first, but she recognized them as they drew closer. They knew her, too.

Officer Amenguale. He had a wife, three kids and, just like she did, a Doberman pinscher. Officer Levitt. A sweet man who sang opera as a hobby.

Levitt turned to his partner, "I'll get her to the car."

Amenguale said, "Right."

Levitt gingerly whisked her out the office and down the stairs and out the side exit Denny had mentioned. He put her in the back of a patrol car, got in the front and started driving.

"What the heck were you doing there, Holly?" he said. "In the manager's office, of all places! That guy's a sleaze bag."

"It's a long story, Ron. But thank you for getting me out of there."

"You ain't out of the woods yet, Holly."

He drove her home and waited in the car while she went up to the door. Her mother pulled it open. The first thing she said was, "Your hair!"

Then she ordered Holly to clean her face, then come back downstairs immediately. She took the opportunity to finally peel the contact lenses off her eyeballs. Her eyes were on fire. She swore to never, ever wear contact lenses again.

And now, here she was, face freshly washed, eyes still stinging, waiting for her execution.

"I don't . . . I don't know what to do with you, Holly."

"Mom, what about my friends?"

"They're all home safe now. I talked to McGuire, and they were released, and there won't be any record of their having been at the club. Their parents are probably giving them a very harsh talking-to. Now you. Just tell me, what were you doing there? And I want the truth."

Holly could not tell her mother the truth. She could not tell her she had been there on the case. Her mother didn't need the aggravation or any complications threatening her promotion, the one the commissioner had mentioned. Holly was so close to solving the case, she couldn't stand the idea of not seeing it through.

"I just wanted to go dancing, Mom." It felt horrible to say it. It hurt to say it.

"Dancing? Dancing?! But I . . . I thought you didn't like dancing . . . anymore."

"Yes, Mom, I still do. I never stopped liking it. I only stopped dancing."

"And you like disco?"

"Yeah. I like it."

Her mother sat down on the couch next to her, quiet for a long time. Finally, she said, "Your father, he was the one who loved dancing. I didn't. I couldn't. Can't dance. Born with two left feet, I guess. We used to go to little r & b clubs all the time. He wanted to dance. I just wanted to be with him. He would pull me up, and I would try. But I would always stop after a dance or two and hang on to a wall. I don't know what the hell he saw in me."

"He saw a beautiful woman with two left feet that he loved."

"That is so sweet. *Wait up now!* Don't try to butter me up, young lady. You were too young to be in that club, and you know it. We can bust that Shabat guy for that."

"Please don't. Not because of me."

"You and your friends weren't the only underaged kids in there. But the commissioner, he wants to get Shabat on something bigger, something that will put him out of business. McGuire really has a chip on his shoulder about discotheques and the whole disco world. It's like he can't stand the future and wants to stop it. *Wait up.* What you did to your hair?"

"Do you like it?"

Her mother's eyes grew watery at the edges. "My little girl. I love it. You look gorgeous. When did that happen? Here you are growing up already, and I don't even know who you are." She covered her face and quietly sobbed.

Holly began sobbing too and put an arm around her mother. "Don't worry, Mom. I wouldn't even know how to replicate it."

"It's not that. It's a little old for you, and that make-up, well, that make-up has to go. Who did that to you?"

"My friends."

Her mother wiped at her eyes. "I guess I never took the time to show you. When would I have time?"

"That's okay, Mom."

"It's not okay! I've been way too busy. And now . . . now I have to go to the precinct because it's all hands on deck going through the witnesses from last night, and apparently these men can't fill out paperwork for themselves."

Holly risked asking: "Where's Mr. Shabat now? Is he in jail?"

Her mother looked at her watch. "At this minute, he's probably making bail. And that doesn't concern you anymore, young lady. Understand? I also had to fire Victor."

"What? But you can't blame him, Mom! I told him he should go home."

"Yeah, but he should've known better than to be tricked by a thirteen-year-old."

"Please don't fire him."

"It's done. Are you giving me the stink eye? Is that what you're doing?"

"No. . . ," Holly said, although she could feel that she was.

"Enough. Go to your room, young lady. Right now."

"Mom!"

Her mother held her hand up, a sign that the conversation was over.

Holly spent the rest of the morning in her room, crying, thinking, moping and talking to Bandit. She picked up the phone to call Victor, but then she felt too ashamed to talk to him. Then she became worried that the girls would be angry with her, so she called Brandy. Brandy answered and said they were more worried about her.

"We didn't know where you went," Brandy said. "We thought you mighta got murdered!"

"Oh, no, no. I was just chasing down a lead."

"Of course, you were! Any luck?"

"A little, yes."

She told Brandy about Larry Dazzle. Brandy said, "So that's why he used to dance up and down the classroom all the time. He had disco in his soul. He couldn't shake it."

"I guess you're right. It's a nice thing to remember about him."

"What now?"

"Well, I need to track down other people who were at the disco that night. I'm not sure where to start."

"The girls and I are ready when you are, Holly. You lead and we'll follow."

"Thanks, Brandy."

"Holly."

"Yes?"

"I just wanted to say, I'm really glad we're friends now. I know in junior high I was totally jealous of you."

"Jealous of me?"

"Yeah. You were always the smartest one in the class. That's who I wanted to be."

"But you were always the prettiest."

"Yeah, but I wanted to be the smartest more!"

The following week, Holly was driven to and from school by a man who smelled like corn chips and who wouldn't talk to her. Meanwhile, her mother was barely home and barely talked to her when she was.

The day before Thanksgiving, Holly got home to find a large envelope waiting for her. Inside was a handwritten note on a slick postcard announcing "Last Dance Contest 1979, November 24th, 1979" with the Mission Venus logo (a purple rocket) on it. Also inside the envelope were a series of black-and-white glossy photographs.

The note read: "HH, sorry we didn't get to finish chatting. Here are some pictures of last year's contest. Ha! Hope it helps! Also, I've included a VIP pass to this year's dance contest. I'm calling it Last Dance because it could be our last one. Please come! Don't bring the cops this time! XOXO, DS."

Holly spread the photos from the 1978 contest out on her desk. Mission Venus was packed with dancers. Even though the pictures were black and white, Holly could still feel the energy and the joy of the people in the photos. She found

Larry Dazzle—Mr. Friedman—easily. He was the focus of every shot. She also found some familiar faces that helped her begin to put the puzzle together. They didn't look like she normally saw them, so it took a moment to make sure it was them: Ms. Barkley, Mr. Baci and . . . she looked closer . . . yes, yes, it was. . . . She recognized her unfriendly face from Gym: Assistant Coach Stephanie Gorney.

She opened up her case notebook while making a mental note to send Mr. Shabat a thank you card.

FORMIDABLE

At fifteen minutes after three o'clock, Xander knocked on Mr. Licata's office door. It was a small office tucked away from the classrooms. Unlike every other room in the school, it had three superior locks on it, one of which Xander hadn't learned how to pick yet.

Licata was sitting at his desk listening to a staticky sports broadcast from a radio on the windowsill. His large frame dominated the tiny desk. He looked up and said, "Oh brother. What do you want?"

Under his arm, Xander carried a plastic chess set, recently liberated from the library. He would return it long before Mr. Gladstone noticed its absence.

"Since we created the story that we had enjoyed bouts of chess, I thought it was important that we continue the subterfuge, in case of suspicious minds or prying eyes."

"What did you just say?"

Xander tried very hard not to roll his eyes or sigh in impatience. "Since we lied and said we played chess that time, we should actually play chess, just in case anyone becomes suspicious."

"Who's going to become suspicious?"

Xander, who still stood outside the door of the office, looked one way down the hall and then the other. "You never know who's watching."

"I don't have any time for games, kid."

"You don't seem particularly busy."

"Always the smart mouth. *I am busy.*"

Something interesting seemed to be happening on the game on the radio. Licata gave his full attention to it for a moment. Then he sighed and said, "You follow football?"

"Not likely," Xander said, walking into the tiny space uninvited. He put the board on the table and said, "Shall we play a game?"

"Is that chess? No, I don't think we 'shall.'"

"Yes. What if I put $20 on it?"

"$20?"

"Yes."

"Let's see the money, chump."

Xander took a wrinkled $20 bill out of his pocket and held it in the air. It had taken him a lot of change finding and collecting to amass this fortune.

Licata smirked. "Sure. Why not? You're on."

As they set up the board, Xander gazed behind Mr. Licata's large, unruly head and saw the object of his mission. Hanging religiously, respectfully, ruelessly on the wall was a circa-1900 school disciplinary paddle. Juanito had not said exactly why he wanted it, only that he did not want it for its monetary value. "It's personal," he had said. "Between me and Licata."

Licata chose white and would go first.

From his briefcase, Xander extracted a large bottle of orange soda. "I also brought refreshments."

"Oh yeah? That's nice. Too nice. What gives?"

"Don't be suspicious. I brought it for me. I have extra to share."

"Yeah. Fine. All right."

Xander poured them both some soda and then quickly moved a pawn.

The security chief's first play, moving his king's pawn, did not surprise Xander. It seemed a random move, a common move. Xander knew he would have to dumb down his chess expertise in order to prolong the game. So he moved one of his own king's pawn.

Then Licata's pushed a pawn out next to Xander's, making it easy prey.

Did he do that on purpose? Does he not know how to play? Or does he know how to play . . . well?

Xander paused. And sweat. This might be more humiliating than he thought.

The game proceeded at the snail-like pace of an MTA bus. Intent on the board, Licata did not notice that while Xander put the plastic cup of soda to his lips, he did not imbibe. Xander had placed a diuretic from his grandmother's medicinal menagerie into the orange soda. He had only to await the results.

"We gotta stop," Licata said. "I have to hit the can."

"Okay, I'll wait here."

"Oh, no you don't, greaseball. Step out. I'll lock up."

Xander stood in the hallway and waited, which gave him time to consider if he should take a pawn *en passant.*

When Licata returned, Xander asked if Licata could turn off the radio.

"Why?"

"It's distracting me."

"Excuses will never get you anywhere in life," Licata said. But he got up and shut off the radio.

In the silence, the game grew more intense.

A few minutes later, Licata said, "Damn. I gotta hit the head again. I'll be right back."

"You want me to step out?" Xander said, as innocently as possible.

"Ah, I'll be right back. Don't you move."

When he returned, they resumed the game, and in a few moments, with only three pieces left, Licata said, "Checkmate. That's twenty bucks you owe me."

Xander was flabbergasted. Licata had sacrificed his queen, two rooks and a bishop to mate. He did not, however, notice that the radio was now on a file cabinet.

"Want to go again, champ?"

"No, thank you," Xander said. "I'm afraid I have to prepare for a Chemistry exam." He handed over his $20 bill with more than a little regret.

"Great," Licata said. "Let's not do this again, shall we?"

In the schoolyard, Xander approached Juanito, who was still hanging with his delinquent crew at twilight.

"Where's the paddle, bro?" Juanito said. "You chickened out, didn't you?"

Xander kept his hands in his pockets. It was getting cold and he was hungry. "If I took the paddle now, Licata would automatically know I was involved."

"No paddle, no Chem test, Jawbreaker."

"His office is on the first floor, right off the street. His window is now open and easily accessed from the side street."

"So what? What about the gate?"

"The gate is no longer locked," Xander said. "But I suggest you retrieve your prize promptly, before he notices that things have been moved. The exam, please."

53

LABYRINTH

Things had been cold, near frozen between Holly and her mother. Then came Thanksgiving weekend, and things fell into a familiar pattern again. As usual, Holly and her mother had gotten up early and gone to Manhattan to see the parade on Thanksgiving Day. They laughed at the balloons but didn't say much to each other. Then they drove to Spanish Harlem to Titi Irma's house and ate turkey and rice and beans with her six cousins. As usual, her mother spent the whole time talking with Titi, and her cousins ignored Holly while she had no choice but to spend hours watching silly TV shows and craving the comfort of a good book (Mom said it was rude to read by herself, and that battle had been waged and lost years ago). The day after Thanksgiving, as usual, Holly did homework and read, and Mom did case work and napped on the couch. Marta had the day off, and they ate leftovers from Titi Irma's house in silence.

Mom had said nothing about Victor, and Holly couldn't find the right moment to plead again for her to hire him back. She wanted to apologize to her mother about Victor and she wanted to apologize to Victor, too. At the same time, she felt her mother was being overprotective and she needed her freedom. For the moment, for those long, silent days, she didn't know what to say to make things better.

What didn't help was that she knew she was going to make things worse. There was more to be done. And Holly knew she couldn't involve her friends this time. The girls were game for anything, but despite Brandy's reassurances, she knew they must have gotten into some trouble with their parents. Holly didn't want to get them into any more. She would have to do this on her own.

On Saturday, when her mother left to work at the station house, which she often did on weekends, Holly tossed off her robe. Underneath, she was already fully clothed and ready to go.

It was rainy and cold outside, so Holly zipped up her purple parka as she left the house. She walked to the F train and took it to Fort Hamilton Parkway. She exited the subway and found herself on a quiet residential street, which according to her street map was only a few blocks from Prospect Park.

Ms. Barkley, Mr. Baci and Assistant Coach Stephanie Gorney were in the photos from Mission Venus. Something clicked for Holly when she saw Coach Gorney's picture. When she had heard her mother and the commissioner discussing Mr. Friedman's dating the "coach," she had immediately, foolishly thought they meant Coach DiGeronimo. It was clear now that Mr. Friedman and Assistant Coach Stephanie Gorney were more than work pals. They were kissing and holding each other close on and off the dance floor.

Holly needed to know more about Ms. Gorney, and she needed to know it fast. If the motive for the murders of Mr. Friedman and Ms. Barkley was what she thought it was, then something bad could happen at the dance contest at Mission Venus, which would take place that night!

Ms. Gorney's house was a two-story structure. There was an empty lot on its right and a boarded-up house on to its left. There was a storefront on its first floor that looked like it had been abandoned long ago.

Holly went in through the crooked metal gate and rang the bell that read "S. Gorney." No answer. She tried again and again. There was no light on in the second-floor window, although she could faintly hear music.

There was an alley on the left side of the house. It led to a small garage and a small backyard with an overgrown garden. There was no fire escape leading to the second floor, but there was a sturdy looking trellis. And they likely couldn't see her. Holly decided to give the trellis a try.

She climbed up easily and stood on tiptoes to examine a back window. She slid one of her father's old credit cards between the frames and slid the lock open. Her mother had told her often that people did not know how to safely secure their houses. Holly realized, of course, that this was breaking and entering, which was not legal in any way. And she knew evidence she found would not be usable in court. Her plan was to find something and then make an anonymous call to her mother. The window slid up with only a slight creak.

Holly flopped onto the floor and was suddenly in the middle of a miniature disco. A mirrored disco ball spun from the ceiling, which itself was covered in mirrors. The walls were also covered in mirrors, floor-to-ceiling, and taped on them in perfectly aligned rows were album covers. Holly kind of knew some of the popular musicians (the Bee Gees, Donna Summer, Peaches & Herb, Earth, Wind & Fire, the Village People) and recognized some from her recent research

(Rose Royce, Millie Jackson, Chic, Goody Goody, France Joli, Kraftwerk). There was a long, modular leather couch and a large red bean bag. *Why in the world did people like bean bags so much?* A glass coffee table was crowded with incense, wine and candles.

"Quite a freaky scene," Holly whispered to herself.

A big stereo system took up another wall. No one seemed to be home. The stereo had been left on, playing Cerrone's "Supernature." Did that mean Ms. Gorney planned to be back soon? If so, Holly had to move quickly.

There was a small room next to the bedroom. What would Ms. Gorney have in there? Holly hesitated, then tried the lock. It opened. Inside were piles of boxes, soccer balls, skis, sneakers, all thrown about. On top she noticed a ski mask decorated with snowflakes. She remembered what Ms. Barkley had said, about being attacked by someone in that kind of mask.

It was circumstantial evidence, yes, but it was piling up.

Holly kept looking. On one wall was a shelf system, and on the shelves were trophies. Lots and lots of trophies. Holly looked closely at the plaques on them. "Second Place Archery Award." "Third Place: Swimmer." "2nd Place Runner Up Volleyball." It didn't take Holly long to realize that not a single award was for first place.

Stuck into the wall next to them was a knife. Unlike Xander's silly joke, this looked like dried blood. Could that be the weapon that murdered Mr. Friedman? Holly needed to take some photos right now. She reached into her purse for her camera.

And then she felt something hard and heavy smash into her skull.

54

VIRTUOSO

After going through the exam and answering all the questions *correctly*, Xander rushed to the lunchroom at top speed. There was not a moment to be lost. He found Daniel sitting by himself and scribbling in his little notebook.

Winded from his mad dash, Xander dropped the filled-in exam on top of Daniel's notebook and plopped himself on the opposite chair.

"There . . . you . . . go," Xander said, struggling for breath. "You have just enough time to fa— . . . familiarize yourself with the answers. There's . . . no time to come up with mnemonic devices, but I'm sure you will be able to pass if you read through it a few times."

Daniel smiled. He took the exam, folded it and nodded at Xander.

"Okay," Xander said, "you're welcome."

Smelling tater tots, Xander excused himself. "I shall return," he said.

When he did return, Daniel was gone. Very well then. *Perhaps he went off to study in silence.* Xander ate his food with gusto, with two hands. He felt he had accomplished many things in the past twenty-four hours and had surprised himself with his guile, gumption and guts.

Then he went to throw out his greasy plate. In the trash, tucked in a wedge of garbage, was the exam he had given Daniel.

"Blue blazes!"

Xander thought about getting upset, then he thought better of it. This didn't change all that he had accomplished. He still felt proud.

Finally, he began to understand Daniel. Or at least as much as he could. There was more to that kid than he had thought.

M. Bascanard, the French teacher, was out sick. The substitute teacher admitted that her grasp of French did not extend beyond "Toast" or "Fries," and that she was happy to sit in front of the class with her feet on the desk and loudly page through *The New York Times.*

"Do whatever you want to do," the sub said. "Just be quiet about it."

Xander was looking again at the picture he had gotten from the library. If only the photographer had stepped back one step, or the photo editor had not viciously cropped her face, Xander would be able to see the face of the woman standing next to Mr. Friedman. He could see her bare shoulder. She had a rather large birthmark or tattoo on the shoulder. He couldn't quite tell because the photo was grainy.

Suddenly, he felt a presence over him. It was Daniel, and he was pointing at the picture "The girl . . . the girl . . . the girl that I used to be."

"Now you're really confusing me."

Daniel beckoned Xander to follow him. With a huff, he got up, and they walked to the stairwell and down the stairs.

"This would probably go faster if you just talked plainly," Xander said, trying to catch his breath. "It's a skill you're going to have to acquire in the real world."

Daniel stopped on the first floor and led Xander to the large showcase in the main lobby of the school. Displayed in the case were trophies and, behind them, pictures of past and present FTHS athletic teams.

Daniel pointed to his SOS badge and then at one of the pictures behind the awards: "Once in a while, this happens to me. I run into the girl that I used to be."

The picture showed the girls swim team of 1976. They were flanked by the coaches, both of whom were baring their shoulders. One of them had a large birthmark.

The caption underneath identified her as Assistant Coach Stephanie Gorney.

"Eureka!" Xander said.

55

GARGOYLE

Holly woke some time later with a sore head. She raised her head, cracked open her eyes and found that she was taped securely to a chair in the middle of Ms. Gorney's living room. The candles were all lit now, and the spinning disco ball shone a million bits of light all over the room. Cissy Houston's "Think It Over" was playing. Loudly.

In front of her was Ms. Gorney, sitting on her haunches, holding a lowball glass and staring at her. She was dressed in a shiny silver sleeveless jumpsuit with a low-cut front. Holly noticed a large birthmark on top of her shoulder for the first time. Ms. Gorney's normally tame hair was teased out wildly, and her face was made up with glitter. She leaned in close and said, "Well, it's the first time I've ever had a burglar in my apartment. I should call the cops."

Holly said, "Ms. Gorney, I know it was you. I know you murdered Mr. Friedman and Ms. Barkley."

"You don't get to call me no goddamned murderer!" Ms. Gorney splashed her drink in Holly's face. It was sweet and tasted of orange juice and almonds.

"I know all about your type. Little Miss Know-It-Alls. Little Miss Perfects," Ms. Gorney said. "Born with a silver spoon in your mouth, weren't you? You never really had to try hard at anything, I bet."

"I wasn't. I have."

"Sure. Well, I had to work hard, really hard. And what do I have to show for it? This lousy apartment in a lousy neighborhood."

Holly regretted not being able to get to her purse and the tape recorder she always carried around. She said, "You work at an elite school."

"Elite! Yeah, sure it is!"

"The best in the city, and, if I remember correctly, the swim team won the finals last year."

"You have no idea what it feels like to be around all you brainiacs every day. Practically everyone there is a god-damned genius. I ain't had it easy, not at all. I work really, really hard. I practice at what I do every day. My hands bleed and my feet bleed, and nobody gives a goddamn."

Ms. Gorney got up to change the record. Holly needed to find out more, needed to keep Ms. Gorney talking. Maybe if she got Ms. Gorney to talk it out and be reasonable, she would let her go and surrender.

"You're wrong. There are people who care. There are always people who care."

"What fairy tale book did you fall out of?"

Holly said, "Mr. Friedman was a kind man. He cared. I could tell. Why did you kill him? Was it because of what happened at Mission Venus last year?"

"Larry. Larry *Dazzle*, you mean. I'll tell you what happened, Miss Poindexter. We won. I won. First place! We won fair and square. Then Larry *Dazzle* threw it away on a couple of PRs. What did he care? Mr. Hippie Dippy. Mr. Mellow. Mr. Intellectual. He said they were better than us. He said the judges were bigots, and that the PRs deserved it more. Can you believe that crap?"

"Were they?"

"Were they what?"

"Better?"

Ms. Gorney smashed her glass on the floor.

"No one is better than I am. I am a trained and experienced dancer, a queen of the dance floor. And for less than a minute the whole world knew it. Then Larry took that away from me."

"What about Ms. Barkley? What did she have to do with it?" Holly took a chance. She had to know that the murders were connected.

"Linda came in third place. Did you know that? She danced with that English teacher, Baci. Did you know that?"

Holly shook her head. "I didn't."

Ms. Gorney laughed. "They were there. They saw me get humiliated. After . . . after Larry and Hector, I knew she would make the connection sooner or later. I had to protect myself. Nobody watches out for you but you. That's how the world works."

Holly wasn't sure who Hector was, but she did want to know about her English teacher. "And Mr. Baci?"

"I'll get him tonight. And the lady Puerto Rican. And then everybody else."

"What are you going to do?"

"Uh, sorry, Miss Hernandez, no time to explain. I gotta split."

Ms. Gorney stuffed a sock into Holly's mouth and covered it with duct tape. Then she bent down and whispered in Holly's ear, "One way or the other, I don't plan on coming back. It'll be too late before they find you."

"You smell that? I turned off the pilots on the stove and closed all the windows good. And that song I just put on, 'MacArthur Park,' that's the 17-minute dance suite. Before it's finished, this place is going to be filled with poisonous gas. Little Miss Know-It-All will be Little Miss Blue-in-the-Face. And then, when the gas hits the candles, Little Miss Blown-Up-Everywhere."

Ms. Gorney turned the music up even higher and left, closing the door with a slam.

56

ACCENTUATE

Xander's mother's current stay at Xander's apartment had been predictably unpredictable. Carmen would appear for a few days in a row, linger in the kitchen, eat and drink aplenty, then disappear for a few days in a row, without a word about where she'd been.

On Thanksgiving morning, to Xander's annoyance, she was still there.

However, Xander was grateful that his grandmother was retaining full control of the stove. Since the early hours of the morning, the small kitchen, which also served as the dining room, the living room and his mother's bedroom, was filled with the smell of *arroz, habichuelas, guineos en escabeche* and rich, redolent, roasted pork. Xander sat in front of the small TV, watching cartoons, game shows, old movies (*King Kong* and then *Voyage into Space*), while his mother, who appeared to be having one of her day-long headaches, sat next to him at the kitchen table, chain-smoking and paging through the day's newspaper.

She had been lingering on one page and then, when she turned it, Xander's eyes popped. Spanning an entire page was an advertisement. The Mission Venus logo was easy to spot. Huge lettering across the top read, "Come to our Last Dance Disco Contest November 24, 1979."

"That's this weekend," he said.

"What?" she said.

"This contest. This weekend."

"Yeah," Carmen said, listlessly turning the paper to look at what he was pointing to, "it sure is."

Xander had been thinking a lot about Stephanie Gorney, the school's assistant coach. Since she was Friedman's partner, and they had come in second, that might have given her a very good motive for murder. Perhaps Friedman had had two left feet that night and made them lose. Or perhaps Ms. Barkley, the guidance counselor, who had been there as well, had stepped on the coach's toes or bumped her or something, making them lose. Revenge was a motive Xander could understand. Now he felt he was closer to solving the case on his own. Maybe there was still time to clear his name and beat Holly Hernandez at her own game. Maybe there was still time to be hailed, be highly regarded, to be—dare he think it?—heroic.

"I need to go to this," he said.

"What?" she said, looking directly at him for the first time that day. "What do you mean? Why?"

"I need to go, and I need you to take me."

"You serious?" For the first time in a long time, Carmen had a big smile on her face.

"Yes. We must go to this," Xander said, tapping the ad. "Can you do it?"

"Yeah, Alex, but I gotta be honest, *I* can get in. But it might be tough to get you past the door."

Xander was immediately incensed by the implication. "Perhaps you would prefer if I wore a mask?"

"No, no, Papi, it's not your face. You should see some of the *caraculos* they have there. No, I mean, what you gonna wear? I bet you a million dollars you don't have dancing shoes."

"Why do I need dancing shoes?"

His mother laughed. It had been a long time since he made her laugh.

She said, "Let me go to the corner and make a phone call."

She went out the door and came back ten minutes later. "Saturday, we're going to my friend Miguel's house." Then she said to Abuela, "Mami, Xander and I are going to the disco."

"*El remedio puede ser peor que la enfermedad.*" Xander's grandmother did not look like she approved.

"You worry too much. Oh my god, we're going to have so much fun."

It struck Xander as strange that he had never seen his mother so happy.

On Saturday afternoon, they walked to a brick apartment building on Berry Street and South 5th, a part of the neighborhood that bordered the East River.

Carmen's friend Miguel had a bushy mustache that seemed to take up half his face. He was also very short, half Xander's height. When he opened the door, he could barely reach around the leftovers Xander's mother brought to give her half a hug.

"This is Alex," she said. "He likes to be called 'Xander.' I don't know why."

"*Hola, ¿qué tal,* Xander?" Miguel said.

"He understands Spanish but he won't speak it with strangers."

"Got you. I'm the opposite. There are some things I only do with strangers. But it's okay, Xander. *Hablaremos inglés.*"

The apartment was filled with plants, religious iconography and paintings of tropical scenes, a lot of them featuring men in bathing suits, for some reason.

"Do you think you can help him?" she said.

"Let me look at you, honey," Miguel said to Xander. "You're a little big around the middle, but I can work with it. I got plenty of left-behind clothes in this house, if you know what I mean."

Xander did not know what he meant.

Then Miguel said to Carmen, "Tell me you got shoes."

"He has shoes, but you don't want to see them."

"Got you," he said. "Whoa! Them feet are big."

Miguel and Xander's mother giggled.

Two hours later, Xander stood in front of a wall covered with mirrors. He had never been fond of mirrors. But he saw himself in shiny shoes, seamless slacks, a white shirt with lapels as large as sails, open almost halfway down his chest and a vest worn open. Xander's mother had washed and blow-dried his hair into a smooth mound as poofy as a cotton swab.

"He's perfect," Carmen announced.

Miguel said, "You're hot to trot, Xander. What do you think?"

Xander decided he did not look too bad, not too bad at all.

57

EFFICACIOUS

You can't be a cop's daughter without learning a few things.

After Ms. Gorney left, Holly counted to sixty before using her weight to tip the chair over. With some effort, she raised her arms up and over the back of the chair. Her ankles were still tied around the base of the chair.

Holly rolled over to where the broken glass was. She reached for the glass, careful not to cut herself. Slowly, carefully, she sawed through the duct tape. When she freed her hands, she sat up and worked on her ankles.

She sat there on the floor rubbing her wrists and ankles. Now what? Ms. Gorney was planning to do something horrible. Holly's instinct told her it would be at the Mission Venus disco. Tonight was the night of the Last Dance contest, and Holly had to get there before Ms. Gorney did. But how?

Holly shut off the gas and considered her next move. She had to get to Mission Venus right away. She found Ms. Gorney's princess phone and considered calling Brandy. Maybe Brandy could get her big sister Dawn to bring her car. That could take a while. Then she had another idea.

She dialed. The phone rang once, twice. She was trying to organize all her thoughts, when she heard, "This is Victor Almodóvar. At the tone leave your name and message. I'll get back to you." *Beep!*

He had an answering machine! How cool! Oh, but she had to speak. As she did everything came out in a blur.

"Victor this is Holly I'm really sorry for lying to you so very sorry. It was the wrong thing to do, but I was doing it for a good reason, and that's why I'm calling because now I have to get to the Mission Ve—."

Beep! The machine cut off. What happened? Had it even recorded?

She called quickly again, but the phone just rang and rang.

"My word!" Time was wasting. She had one other option. She picked up the phone again.

"Hello?"

Finally, a person!

"Steve, it's me, Holly, please don't hang up."

"Uh, okay."

"I need a favor. A really big favor."

There was silence on the other end, as if Steve were taking time to make a decision. "Okay," he said.

"I'm working on a case. It's about Mr. Friedman. I've been trying to find out who killed him and Ms. Barkley."

"Mr. Friedman? Holy cow. He's . . . he was that friend of mine I told you about, the guy who gave me the secret keys to the school. He used to go to Flatbush Tech in the 50s. After taking his class the first time, I found that I could talk to him. He was like a father figure to me then, you know? I would go meet him, whenever I felt bad."

Holly felt herself becoming a little *verklempt*. She held it back. "That's amazing. That's a special kind of relationship. So you'll help me?"

"Of course, I want to find out who killed him."

"I know who it is. And I know how to catch her. Do you know Mission Venus?"

"The discotheque?"

"Yes, in Manhattan."

"The disco?"

"Yes, Steve. I need to go to Mission Venus and I need to go tonight! Right now actually, or very, very soon. The sooner the better."

"But why? My stepfather goes there. It's for old people."

"Okay. What kind of music do you like?"

"Heavy metal!"

"Very good. I'll take you to a heavy metal place or concert or show next week. But tonight I need you to take me to a disco. Do we have a deal?"

"Deal."

"Good. Can you pick me up now?"

"Right now? I was just having pizza."

"Bring it with you. It's a portable food."

"I guess. Where are you?"

"I'm at Ms. Gorney's house in Windsor Terrace."

"The gym lady?"

"Yes. It's a long story. Hurry, please."

Twenty minutes later, Steve pulled up in a brown and battered Ford Pinto. It looked like it hadn't been cleaned in years.

"So this is your father's car?"

"No, it's my mother's. My stepfather has his car tonight."

"Did you tell him where you were going?"

"We don't really talk. He went out just before you called, anyway. What's all this about?"

"Ms. Gorney killed Mr. Friedman and Ms. Barkley. She's going to Mission Venus tonight to kill more people. I know she is. And I have to stop her."

≫ ≪

There was a long line at the door, much longer than before. Holly went straight to the front of the line. She knew that in her purple parka, pink blouse, old blue jeans, ponytail and total lack of glitter, she wasn't dressed appropriately.

The bouncer was different from the last time Holly had been there, but he was just as big. He started shaking his head and saying, "No, no, no, no," as she approached.

Then she pulled out the VIP card that Mr. Shabat had sent her. Without a word, the bouncer picked up the rope and let her and Steve in.

"Wow, I guess you know the right people," Steve said.

"It's important to be friendly and make friends," Holly said. "Remember that."

Inside, she was glad to finally be able to *see* Mission Venus. She had missed the vastness of the vestibule the first time. The delicate Art Deco sconces, the lovely trim along the walls, the elaborate herringbone pattern of the floor tiles.

Past the vestibule, the bar area was colorful and smoky. The room was filled with energy and the smell of cologne and cigarettes and sweat and something that reminded Holly of a skunk.

"I can't believe I'm here," Steve said. "Disco really makes me want to puke."

"Stop exaggerating. But if you do puke, please don't do it on my shoes."

They waded into the crowd, not checking their coats. She told Steve to stay close. With the moving multi-colored lights and everyone in constant motion, it would be hard to spot Ms. Gorney first. *What will she do?* Holly wondered. *With this many dancers in such a tight space, she could hurt a lot of people.*

They stood with their backs against a column and scanned the room.

"Keep a lookout for her," Holly yelled. "She looks a little different. She's all made up."

"Um, okay!"

"Hmm, it looks like our best option is . . . to dance."

"What? I don't want to."

"I'm not crazy about it either. For more reasons than I can tell you. But the dance floor gives us the best vantage point. C'mon." She pulled Steve onto the dance floor.

He stood there motionless. "I can't dance. I told you, I like rock music. What do I do?"

"Just move your feet to the beat a little and keep looking as we turn."

"Turn?"

He looked scared, and she felt a little bad for him. She took Steve's hands and allowed herself to remember her father teaching her to dance, so long ago she had to stand on his feet.

What dance should they do? A tango didn't seem appropriate. She had heard of the hustle but had never gotten to practice it. Then she remembered: *Mambo!*

She led Steve, trying to remember the mambo steps her father taught her. Her body began to relax, began to recall the moves as she thought of her father's gentle voice, the way he smiled as he spun her around.

"What are you doing?" Steve said.

"Trying to spin you."

"No way."

Holly shook her head. "Yes way."

"But I'm a guy."

"Guys can spin. Look at those guys over there."

"Are they dancing together?"

"Yes. Now follow me."

Holly led him the way her father would lead her, and soon they seemed to get into a rhythm, in sync with Walter Murphy's "A Fifth of Beethoven."

"This ain't bad," Steve said. "How'm I doing?"

"Not very well, I'm afraid. You do show enthusiasm, though. And you haven't stepped on my feet for over a minute."

As they danced, Holly scanned the room. From the middle of the dance floor, she could see all around the club, and she had a good view of people standing in the upper balcony. But there were columns and the balcony went way back.

"Listen," she told Steve. "I'm going to have to do reconnaissance. Please stay here and keep a lookout."

"On the dance floor? By myself?"

"Dance with somebody! You know one dance now. Make friends!"

Before he could protest, Holly squeezed through the crowd. It was tough going, and she had to lead with her elbow to get through. She found the hallway and the stairs to Mr. Shabat's office again. This time there was no security. She knocked and knocked and got no answer. And the door was locked.

She went back down and waded into the crowd again. On her way to the dance floor, she saw Steve coming toward her. He was covered with sweat.

"You seem to be getting into the swing," she said.

"It's not so bad, I guess."

Just then, they both saw Mr. Baci moving through the crowd.

"It's Mr. Baci!"

"Oh no!" Steve turned.

"What's wrong?"

"That's my stepfather."

"Mr. Baci? Of course!"

"I should have known he would have come here. He's a disco maniac. I gotta go."

"Mr. Baci is a disco maniac? Wait! I was hoping we would see him. I have to talk to him." She turned and could not find Steve anywhere in the crowd.

He was gone.

꘎ ꘏

"Oh great," Holly said.

She could still see Mr. Baci. She followed him into a corridor. Before she could stop him, he went in the men's room.

"Well," she said, "this is for justice," and walked in after him.

To her surprise, there were other women there as well as at least one man dressed as a woman.

She found Mr. Baci combing his long hair into a ponytail in the mirror. He was dressed very differently from the way he dressed at school.

"Holly Hernandez?" he said. "What are you doing here? My god!"

"I don't have much time. I'm here with Steve, your stepson."

"Steve?! Where is he?"

"Actually he took off when we spotted you."

"That's par for the course, I'm afraid. But why are you here, first of all, in this disco, and second, in this bathroom?"

"I don't have time to explain. Please listen! Ms. Gorney is the one who killed Mr. Friedman and Ms. Barkley, and she is coming after you. You have to get out of here."

"What? How do you know this? Why would she?"

"Because Mr. Friedman stopped her from being number one last year. So she's here to take her revenge."

"That's insane."

"She's insane. And you're next in line."

"I can't leave."

"Why not? You're in danger."

"I'm here to honor Linda and Larry and Hector. I'll be dancing with Hector's wife, Marie Chevres, and we plan to win. We've been practicing for months, since he was killed."

"Hector?"

"He was the lead male dancer who won. Marie is, *was* his wife."

"If he was killed, then it's likely she killed him, too. Mr. Baci, she's going to kill you. She probably wants to kill Marie, too."

He shook his head. "I have to say I suspect you're over-thinking this. I know Stephanie, and while she's a little neurotic, I don't think she would kill anyone. Anyway, we can't live our lives in fear. I can't. Besides, with a crowd like this, what can she do?"

"That's what I'm afraid of. We're all sitting ducks here."

"Disco ducks," Mr. Baci said.

"That's funny."

"But I'm not laughing."

58

OSTENTATIOUS

A large man who looked like what Xander imagined an Uruk-hai would look like in a leather jacket, with red hair and scars across his serious-looking face, blocked the front door of Mission Venus. He seemed to brighten when Xander's mother approached.

"Hey, little one, it's good to see you," he said. "But it's a packed night."

"I got my cousin here from out of town," Carmen said. "I want to show him a good time."

Xander was flummoxed. *Cousin?*

The large man looked Xander up and down and his bright mood vanished.

"Yeah, he's never been, and this is the place to be," she said. "You going to let us in?"

"You're looking sweet tonight."

"I don't just look it. What do you say? Maybe we can get some White Castle after, you know?"

Smiling, the large man smiled opened the velvet rope. Xander wondered where the man had acquired such a complex skill set.

Inside the club, Xander was astounded by the sound, the smell, the sheer volume of humanity. Why would so

256

many people willingly cram themselves into a space only to be assaulted by smoke and cologne and that constant thumping bassline?

"It's loud in here," Xander yelled to his mother.

"What?"

"It's loud in here!"

"What?!"

Getting close to her ear, he said, "Never mind. I don't like White Castle, it gives me Montezuma's revenge."

"Alex, we're not going to get White Castle, don't worry. I just had to say that to him so he would let us come in here. You're going to have to learn that it pays to be sweet to people to get what you want."

"Are you teaching me to lie?"

His mother chuckled. "It's not lying. It's getting what you want."

She led him through the thick crowd to a massive dance floor filled with vibrating, pulsating, gyrating bodies. Did no one in here prefer reading for fun?

Xander tried to look for Gorney, but with the lights and the constant moving it was hard to focus.

He was wondering what she would do here. How would she exact her revenge? Then he felt his mother tugging on his arm.

"C'mon, I love this song."

His mother dragged him on to the dance floor and seemed surprised that he didn't move once he got there.

"Don't you even know how to dance?" she said. "No one taught you?"

He looked at her, without blinking.

"Oh, I guess that was my job. Well, c'mon."

She put Xander's right hand on her waist and took his left hand in hers and raised it up. "Listen to the music. You follow me first."

Xander had no idea what she was asking.

"Pay attention," she said. "Quick-quick-slow. Relax. Relax! Don't look at your feet. Let the music take over. Let it play in your head. Let it get into your body. You can't dance and stay uptight."

He was going to ask what she meant by that, but he was too busy trying as best he could not to look the fool. He glanced at the others dancing near him and tried his best to emulate them. His efforts felt awkward and clumsy.

"I give up," he said, standing still.

"C'mon, don't be like that," Carmen said.

"I will never be Fred Astaire."

"That's not the point, Xander."

They walked off the floor, and his mother said she was going to get them some drinks if she had any money left. Just then, there was an excited voice calling her name.

"Oh my god!" she said. "Look who it is."

Xander turned and his mother was hugging a woman in a long red dress with some flowery something sticking out of her long, dark hair. They said something in Spanish, and then Carmen turned to him.

"Remember the friend I told you about whose husband died? This is her. This is Marie. She was the champion last year."

"*Hola, mucho gusto,*" Marie said.

"Marie, this is my cousin Alex."

Xander had had enough of subterfuge. "I'm her son," he said. "I'm Xander."

"Okay. Fine. He's my son."

They started chatting about hair, but Xander had no patience, had something to say and had already had enough of this disco. "I know who killed your husband."

"Xander!"

"What do you mean?" Marie said. "Hector got pushed in front of a train. The police said it was probably a crazy homeless person."

"They're wrong. It was Stephanie Gorney. She works at my school. She did it because she was denied the first place award at this contest last year."

"Was that the lady's name? Yes, she was upset that we won. She was killing me with her eyes. Her boyfriend was very nice to give it to us. I think they broke up after that, though. Do you think she really was the one who killed Hector, for that? I can't believe it."

"You should. And she will be here tonight," Xander said. "Looking for more revenge."

"You're scaring me."

"Xander!" Carmen said.

The women talked and Marie walked away, looking back at Xander as if he were a harbinger of doom. Which of course he was.

Xander's mother turned to him. "This is too crazy. Is this why you wanted me to bring you here?"

"Yes. I have a mission at Mission Venus."

"Xander, I don't understand you. I can't! How the hell did you end up so goddamn weird?"

Xander had been called "weird" a million billion times before in his life. He had learned to accept the adjective with pride. It meant he wasn't part of the crowd, not one of the sheep, a standout from the masses. But when his very own mother called him "weird," he didn't know what to feel.

"If I'm so weird," he blurted out, "some of it had to come from you."

She looked at him as if he were dirty, as if he were wrong, as if he were a stranger. She turned and melted into the crowd of dancers, instantly finding a partner. Xander watched as she spun farther and farther away.

59

INSIDIOUS

Mr. Baci refused to leave the club and promised Holly he would be careful. She would have liked to look for Steve or Mr. Shabat, but they could be anywhere. What she needed to do was find Ms. Gorney and stop her before she did whatever it was she was planning to do.

Holly continued to scan the crowd. She spotted famous people: Brooke Shields, Andy Warhol, Liza Minnelli. No one she really wanted to meet. Now, if Carl Sagan walked in, she would walk right up and introduce herself.

She felt very warm in her parka and was surprised at how little other people were wearing, some were in what looked like bikinis, some were just in shorts.

Still, no sign of Ms. Gorney.

The volume of the music lowered and lights went on at a small dais near the deejay. The dancing on the floor slowed down and two people in Mission Venus jackets moved people away from the center of the room.

There was a spike of applause as Denny Shabat came out, wearing a circus ringmaster costume. He doffed his hat and said into the microphone, "Ladies and gentlemen! Unladies and ungentlemen! *Mesdames et Messieurs!*

Madames and masseuses! Welcome to the greatest disco in the world: Mission Venus!"

The crowd roared again with applause.

"Tonight is our world famous disco dance contest! The Last Dance! Maybe our last, Who knows?"

Holly found a spot by a column and stood there with her arms crossed. Mr. Baci stood on the opposite side of the dance floor next to a tall woman with long, dark hair and a red dress. So that was Marie Chevres. They were surrounded by people. What could possibly happen to them?

Maybe Mr. Baci was right. Maybe she was overthinking this. Ms. Gorney's M.O. had always been crimes of opportunity, using weapons she found at the scene. Maybe Ms. Gorney had chickened out and was long gone, in some other country with a new identity.

No, after their encounter this afternoon, Holly was convinced that Ms. Gorney would find a way to get revenge, maybe not here, but afterward when people were going home. She would have to stay sharp.

Shabat announced one couple at a time, and each took their turn on the dance floor. The fifth couple he announced were Mr. Baci and Marie Chevres. "You're in for a real treat, ladies and gentleman," he said.

On the dance floor, Mr. Baci looked uptight, worried. He kept scanning the crowd, his eyes more on them than on his partner.

Now his dancing might be ruined and he'd lose the contest. Holly felt awful, but he needed to be told the truth.

But then the music began, and something seemed to change in him. He wasn't the surly-looking English teacher anymore. He seemed transported, transformed. It was as if the dancing took him over and he had no choice but to concentrate. Soon, Mr. Baci and Marie were turning in small circles, moving as one. Then he took her hand suddenly and twirled her one, two, three, four, five, six, seven times. Then they stepped back and forth, their bodies perfectly mirroring each other. It was harmony. It was beauty. Holly envied them.

And the crowd was with them, watching every move, clapping or swaying along. All these humans in sync. It was scary, but it also felt natural and human and alive. Holly realized what made disco so attractive to so many people: the chance for people to be fully alive together. Besides all the bad stuff that made Commissioner McGuire go ballistic, there was good stuff here, too.

The girls had said that disco was dying. If that were true, she would be sorry to see it go. Then she thought it would turn into something else, something new. It made sense, here near the end of the decade, that the things that people loved would change, that in a year hairstyles and pop music could be completely different.

As Holly was looking around, someone on the balcony caught her eye. Someone who stood out, not part of the community. Holly recognized the hairstyle, the barrette, the silver jumpsuit. That was her, no mistake: Assistant Coach Stephanie Gorney.

Ms. Gorney's eyes were focused on the dance floor. Everyone's eyes were focused on the dance floor, but for Ms. Gorney it was different. She wasn't looking down with joy and camaraderie. She was looking down like a hunter, dead-eyed, joyless, intent.

She was in a corner, slightly away from the crowd. Her shoulders moved, and Holly saw that Gorney was moving something out of her coat, first one thing, then another. It took a moment to realize what it was, since it was so out of context here. First the stock and then the barrel of a rifle.

Assistant Coach Gorney snapped them together.

"Rifle!" Holly yelled, but then she realized her words got swallowed by the loud music.

Ms. Gorney rested the rifle against the railing. Holly imagined a beeline and saw that she was focused on Mr. Baci and Marie. *Oh no!*

Holly yelled as loud as she could: "Gun! Gun! Gun!"

She pushed her way through, suddenly clearing the crowd and finding herself on the dance floor, in the space where Mr. Baci and his partner were spinning. Because of her momentum and without people around her, cushioning her rush, Holly lost her balance and began slipping.

Ms. Gorney was raising the rifle. Did no one else see her? Why was no one else stopping her?

Holly was still yelling, "Gun!" In slow motion, Mr. Baci and Marie were turning their heads to her, looking puzzled, and the people in the crowd were looking both at her and where she was pointing. She kept slipping until she hit the floor with a bounce on her butt and looked up to see the rifle muzzle turning toward her. *No no no!*

Then, there was a shot, and Holly felt the air pressure change around her. She was sure she was dead.

60

INEXORABLE

Xander's mother never returned. He spotted her once at the bar, talking to a man. Later, he caught sight of her on the dance floor again. After that, it seemed she had disappeared. He found a spot against a wall and stayed there for an hour. Then he had to go to the bathroom and, afterward, saw a stairwell leading to the balcony and decided to go up there where he could watch the decadent display of *la danse* from above, lost in the shadows.

He situated himself by a column in a corner and watched the dance contestants come on and get off. He did not applaud.

He was getting overly warm, bored, sleepy even, when he saw Holly Hernandez down at the edge of the dance floor. So, she had sussed it all out, too? Of course, she had. She was pretty smart, after all. He had given her the vital clue, hadn't he?

There was no sign of Gorney. Maybe she wasn't coming. Maybe she had chickened out. Maybe he had been wrong.

He looked down, and there was Mr. Baci and that woman friend of his mother's dancing. The crowd seemed to love them, cheered them along. Xander was wondering what to do next, maybe get himself an overpriced soda, when he saw, down at the far end of the balcony, not even trying to hide but somehow not seen by anyone else: Gorney holding a rifle. She had it pointed straight at Holly.

Xander could stop her. He took a step, but then stopped. He felt a weird, a momentary sensation of happiness, hate and hesitation. Holly would be gone. His rival would be vanquished. All he had to do was do nothing. Gorney aimed.

No. He couldn't stand by. He had to do something. And imagine. They'd say what a good person he was. They'd hail him as a hero.

He stepped forward.

As he did, Gorney pulled the trigger. Xander turned.

On the dance floor, out of nowhere, a large old man had come flying toward Holly and shielded her with his body.

A bullet struck the man. There was a mist of blood. Xander's eyes went wide. People screamed, barely audible above the still-playing music.

Before he could do anything else, the balcony filled with police. Police in vests. Police carrying guns. They flew toward Gorney, guns drawn and pointed at her.

She must have sensed them. She turned her head slowly and seemed to make a decision. She turned her body, raising the rifle. Before she moved another inch, she was shot once, twice and again and again.

Xander lost count.

She collapsed against the railing and then slumped back onto the floor. Her eyes were still open. Her feet twitched.

Xander wanted to see, wanted to witness this terrible thing. But he found himself stepping back, turning his head into the velvet-covered corner and sinking to the floor.

The cops didn't see him. They stood around their kill and chatted amongst themselves. Some laughed.

Xander sank back further to a darkened area at the far end of the balcony.

He was there, staring at nothing, when someone shook his shoulder.

"Jawbreaker. Hey. Hey! Jawbreaker! C'mon, I'll get you out of here."

It was one of the Mission Venus workers. He wore shades and a smooth haircut, much like Xander's fetching current one. Xander thought it looked better on himself than on the worker.

"Gadzooks! Who are you?"

"Call me Pito. Let's go, bro."

Xander allowed himself to be pulled up and led down a back staircase and through an exit door. Suddenly, he was on the street, on the opposite side of the entrance. He began walking away quickly.

"Jawbreaker! Train's that way," Pito said, picking up Xander's hand and putting a token into it. "Watch out for yourself now."

The train took a long time to come. When it did, it sauntered into the station like a sleepy Model-T. Three homeless men slept in the car and smelled like onions, urine and a thousand locker-room socks boiled into stew.

Carmen would not be home, he knew that. He did not know if he would ever see her again. He realized that he did not mind that. Abuela would be home. Abuela would take care of him. He hoped he had not angered her so much that she didn't love him anymore. He sighed, and his chest felt pain.

He got off at the Canal Street station and walked through a series of empty stairways to get to the J and M platform. There was a strange man in a long raincoat nervously rocking back and forth, hiding behind a column and then peeking out every now and then.

The J train came surprisingly quickly. There were a lot of people in the car. A large group near Xander still carried the party atmosphere from wherever they had been. They were loud. They smelled like skunk. They were looking at him.

"What are you looking at?" one of them said to Xander.

"Oh my god. Look at that big dude."

"What a face!"

"It's Frankenstein's child!"

Xander moved his stare to outside the window. They kept talking at him. The train moved out and over the Williamsburg Bridge, crossing the East River. He kept staring until he couldn't hear them anymore.

61

ADUMBRATE

Holly sat on the floor of the disco. She was covered in cold sweat and shivered under her parka. There was still a crowd there, but it was different now. Not dancers and divas, but police officers, detectives, EMTs, photographers. Her mother sat next to her, with a warm arm across Holly's shoulders.

A paramedic finished checking Holly and said, "Just a little bruised, but she's going to be all right."

"I should be mad at you," her mother said. "But I'm just glad you're alive."

"Thanks to Victor. How is he?"

"I don't know. He had a vest on, but he still took a pretty bad hit."

"For me." Holly couldn't hold back anymore. The idea of Victor saving her broke her heart. "He did it for me." Her face mashed up and tears poured out.

Her mother held her, *shhh*ing her gently. "Why didn't you tell me right away, Holly? Why didn't you let me know?"

"You would have stopped me," she said, wiping the snot from her nose. "It's something I needed to do. To make things right."

"Oh, Holly. My little girl is no little girl anymore. She thinks she's a detective. I guess you are a detective."

"And then Steve left, and I had no backup."

"Steve?"

"The boy from school."

"A boyfriend?" her mother said.

"He's a boy and he's a friend. That's all. He knew Mr. Friedman and he helped get me here tonight."

"So what was your plan then, detective?"

"Um," Holly said, sniffling. "I just knew I had to stop her. When I saw her, I did the only thing I could do at the moment: Yell! I'm sorry, Mom, about all of this. I guess I wasn't thinking it through all the way. I knew I wanted to solve this case on my own, and then in the back of my mind I figured I would turn the evidence over to you, and you'd arrest the killer."

"But you almost got yourself shot. This is not some game of Clue, Holly. This is real life. It's dangerous."

"I know, Mom, but the danger didn't matter to me."

"Well, it matters to me. So I don't want to hear anymore about you skulking around and tracking criminals. I can't lose you, too. Do you understand me?"

Before she could answer, Mr. Baci came over. He had an arm around Marie, whose make-up was smeared from sweating and crying.

"We wanted to thank you," he said.

"You don't have to."

"Holly, you're a hero."

"I'm not."

"Think about it. You went out of your way to put yourself in a place you knew there would be danger. You could have just been at home listening to your Carpenters records."

"How did you know I love the Carpenters?"

"You mentioned them in two of your essays," Mr. Baci said. "But, listen, you came out here. How the heck they let you into this place, I don't know. But you drew her attention away from us, and you saved our lives."

"But!"

"Holly, a good hero accepts gratitude with humility and grace."

"I get it," she said. "I understand."

"But this doesn't mean you get to pass my class automatically. You still have an essay due next week."

"Mr. Baci, about Steve . . . he's very smart. He loves literature. I don't know why he doesn't let you know who he is."

"I don't know if he told you. I married his mother, and then a year later she passed away. So he was stuck with me. We were stuck with each other. It hasn't been easy on either one of us. I don't know how to talk to him, I really don't. I rarely see him now. Maybe some day, Holly, you can come over for dinner. I know he'll be there if you're there. Maybe you can help me, help your teacher."

"Let me know the date and I'll be there."

"Come on, Holly," her mother said, "we better get home. I'm driving."

"What time is it?"

Her mother looked at her watch. "Eight in the morning."

"We haven't been to Tom's in a long time."

"In Prospect Heights? That was your father's favorite place. What made you think of that?"

"No reason."

CONVERGENCE

"¡Desayuno!"

Xander awoke smiling to the sound of his grandmother's voice. He could have used another three days of sleep, but for once he was not complaining. Besides, he would take a generous nap in the afternoon. He put on his robe and slippers and performed his ablutions. Then he padded into the kitchen.

"Good morning, Abuela."

"Siéntate, niño"

He sat down at his usual seat at the small table. Waiting for him was a big glass of orange juice and a small *café con leche*.

It was no surprise that his mother's seat at the table was empty. He didn't say anything about it. He knew his grandmother wouldn't either.

In short order, there were four fried eggs in front of him, fried *maduros*, six slices of bacon, three thick slices of fried Spam and toast. His grandmother had already eaten, but she sat with him, drinking her own coffee.

"Thank you, Abuela."

"Come antes de que se enfríe."

On the table was also the fat Sunday edition of the *Daily News*. The funnies were always on top. Xander peeked under them.

DISCO FRENZY!
Mission Venus to Close after Melee
Teen Saves Day

The large front cover picture was of Holly Hernandez. So she had won. This time.

Xander refused to let the news spoil his appetite. There would be other encounters with Holly, other contests, other chances to prove his superiority. He dove into his breakfast with gusto.

His grandmother left to go to church, and Xander got out of his pajamas and dressed for the day. He got his briefcase and proceeded down to the basement, his lair, his Hall of Xander.

It was damp but warm down there near the hot water pipes, and he liked the slightly musty smell. He got out a writing pad and a marker. It was time to begin.

At that point the building's front doorbell rang. Xander looked at his empty wrist out of habit. He knew what time it was anyway, without looking.

He stomped up the stairs. It had snowed the night before, and the cold rushed in as he opened the door. Daniel stood there, holding his schoolbag.

"I want to open your head, like a can of tuna," he said. "Uh oh, here comes a wave, the big kahuna!"

"Daniel, *mon ami. Entrez s'il vous plait.*"

63

PUGNACIOUS

The weather had suddenly turned cold, so Holly wore a black turtleneck sweater and corduroy jeans. She put on her parka and matching scarf and earmuffs and went out to the car, where Officer Levitt was waiting.

He drove her to Bay Ridge and said, "Five minutes. No more or you'll be late."

"10-4!" Holly said.

She rang the bell and the buzzer let her in. The apartment door was open.

Victor sat at the kitchen table, looking better. He wore a sling on his left arm and a big smile.

"Marta made you muffins," Holly said, handing over a big paper bag.

"Right on, Ms. Holly," he said. "You're the best."

"I want to say again how grateful I am, Victor, for what you did at Mission Venus. I'm so glad you got my message. I guess I do need a bodyguard."

"You do if you're going to keep being a detective. It'll be my pleasure. And you don't need to thank me."

"Okay," she said, "but expect something really nice for Christmas! Something freshly baked."

"Don't spoil me, miss. I can barely fit into my suit now."

She ran downstairs and Levitt drove her to the school. She wasn't sure what to expect after the incident at the disco. It had been in the local newspapers and on *Eyewitness News.*

Officer Levitt pulled up to Flatbush Tech and she hesitated opening the door. The students, dressed up like Eskimos, were gently queuing into the school.

She got out of the car and walked to the entrance. Maybe it would just be another day at school.

"Holly!" "Holly!" "Holly!"

Beth and Sharona and Brandy surrounded her, hugged her.

"We didn't know if we should call," Sharona said. "Should we have called?"

Beth hugged her and said, "I love that sweater."

"Thank you, guys."

Brandy hugged her. "You're okay?"

"I'm fine."

"Did you solve the case?"

"Well, yes. But it wasn't just me. You all helped me."

"I told you."

"I can't wait till our next case!"

"Who doesn't love being a detective? Don't you?"

"I have to confess," said Holly, "I really do."

Later that morning, she was walking to class when she saw Christina. She was thinking about talking to her when suddenly there was Xander coming down the hall headed toward their English room. She had forgotten how tall he was. He was pounding down on those fourth row tiles as he came toward her. His face was completely unreadable.

For a second there, she thought he would walk past her. She had grabbed all the headlines. He remained unknown and unheralded. She hoped they could at least have an interesting conversation once in a while, maybe they could even be friends. There was something good in Xander, and she didn't know if he knew that. Somebody would have to tell him that some day.

She stopped in place outside the door of the classroom, her books against her chest like a shield, and waited for him.

"Xander," she said.

And he stopped. He didn't look at her, but he stopped.

"Ms. Gorney would not have been caught without your help. You know that. I know that. I spoke to my mother, and she's going to see what she can do about getting your criminal record expunged."

She got the words out as fast as possible before he could disappear inside the classroom.

Xander didn't say a thing. *Is he going to give me the stink eye? Maybe a grunt?*

Instead, turning to look at her, he let out a big, windy "Hmmphhhh." *And was that the tiniest hint of a smile?* Then he turned and ducked away.

Was that progress? Yes, that seemed like progress. One day at a time, then.

Holding her books close and anticipating an exciting lesson on Edgar Allan Poe, Holly turned and walked into class.

APPENDIX A

From Daniel Calara's Spiral Notebook
Top 10 Desert Island Songs List #17

"The Ballad of No-Neck Bradley"
by Bruce Springsteen
From the LP *Sure, Jersey City, Why Not* (1975)

He was seven inches shy of six feet tall and they called him
No-Neck for no reason at all.
Not a hero or a villain like they teach you in school, no, No-
Neck Bradley was just another fool.
That's right, just like you and me, boys and girls.

No-Neck Bradley was a burly burly man with a curly curly beard
of all the things on Earth there was nothing that he feared
'cept his mom maybe, chatty toddlers and bad cheese . . .

He made it out of school by finally passing gym, a year or
    two later the railroad called him: the old choo choo.
Bradley found work with the N-J double R, punching tickets
    all day, walking from car to car.
Next stop: Cranford!

No-Neck Bradley was a burly burly man with a curly curly
   beard
Of all the things on Earth there was nothing that he feared
'cept escalators maybe, microwave ovens and them tiny
   dogs look like Dobermans.

There came a hot summer day on the Morristown line
   Bradley's in his blue duds, wasn't feeling too fine.
The commuters piled on at Penn Station, packed them-
   selves in as if space were a sin.

As the train came to a rest in Dunellen, No-Neck had a real-
   ization:
"This is all I am," it was, "this is all I will be." Now I know
   what you think, but it made him feel free.
At the end of the day, no, he didn't feel down as he drove
   on home through his cancer-cluster town—
smiling, that boy was, whistlin' Buck Owens . . .

No-Neck Bradley was a burly burly man with a curly curly
   beard
Of all the things on Earth there was nothing that he feared
'cept handshakes, public displays of affectation and small
   talk.

"The Girl That I Used to Be"
by Suzie Quatro
From the LP *The Engine of the Band* (1974)

Once in a while
this happens to me
I run into the girl
that I used to be

I'm at a movie
standing in line
Then from behind me
I hear a whine

Whine whine whine whine whine

I'll be at a bar,
just drinking a beer
and then this teen mess
in a dress will appear

There's me spitting spitballs
annoying my date
Should I tell him I'm no good
before it's too late?

Late late late late late

Once in a while
this happens to me
I run into the girl
that I used to be

I got to admit it
I'm getting that a look
from a face on the subway,
eyes over a book

I wonder why that girl
is staring at me,
And it's then that I see that
She used to be me.

Me me me me me

"Upon the Shadow"
by Led Zeppelin
From the LP *Led Zeppelin II.V* (1974)

Gaze upon the shadow
find your true name
All the luck you've had, oh
find your true name, boy

Surging through the open sea
is that you? Is that me?
To the open sea
is that you? Is that me?

Gaze upon the shadow
say the word of the unbinding
Look upon the shadow
see your destiny unwinding

To the open sea
where you'll meet you
To the open sea
where you'll meet me

"The Lonely Guy"
by Harry Nilsson
From the LP *Pandemonium Fandemonium* (1971)

I am alone
the lonely guy
I am alone
nobody's home
I think I'll go
away, far from home
Alone

I walk the road
with my thumb out
I have a backpack
with books and some clothes packed in there

The big green thing
it's—it's always near
inside me here

I am alone
the lonely guy
I have my books
I read them all
I think I'll roam
with all my books now
Alone

"Modern Girl"
by ELO
From the LP *How's Your Father?* (1976)

I see you on the steps in your new blue jeans
I see you reading a book I dig what it means
I have a nice place I pay to keep clean

Modern girl, Modern girl
Modern girl, in your crimson and clover
Modern girl, Modern girl, can I come over?

I wish I could play guitar or at least knew how to sing
I could give you a song instead of a ring
If you threw a party, I wouldn't know what to bring

Modern girl, Modern girl
Modern girl, in your crimson and clover
Modern girl, Modern girl, why won't you come over?

I see you in the park in your protest clothes
I would go to protests but I don't go to those
I have some nice stuff to pacify my woes

Modern girl, Modern girl
Modern girl, in your crimson and clover
Modern girl, Modern girl, why won't you come over

"Office Romance"
by America
From the LP *Hubbub* (1978)

Eat a pickle in your cubicle
just another one of those days,
praying for your fate to be fickle,
have your turkey sandwich with a spread of malaise.

In accounting there goes Claire
down the hall and to the right.
In the elevator she gives you a stare
and now you dream of her at night.

At a team meeting she laughs at you
breaking your day from its routine.
Work becomes the smell of sweet perfume
daydreaming by the copy machine.

One Happy Hour with the office crew.
Margaritas flow on till way past eight.
Everyone leaves and it's just you two.
You start thinking, Ain't love kinda great.

You hit it off, you're two of a kind!
You thank god for a change in your life.
Then sober reality enters your mind—
You're going home to a dear little wife.

You wait for your train alone at First Ave
stare at the gum on the concrete floors.
There are things in life you just can't have
"Stand clear of the closing doors."

Eat a pickle in your cubicle
another one of those days
praying for your fate to be fickle
eat your turkey with a spread of malaise.

"Johnny, Roll Your Eyes Once More"
by AC/DC
From the LP *Brutal Lesson* (1977)

Johnny, roll your eyes once more
and they'll roll out your head on to the floor
you'll only hear them rolling out the door
because you won't be able to any no more.

Oh Johnny, Oh Johnny

Johnny, go say that word again
that's a grown-up word to use when you're ten.
That word's going to be your only friend
and you'll be alone with your word in the end.

Oh Johnny, Oh Johnny

Johnny, keep teasing the dog that way
there's no need to listen to what I say.
I can't even get the dumb dog to obey
so he'll probably bite off your hand one day.

"The Silver Tree"
by Queen
From the LP *Duck Soup* (1976)

When I was a young lad of only three
my dear old daddy came to talk to me.
Sorry and sad faced, he said he was dying.
He said just to listen. He said to stop crying.

He said he was going to leave a gift just for me
He said, "Look outside and see that old Silver Tree."
He told me I'd never, ever need fear
that this precious tree would always be here.

Oh Silver Tree, my Silvery Tree
poor, hungry, or sad I'll never be
because I'm always gonna have
my Silver Tree.

For years I watered that tree every day
when dogs came around I shooed them away.
I dreamed that its treasure was its bright shiny fruit
or that riches were buried deep under its roots.

And then one day, dear Daddy was gone.
Uncle Gower took me from the funeral home.
On the bus going back, he patted my head
he said it's sure gotta suck with your dad being dead.

Oh Silver Tree, my Silver Tree
poor, hungry, or sad I'll never be
because I'm always gonna have
my Silver Tree.

I told my uncle nothing would happen to me
Daddy has left me the great Silver Tree!
I looked up and Uncle followed my gaze,
and his eyes, for a second, lost their usual glaze.
What happened next, you must listen to most
'twas then uncle said, "You mean the stupid lamppost?"

Oh Silver Tree, my Silvery Tree
poor, hungry, or sad I'll never be
because I'm always gonna have
my Silver Tree.

"Zombie Surfer Boy"
by the B-52s
From the LP *Mad Monster Party* (1979)

All the guys and the gals
party on the sand
but I'm all by myself
looking for my hand

I want to take your bikini
on a wild ride
there goes my left foot
going out with the tide

No one loves a Zombie Surfer Boy!
He wants to eat your brains
He wants to eat your ends
He wants to eat your brains
He wants to eat your friends

I just have to eat
I tell you I gotta
just give me a taste of
your medulla oblongata

I want to open your head
like a can of tuna
uh oh here comes a wave
the big kahuna

No one loves a Zombie Surfer Boy!
He wants to eat your brains
He wants to eat your ends
He wants to eat your brains
He wants to eat your friends

"Star Wars Theme/Cantina Band"
by Meco
From the LP *Star Wars and Other Galactic Funk* (1977)

APPENDIX B

abject: in a low state or condition; wretched
abstruse: hard to understand; esoteric
accentuate: to make more prominent or noticeable
adumbrate: to sketch or foreshadow
adversity: difficult times; unfortunate circumstances
alacrity: cheerful readiness; eagerness
arcane: mysterious, obscure
beguile: to mislead by trickery or flattery; hoodwink
brazen: shameless or impudent
calumny: a lie intended to harm someone's reputation
camaraderie: the spirit of good-fellowship; comradeship
circumlocution: speaking in a roundabout way; evasion
cognominate: to give a nickname to
conflagration: a destructive fire
confluence: a flowing together of two or more streams; a
  junction
consensus: general agreement; solidarity
conspire: agree to do something together, usually something wrong or illegal
convergence: the act of moving together toward unity
decorum: dignified behavior; good taste in conduct or
  appearance

discomfit: to embarrass or confuse

dissipate: to spread thinly or scatter; disperse; deplete

divergent: different from each other; moving in different directions

efficacious: able to produce a desired effect; effective

emollient: something that softens or soothes pain

empathy: the ability to understand and be sensitive to another person's feelings as if they were your own

equanimity: stable in composure; calmness; having balance

exacerbate: to aggravate; to make something bad worse

formidable: inspiring awe, discouraging attack

fortuitous: lucky, or accidentally successful or pleasant

gargoyle: a grotesque person or figure

garrulous: loquacious; annoyingly talkative

hapless: luckless, unfortunate

inexorable: relentless; unstoppable

insidious: treacherous; intending to entrap

insurgent: a rebel; a person in opposition to authority, especially in armed resistance against their own government

introspection: looking at one's own thoughts and feelings

knell: the slow sound of a bell sound made by a bell rung slowly, especially for a death or funeral

labyrinth: a place of intricate combination of paths or passageways; a maze

lionize: to treat someone or something as important or famous

multifarious: occurring in great variety; diverse

oration: a formal public speech or elaborate discourse

ostentatious: being pretentious or conspicuous in order to attract and impress others

pariah: someone despised or rejected; an outcast

paucity: a small amount; scarcity

pellucid: easy to understand; translucent

pertinacious: holding to a purpose, course of action or opinion; stubborn; resolute

profligate: shamelessly immoral; recklessly extravagant

pugnacious: inclined to fight; quarrelsome; combative

quixotic: extravagantly chivalrous or romantic; unrealistic and impractical

quaint: old-fashioned or peculiar in a pleasing way;

recalcitrant: resistant of authority or control; hard to manage or control

requiem: a chant or song in honor of someone who died

semaphore: an apparatus for visual signaling

stupendous: awesome, impressive

trenchant: incisive, keen, sharp, as in a remark or a person

torpid: sluggish or inactive

ubiquitous: widespread; existing everywhere

vicissitude: a change or alteration in the state of things

virtuoso: someone who has special knowledge about or is extremely good at something

voracious: having a big appetite; ravenous; avid

wily: crafty, full of cunning

wretched: very unhappy; miserable

zealous: ardent, diligent, often overly so

APPENDIX C

Arresting Silence
by Holly Hernandez

Sundays Daddy yelled, *Pancakes*
Banging on doors, scaring the dog, *Pancakes!*
broadening his Brooklyn accent, *Pancakes!*
til he sang like a Coney Island barker

Holly! he'd say, squeezed into seats at Tom's,
tell me these are not the best pancakes in the world!
Every bite proved he was right

And then someone
We never found out who
shot him

Sundays now the rooms echo
the scratch of doggy nails,
rings of telephones, then
the opening and closing of doors
the barker's song gone now, the accent
silenced

ACKNOWLEDGEMENTS

The lyrics and album names in Appendix A were made up by me, so apologies to the singers and groups mentioned; it was done with geekiness and admiration. My teachers in Brooklyn guided me to a lifelong love of reading and writing. Deep, sincere thanks to all of them, especially Helen Jewells, Robert Quinn, Sharon Ribak, Sydney Rotter, Paul Boccio, Leo Lieberman and Ellen Finnegan. Thanks to my good friend Ardi Alspach for her great suggestions on an early draft of the text. Thanks also to New York Police Department historian Bernard Whalen for background on 1970s police procedure, to Arte Público's Marina Tristán for her endless support of Holly and Xander. Thanks to my sister Yvette and my brother Ray, who can recall the Disco Era better than I can. And as always thanks to my sweet wife Denise for her proofreading and her inspiration.